Stitches

A Novel

Courtney Pierce

DEDICATION

To my mom, a dreamer through great books; my dad, a dreamer through great deeds; and my husband, a collector of books about great dreams and deeds. And to all the kids who were told to stop staring out of the window—but who aced the tests.

The miracle is not to fly in the air, or to walk on the water, but to walk on the earth.

—*Chinese Proverb*

Cover Photo:

Irwan Hadiyanto

ACKNOWLEDGMENTS

A special note of thanks goes to my husband and family. It takes patience to live with a writer and endure the obsessive, long hours of silence. Since my mom was the very first reader, a thumbs-up from her meant a lot. My sister was a constant source of inspiration. Thanks also go to my two aunts, who were enthusiastic early readers. My uncle is an inspiration to me for the possibilities of a life filled with passion, obsession, and determination.

My family of early draft readers across the country helped to shape this book. Many of you are in the souls of my characters. In particular, extra kudos go to Joanna Minerley, Eric Boardsen, Chante Moore, Jan Pierce, Doug Pierce, Ann Pierce, Susan Welli, Gerrod George, Steve Winton, Susie Krajsa, Katie Jackman, Linda Montgomery, Mary Jo Daly, Alison Davidow, and Carole Florian for their suggestions and constant encouragement.

Kristin Thiel at Indigo Editing & Publications is more than an editor to me. Her pen sparkles with magic.

PROLOGUE

Richmond, Virginia, 1928

Birdie wished Wiley could live forever. That jet-black bird dog of Doc's snatched her heart seventeen years ago and held on with a tight grip. Until finding him under the porch steps as a tiny pup, she'd never heard so much crying and carrying-on. Doc fixed him up, named him Wiley, and ever since his tongue's been licking at someone's hand; tail knocking at something.

Now Wiley's too tired. But Doc has healing hands. After forty-seven years of working in his house, Birdie and her husband, Jess, had seen him fix everybody in town; if he couldn't, well, Doc would make folks feel better about not feeling good. He'd know what to do. Doc always knew what to do.

She and Jess had been working for Doctor Gaines and his wife, Charlotte, since 1881. They were only teenagers when Doc fixed her up too. Just starting out in his practice, the paint wasn't yet dry on Doc's sign outside the day Jess brought her here. She had a bad burn on her arm, and both of them had lost their work situation. Curtains in the old Whitfield place caught fire from the gaslight and burned it to the ground. Birdie hated gaslight. It was one happy day in Doc's house when she flipped on the switch with the new electric lights. He and Charlotte wired this house just for her when she and Jess got hired on.

Doc sounded older now; lost some lilt after Charlotte passed on a couple of months ago. Only sixty-eight she was; same as Doc. Such a shame. Heart too big. Never was a kinder lady; she had wise eyes like blue crystals. Used to wear her dark hair in a fancy twist with a sparkly comb; didn't even need to try to look pretty.

The roast for supper rested in the oven; shortbread all done; the gravy bubbled in a pan on the stove, fussing for a stir. Leaning over the sink, Birdie spotted Jess through the kitchen window. She knocked on the pane and whirled her hand in a circle. An impressive man, Jess hadn't lost his muscles as he aged. Seemed to get taller while she got rounder. And he'd hung on to his heart too. She'd seen Jess sulk for days even if he found something dead in the road.

Jess waved back, and so did the flowers. Charlotte's hyacinths, planted years ago, stretched out of the ground in the late-afternoon glow after he spread the mulch. Those fragrant bells rang out in celebration of spring's arrival, and along with them came cool mornings and warm twilights. Some things change; some things don't, but one thing stayed steady: When spring comes to Richmond, Virginia, all is right with the world.

"Law, we need new life in this big, old house," she muttered, wiping her hands on her wide, white apron, her partner in the kitchen over the years. Birdie stepped to the dining room and pulled a table cloth from the drawer in the breakfront. Snapping open the linen, she broke into a toothy smile. "Why look a there. Charlotte, sometime I think you still around. I tried and tried to get that stain out last night. Stain's all gone. I'll be."

Birdie smoothed and straightened the white linen, and then peered through the doorway to the parlor. She put her hands on her wide hips and shook her head. A dime wouldn't fit under that old dog's head these afternoons, owing to how stuck he was on Doc's lap. That wild, wavy hair of Doc's peeked over the sofa. All quiet. He dozed. Wiley sound asleep, like he had no bones; breathing heavy too. She didn't want to wake them, but Doc liked his tea a half hour before supper.

"Doc? You best not let me catch you and Wiley sleepin'. Tea's ready."

"I'm awake, Birdie. Resting and thinking, that's all. Fire's dying out. Can Jess give the logs a poke?" Doc pulled off his glasses and squeezed his eyes. "Smells like roast; shortbread too. You spoil me." He patted Wiley's ribcage. "We might need some time before we eat. I have something important to talk with you and Jess about for our Wiley here." The dog's gaze rose to Doc, but his head didn't move.

"He don't look so good. I'll get Jess from outside." Birdie quickened her heavy steps to the kitchen. Something wasn't right.

The squeal of the back screen door made her turn when it stretched open. Birdie raised a finger to her lips and pointed down the hall toward the parlor as Jess wiped his work shoes on the sisal doormat.

"Sure smells good in here," Jess said and lowered his voice when she pressed her lips together. He paused to decode her expression. "Doc all right?"

"Mmm-mmm. Doc's fine."

"Wiley then?"

Their dark eyes locked in silent conversation. She turned to the stove and stirred the gravy. "Fire's dyin'. Wiley needs some heat on his bones, and Doc's got somethin' to tell us."

As Jess changed his shoes, Birdie sensed his gaze on her back. Could have rearranged the flowers on her print dress with how hard he was looking at her. "It's Wiley," she said, without turning. Birdie took a breath to hold back tears and arranged the shortbread in a symmetrical stack on the plate. She picked up the tea tray and nodded toward the parlor. "Better find out what this all about."

The floor creaked as she followed Jess's long steps into the front sitting room. Every step filled her with trepidation. Maybe Wiley would liven up if he got a whiff of the garden on Jess's clothes.

"Here we go." Birdie kept an eye on Doc as she set the tray next to him.

"Still chilly outside, Doc," Jess said, adjusting the logs in the fireplace. He settled his gaze on Wiley. "Spring's not got here all the way yet."

"No more work this afternoon. This is Wiley's day." Doc's soul was magnified when he gazed up at Jess from behind his reading glasses.

The revitalized flames resumed their lick of Wiley's paws. His eyelids fought their weight until he gave up and lowered them. Eyes disappeared. Doc stroked the patches of thinning fur over Wiley's brows.

Birdie and Jess exchanged glances as they each took a seat across from Doc. All was quiet, except for the tick of the old farmhouse clock and the crackle of the fire. The faint linger of Charlotte's sweet, floral fragrance drifted from the upholstery of the sofa cushion. Doc sat in her spot now. Wiley's nostrils billowed in and out as he picked up the scent. As if reading the dog's thoughts, Doc whispered, "Yes, that's her perfume, dear boy. She's right here with us. I know she is." His fingers slowed and rested still between Wiley's ears. "Don't you worry...I'll never let Birdie clean these cushions."

"Wouldn't dare try, Doc." Birdie studied his deep-brown eyes, kind eyes. The lines around them turned his expression serious.

"Wiley's starting to breathe heavy. Time is short."

"What is it, Doc? Bad?" Jess's deep voice matched the concern on his face.

"I must share something with you both, which will be very important for Wiley. In my bedroom, you'll need to retrieve a package. Open Charlotte's chest at the foot of the bed and remove the wedding ring quilt, and then pull up the bottom piece of wood. Bring to me the wrapped bundle, tied in twine, you'll find inside." He used that doctor voice, controlled and calm.

"I'll get it, Doc. Can't keep still. No, I can't." Birdie stood and started her half walk, half run up the stairs. "Oh, Law, we got to talk about this..." Unable to get enough air in her lungs, she stopped and held the banister. *What's Doc up to?*

The chest groaned as she lifted the lid, the noise announcing her intrusion into Doc's private space. After she removed the quilt and set it on the bed, Birdie smoothed her hand over the pine-wood base. As many times as she'd put away that quilt, she'd never noticed the bottom piece wasn't attached. Her thick thumbnail did the trick to pry it out. A wrapped bundle waited inside, begging to be touched. She plucked it from the chest and rushed down the stairs, the package balanced as if secrets might spill.

The cushion on the overstuffed chair *whooshed* as she sat; her heart too heavy to stand. The tissue around the bundle crinkled when she leaned forward, raised her dark hand to her chest, and turned to Jess as though he might save her from bad news.

Doc took a long sip of his tea and rattled the cup back on its saucer. He slipped off his glasses, rocking them as the music of his voice started again. "Before you open this, you must know I can't explain what you are about to experience. I am a man of science, but our home is filled with heart. I've kept this secret for many years. No more. Open that package, Birdie, and marvel at what you'll see."

She eyed Doc, and then eyed the twine. She pulled the ends and it fell to the rug. The folds of the paper opened with ease—the room went quiet as the paper, too, drifted to the floor. The fire silenced its crackle. Wiley shifted his gaze to the grate, waiting for the snap and pop to start again.

Images of three birds emerged as she unfolded the fabric across her lap, big birds with glittering plumes and crowns of bright red, iridescent feathers. They seemed to shift their eyes to Wiley—*so alive.*

"I...I never seen nothin' like this before."

"Doc—" Jess stopped and stared at the fabric.

"This came from Charlotte's father, the day he died and went on to live again in 1913." Doc paused and dipped his head with a sly smile. "Yes—live on again." He placed his glasses on the tea tray and rested back against the soft cushion. "A wonder—ancient beyond comprehension. I've tried to make sense of this myself, but some things are too wondrous to explain. We all have our time—as Charlotte did. Now, magic will be part of your lives after this day."

Doc closed his eyes. "You and Jess each set a hand on one of those magnificent birds, and I'll put mine on the third. Experience what happens for our Wiley. You both will be keepers of this secret."

Heavy and smooth; not a frayed thread to be seen. Birdie's hand trembled as she touched one of the pheasant-like birds on the fabric. A tingle, much like electricity, engulfed her fingers. The reflective surface caught the sunlight and released a shimmer of vivid colors. She grazed her palm over the images on their soft cream background. Brilliant green vines with tiny white flowers wound around the birds in an endless loop. She glanced at Jess, a signal for him to reach out his hand, and nodded to Doc for confirmation. A secret knowledge washed through her; how she understood it, she'd never know. She just *knew*. Wiley would live forever.

As instructed, she set her hand on one of the birds in the fabric; Jess placed his on the second. Doc reached over, being careful not to jostle Wiley, and lowered his fingers on the third.

Birdie's chocolate eyes warmed and opened wide, wider than ever before. The birds stirred and began to undulate. Their wings stretched and strained from the fabric's surface. Her thick, work-worn fingers rolled in waves with awakened energy. She sucked in a breath as all three came alive, and then disappeared from beneath their hands. Jess gasped. She smiled with no hint of fear.

Doc turned his gaze toward the light-filled, arched window across the room. Wiley's eyes shifted to the destination, his breaths mere shallow puffs. They were there—Doc confirmed it when he smiled. Birdie stared at the bird bath in the garden, framed with velvet curtains the color of rich claret. Its cool, fresh water twinkled through the rippled glass. Perched on the rim were three glorious birds—the very same wondrous creatures under their hands only moments ago. Long, graceful tail feathers brushed the ground; their wings extended to reveal brilliant sprays of electric-blue, deep-turquoise, and luminous gold.

One after the other, the massive birds launched high above the trees and into the intense setting sun. The ripples in the water of the empty bird bath settled. Birdie trailed her gaze back to Doc, Jess...and finally to Wiley.

"Don't you worry, sweet boy," she murmured, handing the heavy cloth to Jess. His ebony eyes welled with shiny tears as he stared at it. His garden companion was leaving him. A single drop tipped and spilled on the vacant fabric. Only the winding vines remained, poised to rope back their wards. Birdie knelt on the floor and inched her way over to Wiley.

Leaning in for one last soft kiss of his head, her lips brushed the velvety flap of Wiley's ear. "Go see Miss Charlotte." She rested one hand on his rib cage as it rose for its final descent; Jess placed his on the top of Wiley's head, next to Doc's healing fingers.

"Run now. Fast as you can." Doc's firm words raced with heated energy. He inhaled, as if his own final breath, and closed his eyes.

Wiley melted under the tingle of loving hands. Maybe the family could go on without him. He wasn't sure yesterday, but today his work in this life was done. He'd be back.

A warm surge of liquid heat coursed through him. Voices, like the ring of flower bells, trailed away. The scent—hyacinths in the garden—became stronger and stronger. He was light as a puppy, bounding toward the scent and into Miss Charlotte's welcoming arms.

CHAPTER 1

Taking Flight – Present Day

Houston doesn't seem so bad from this vantage point, Jean Collins thought, staring at the twinkle lights in the perfectly manicured trees on Post Oak Boulevard, sixteen floors below her office window. The branches swayed under the weight of their lazy light strings in the humid breeze. To this Northern girl, running the air conditioner a week before Christmas was a crime, but it was a crime she'd gotten used to after so many years. Her gaze shifted to different lights of the season: taillights of status cars filled with coiffed fodder lined up to endure the hunt for a parking spot at the Galleria. She and Spence had their shopping done, and what they'd found wouldn't fit under the tree. This year's gift was about to be unwrapped in a meeting with her boss.

"This is finally going to happen," she whispered. The darkening sky transformed the floor-to-ceiling office window into a mirror. After twenty-five years of slogging through all the company's trans-formations, she still looked pretty darned good, still professional for turning fifty-three. She wore just enough makeup to accentuate her best features, mostly her penetrating, light-aqua eyes, and hide the small flaws that seemed to crop up faster and faster. The last trickle of estrogen in her body kept her skin soft and relatively unlined. Only her hair had altered drastically over the years. She made a radical change in cut and color every time the company was sold. It was her way of reinventing herself to meet the expectations of each new regime. Roy Welton, her boss and the company's president, would laugh on video conferences and welcome Jean's hair to the executive staff meeting. She'd quip back, "You'll have to dig me up six months after I'm dead to know what's under here!" She was happiest in her blond pageboy, though, and that's what the style would be from now on.

Roy was a survivor. He knew how to play the chess game of making new owners happy. Convictions changed overnight. She wasn't nearly as adept at cutting in line to christen the freshly painted fire hydrant in the rookie CEO's redecorated office. Instead, she dug in her heels to protect the balance sheet from becoming the fire hydrant. Yes, it was time for this meeting.

For so many years, she'd helped to lead change in the company. Starting today, she would lead change in her life. The belt of pudge she'd developed from stress had to be addressed when this was over. The survival of each merger and acquisition added a layer to her shell of success. That was a polite way of looking at it.

She and Spence had never wanted to move to Houston, but the decision had been a boost to their careers—at one time. Now her company seemed to be bought, sold, split, and merged with the speed individuals changed underwear. Changes were duly paid for by the loyal staff, who took on more and made less. Spence, too, complained about his work these days, bitter over the politics and lethargy within the education environment where he'd worked as a Program Manager for the past ten years. While Spence seemed to let the stress roll off his back, he showed fissures with magma seeping to the surface. Blood pressure pills held it at bay; she kept hers down with resolve.

The game she and Spence played each morning strengthened their decision to make a change. Drumming the roof of his Mini Cooper, Spence would grin and call out, "Have a wonderful day, sweetie, and if you want to quit today, go right ahead. I'll buy you a drink when you get home." Those words were like buckling a second seat belt as she drove off, even though she knew she wouldn't act on them that day.

Now that day was here. The most recent plan was for the company to centralize all of its operations in Boston. She had been asked to make the move. Of course, they didn't want her to accept the offer any more than she wanted to. The offer was just a non-litigious way of saying, *You're too old; you make too much money.* They were really saying, *We know you won't move. This allows us to get rid of you without you suing us.* She'd take the severance check. Make nice, keep up appearances, and nobody gets hurt.

Home would always be Portland, Oregon. Going to Portland had been their first move together when they left San Francisco after the wake-up call of the Loma Prieta earthquake in 1989. This time they didn't need an earthquake to shake things up. A new start, within the security of the familiar, mitigated the risk of walking away.

She and Spence now had an opportunity to find out what they really wanted in life—and what they could still attain. In anticipation of making the move, they'd purchased house in Portland when the market dipped. It waited for them. The renters had moved out. Plus, its modern style would kick-start the downsize process they both dreaded and welcomed. Her Mercedes, a must in Houston, would be a joke when they moved to Portland. Something more practical and efficient was called for, like a Volvo.

Roy knocked on the metal frame of her office door. "Hey, girly girl!" he said, setting down his overnight bag to give her a long, warm hug. Roy would always be her friend first and boss second.

"Hey back. Come on in, Roy. Have a sit." She returned to stand at the window to tower over the shoppers, the lights, over Houston itself. She held up her hand. "Don't even ask. The answer's no—Boston is on the wrong coast for Spence and me."

"Are you sure?" Roy asked. "This is a great opportunity." He had that tone, which coughed up as obligation. He was even more miserable than she was. They'd discussed the situation numerous times. At least she and Roy had a friendly, respectful relationship where brutal honesty was a comfort to both of them.

"C'mon Roy, you know those guys up there don't want me to accept the offer. You should tell them I'm coming, just to see the look on their faces. Priceless."

"I know, I know," Roy lamented. "You shaped much of this company. I'm so sorry this is happening."

"This isn't your fault. We've been through this duck-and-cover game so many times." Her feeble attempt at humor came out more bitter and caustic than she had intended. She tossed her reading glasses in the drawer and sat; her shoulders gave up the balancing act. Responsibilities rolled off all over her desk, making her lighter—*free*.

For nearly an hour, she and Roy reminisced about their most ridiculous moments, gaffes in meetings, others' career-ending scandals, and the ever-revolving door of senior executives. The discussion was actually quite pleasant. In fact, they'd belly-laughed through the most tragic incidents. These stories had shaped her as a person. Who was she after today? Strange to have started out as the company's young whippersnapper twenty-five years ago, invincible and lunging into uncharted territory to come up with the next brilliant idea. The company had been a start-up back then. Now, she was usually the oldest person in the room, mentoring younger staff, not about new ideas but on basic things: how to run an efficient meeting, teamwork, and communication skills. Many of them were more focused on updating their personal social networking pages than getting the job done.

Jean wanted to feel again—really feel. It seemed ridiculous that one-way commands eclipsed respectful discussion, capital letters shouted out anger, and emoticons replaced a real smile. At least Roy made the effort to discuss her decision in person. So many conversations about company changes had taken place behind the coward's wall: video conferencing.

After Roy left, Jean picked up her purse and fished out her keys. Her laptop and briefcase remained behind. Taking them home tonight would be a charade, just a habit, even though she'd be back in the morning. The new owners wanted a six-month transition for her to train the to-be-determined replacement. But the computer, along with all of her accomplishments, would be handed over to someone else—younger and less jaded, for sure.

Jean switched off the green-shaded library light on her desk and made a special gesture of plucking the sleek silver pen from the desk blotter. Spence had given it to her when the company was last sold. The door shut with a soft click.

Now that pleasant anticipation had turned to certainty, her body ached. As she descended in the elevator to the lobby, she hadn't banked on sadness taking over her emotions. Peeling off every stitch of her black pantsuit and tossing the pieces on the floor behind her seemed like a good idea as she walked out of the elevator. She didn't, of course. Her heels clicked through the shiny marble lobby toward the parking garage.

"This is ridiculous. Go home and celebrate, you idiot!" she muttered and pushed open the heavy glass door. Today, its weight descended like a glass ceiling. For years she opened the lobby door on the right side; today she went out through the left. Every single thing should be new. There had to be more to life than this.

As her clipped steps took her closer to her reserved spot, number 3465, Jean rehearsed her first words to Spence. She dropped in the leather seat and shut the car door with a quiet *phoomph*, glad now she'd backed into the space this morning. She could just take off. The engine of her Mercedes SL-550 thrummed with anticipation. She pressed the button to indicate the third CD, track three, reserved for this moment. To the beat of Paul Weller's "C'mon Let's Go," she put the car into drive.

Spence normally arrived home from work before Jean. There was comfort in his private greet-and-feed session with their Maine Coon cat, Mycroft. They talked to each other about their days as he pulled the evening's dinner preparations out of the refrigerator.

"Momma's got news for us tonight, big boy. Let's turn on the light so you can go out and wait for her," Spence said. Mycroft hung on his every word and marched to the door.

The back patio light flooded the small, fenced courtyard between the house and the garage. He let Mycroft out to wait for Jean. She'd be late, so he could take a little extra time with the Christmas routine tonight: turning on the icicle lights, inside and outside, and stopping for a moment at the tree in the living room to admire the mementos of their thirty-two years together. All white lights this year, with cascading see-through, chestnut-colored ribbon. Their favorite ornaments, of course, were the petite framed pictures of their Maine Coon kids who had shared their lives.

They never regretted not having real children. Sticking to the fuzzy variety fulfilled their parenting instincts. Their freedom was more important; entrepreneurs grabbing hold of what life could offer without encumbrances. It took decades to build the walls around themselves they'd now vowed to shed. In recent years, drudge and routine had become the main ingredients of their security recipe. Happiness was their early days in Portland, Oregon, when they struggled and took a dive into the unknown. Jean's company was only a start-up in the nineties. Their goal was to run back to the new.

Mycroft's picture inside its silver-frame ornament drew Spence's gaze. Mycroft had a wide, white face with splotches of orange around his nose and wise green eyes. The feathers in his ears were so long the frame cut them off. They adopted him right after losing their two previous Maine Coons after eighteen years. The house, quiet and lifeless, produced tears at unexpected prompts: a long hair pulled off a wool jacket, a glittery ball found under the furniture, or an ejected whisker poking out of the sofa cushion. The house needed a boss. Mycroft became their Velcro kitty—he stuck.

They chose Mycroft because he seemed full of life, so, antici- pating a kittenish play session after they got him home, they were baffled when Mycroft marched out of the cage, surveyed where his food, water, and litter box were, and then promptly went to sleep for nearly two days. He only wanted to be cuddled.

Reluctant to release himself from the memory's grip, Spence glanced at his watch and climbed the stairs to change into his jeans and favorite yellow sweatshirt. He grinned at the bathroom mirror. Welsh through and through, his clear brown eyes and full head of dark hair, now streaked with gray, seemed to radiate hope and promise. Younger inside than his sixty-one outer years. *Do I look like we're starting a new life tonight?*

The rumble of the garage door made him quicken his steps to the kitchen. He rushed to pop the cork from the celebratory bottle of wine, a special one he'd picked up for this moment, and pulled two glasses from the cabinet. The patio door squeaked open. The melody of Jean's familiar greetings with Mycroft filled him with light.

Spence watched Jean rub Mycroft's long, muscular orange-striped torso. Unusual for her not to have brought home her briefcase. While he was excited to hear about her meeting with Roy, he enjoyed the chance to savor this scene for a minute longer. He admired the back of her blonde pageboy cut; his favorite. And when she tucked one side behind her ear it gave her the same look as when she'd kidnapped his soul in 1979.

Jean finally came through the door pulling several long, cinnamon-colored cat hairs from her black slacks. Her smile released an odd combination of elation and sadness. She took a deep breath and said:

"I'll take that drink now, Mr. Collins!"

June came with minimal fanfare. Jean expected the transition to be more dramatic and traumatic. She slowly faded away. The last week on the job left her standing in a bucket of boredom. Colleagues stopped calling about work and meeting notices never showed up on her calendar. New projects ceased to be discussed. Her limbs had been cut off. A useless stump with a big check in her hand. Hugs had long been dished out. At this moment, she would have given the check back for one more helping.

On her first morning of freedom, she checked her Droid. She had been deleted as of close of business yesterday.

"Are they still bugging you?" Spence asked. "I'm sure they're already missing you like crazy."

"No, not really," she said, whisking her finger through old e-mails on the small screen. "Well, enough of this, how about you?"

"Couple of loose ends. I'll call them back later. They're all in their Monday morning meeting right now." Spence sounded left out of life too.

"Let's tackle the job we have ahead of us."

Jean turned and walked around the open kitchen-and-den layout and appreciated the abundance of built-in space they had in their Victorian. Her gaze trailed along the shelves of mementoes and inherited heirlooms collected over the years. She opened some cabinet doors.

"We've gotten a start on the packing, but we haven't touched these cabinets. I can't believe there's a beta hi-fi machine under here. You can't even buy the tapes anymore."

"But beta is still better technology than what's available now." Spence took a sip of his coffee with narrowed eyes.

"You haven't plugged it in for twenty-five years. Time to let go."

"What about all the fabric in the closet upstairs?"

"I know, I know. I'm just as guilty, but I'll never be able to find some of those designs again." She pointed to a shelf in the cabinet. "Let's take these tapes of the Kinks. You have albums of the American and European releases of *Schoolboys in Disgrace* upstairs in the office...on beta, on a cassette for the car, and on CD—also for the car. And you've downloaded most of the songs on iTunes. That's just one title. You have thousands of albums, Spence. I totally get you want to keep those, but can't you shed some of these extra versions? You *never* play them."

Spence stayed silent for a few moments. "But I know where they are if I want to."

Jean studied his face. If anything more were said, her words would stick like poppy seeds in his teeth. His rock music, in all its forms, documented the milestones of his sixty-one years in perfect freeze-frame. "Let's compromise. I'll donate the old bolts of fabric. I'll only keep the modern ones I'm going to use for the house, and you get rid of the old tape versions of this music. Deal?"

"All right, that's fair. But not if it's a live version that I don't have anywhere else."

That was fair—"only" the modern fabrics were still ten bolts' worth.

Stuff. Treasures quickly became junk with no place to put them. It was going to be liberating to move into an open mid-century house when they got to Portland.

"None of this furniture will work, either. All of these old knickknacks...I'm kind of sick of them ," she said and swept her hand around the room. "I poked in the attic, and there are boxes we never unpacked when we moved in here. I don't even know what's in them. And we need to do something with those plates from your mother and the bedroom furniture from my parents. What the hell are we going to do with a pewter maple-syrup pitcher from 1850? I'm sure all of these things have some value, but damn! Who has time to deal with them? I don't." The long to-do list was getting longer.

"Don't get all worked up. We both want to start new, so let's do it."

Frustrated and overwhelmed, she was sure their mental shift was the real issue. The storage problem was an excuse. Divesting of many tangible reminders of their journey together, of their identities both individual and as a couple, seemed like a betrayal.

"Here they come," Spence said. "We've never moved without a thousand lists."

It was true. She'd break through the emotion with lists: the types and quantities of moving boxes, heirlooms to be sold, short-term grocery items divided into perishables and non-perishables, appliances to be cleaned out, last-minute repairs, lists of lists she needed to create and, finally, the list of what was to be loaded in the car for the long road trip to Portland. All would be organized, categorized, marked on a timeline, and designated on a countdown calendar to moving day. Spence joked about her meticulous organizational skills, but he secretly counted on them. Every move—California to Portland, Portland to Minneapolis, and Minneapolis to Houston—ended up being a frantic circus of pulling up stakes to grab the swinging ring of a promotion. This time, the house waited patiently for their arrival.

"Yep, I've already got them started. Oh, and Little Magic is coming this afternoon to do a walk-through of the house." Jean squinted her eyes, waiting for his reaction.

"Board up! Hurricane Fannie's coming," Spence said, laughing as he struggled to replace the spotlight bulb in the stairwell.

Little Magic was the pet name they had for their realtor, Fannie Walters. A Houston Heights institution after decades in the business, she had a spitfire, unyielding personality. Fannie was all of five feet tall in her brightly colored Manolo Blahnik sandals and matching bag. The shoes were authentic, the bag a knockoff, and the jewelry always jingly. She was a true Texas gal. Their Little Magic—and she wouldn't pull any punches.

"Hey, girl! Hey, Spence!" Fannie called out as she click-clacked through the front door and jingled her way past the dining room, den, and into the kitchen. "I thought you were never going to call me to get this house sold. What took you so long? We've been talkin' for months."

"We had to wind down our jobs," Spence said, somewhat defensive. "The landscaper just finished yesterday, and Jean's been cleaning like a fiend."

"Well, the place is a prize winner. Let's walk through, startin' at the top," Fannie said as if entering battle. "Oh. All the rugs need to go. You can't cover up these beautiful antique pine floors. And I love y'all's window coverings on the first floor, but they have to come down. People want to see the bones. The house has to be all bright and airy." Fannie whirled her hands in circles as she ascended the stairs.

As they followed Fannie, Jean tugged on Spence's back pocket. He turned to her. The stunned silence blared as loud as an ambulance racing past their house. Fannie talked to the air at the top of the stairs, and still talked as she rounded the corner into the master bedroom. Spence shook his head as if to say, *Not here. We can talk about this later.*

They caught up with Fannie in the bright, sunny front bedroom, which had been turned into the office. Tall bookcases lined the entire room. Framed vintage rock concert posters adorned the wall between each one. They were stuffed with books on rock bands, pop-culture retrospectives, and antique poster art. The bottom cabinets were lined with record albums, all carefully inserted into plastic sleeves. Spence's personal lair.

"Spence, you need to take at least half of these bookcases out. They make the room small. You should take down the picture of that eyeball cartoon too." Fanny grimaced. "That's kinda creepy. People will think you smoke pot in here."

Jean watched Spence's face fall like the Hindenburg.

"What are we supposed to do with them?" Spence said. "That poster is a Bill Graham-105—a Rick Griffin—Hendrix, John Mayall, and Albert King. And a first printing too!"

Fannie gave Spence a tired scowl. "Okay...I get it, but you'll need to rent a storage unit until the house is sold. This is some tough love. I don't want you telling me it's taking too long to sell. Nobody cares about your stuff the way you do."

They had anticipated Fannie would ask them to change a few things, but Jean hadn't counted on this. The rugs they could live without; her window coverings and Spence's record albums struck a low blow. She sewed nonstop on weekends while Spence played DJ with hidden gems from his album collection. Their collaboration transformed over fifty yards of imported Dupioni silk into soft frames around their Victorian sanctuary. She could turn on a lamp and change the fabric's color and sheen—always moving forward and alive.

Jean calmed down as they escorted Fannie to the front door, resigned to making the changes. Fannie was right. Their home had to appeal to somebody else.

"If you can get the house spiffed by tomorrow, my photographer will be here on Tuesday morning. Hold on to your hats kids, you'll be off to O-rah-gon in a jiff. We'll do an open house on Sunday, startin' at noon. That's when all the looky-loos are unleashed after church." With that, Fannie clacked down the steps, clicked along the sidewalk, and threw her handbag on the passenger seat of her big, beige Cadillac Escalade.

As Spence continued to wave at Fannie, he leaned over to Jean. "This is going to be a pain in the ass. I can't believe we have to take all this stuff to storage."

"Yep, big ole pain in the ass," she said and turned to go into the house to tackle the window coverings. Spence followed her, his steps heavy up the stairs on his way to the office to empty three of the bookcases.

The first valance made a ghastly sound as Jean ripped the fabric from the wood frame over the living room window. She had attached them with Velcro so they were easy to pull down for their annual cleaning. "Silk doesn't hold up, anyway," she muttered, noticing the beginnings of dry rot on the inner edges. The relentless hot sun had baked them to a crisp. She pulled the drapes off the rods and threw them on the floor. A hairy black spider raced away from the hem, seeking safety somewhere else. She stomped on it with her sneaker and scraped the remains across the silk.

Spence made twelve stacks on the floor of the office as he pulled the albums out of the bookcases. At least he could keep M through Z intact for now, but A through L would need to be packed up. He pulled one album out of a stack of Bs and inspected the cover of David Bowie's *Pin Ups*. Humming "Don't Bring Me Down," he slipped the album from the sleeve and scanned both sides for a scratch. He took a deep whiff of the woody aroma inside the aged cardboard cover, remembering the moment when he rested the needle on this album for the first time in 1973. He slid the vinyl disk back in its protective paper sleeve.

Spence stood, lifted his Bill Graham *Flying Eyeball* poster from its hook, and stared at the signature. The warmth of Rick Griffin's handshake radiated in the gold ink. He'd met the artist at a record show in San Francisco just before being killed in a motorcycle accident in 1991. What a privilege to have the poster in his collection.

Needing a break, he went downstairs to check on Jean's progress with the window coverings. As he came through the dining room, he spotted her folding the last drape. The rest were stacked in a pile by the front door.

"Wow, what a difference!" His voice echoed off the bare windows and sailed around the walls. "So much light in here. The living room seems twice as big. I think I like—" He flinched when Jean threw the drape on the floor and covered her face with her hands. She hadn't cried in years. He hurried to her and wrapped his arms around her shaking shoulders.

"All that work. Now we're just throwing them away," Jean sobbed. She buried her head in his chest.

"Honey, we talked about this. The curtains were...*are* beautiful, but people are buying the house, not the curtains. I'm doing the same thing upstairs." He ran his fingers through her hair. "What's going on here? Talk to me."

"They threw me away."

A surface crack. She was right; they had thrown her away. This smart, accomplished businesswoman—his wife—was today transformed back into the young girl of twenty he'd married thirty-two years ago. She had returned to him, needed him, and counted on his strength. As he let her cry, Spence gazed out the curtainless window. He wondered whether, at sixty-one, if the door was locked to him too. Was he holding her, or was she holding him? This next chapter in their lives held so many unknowns.

"Can you take these out? I can't—" She wiped her eyes on the sleeve of his sweatshirt.

Spence released her to pick up the curtains piled at her feet. On one side peeked out a fluffy, orange-and-white striped tail.

"Tell Mycroft you're all right. You know how he worries when either of us gets upset."

By sunset, the fabric spilled out of the garbage bin on the side of the house. The silk had given up the fight to crawl back to the safety of the windows.

The following Saturday, Fannie pushed the For Sale sign deep into the ground in front of their house, accompanied by its little companion, Open Sunday. Her delicate sandals doubled for work boots considering how hard Fannie jammed those signs into the parking strip.

"Oh, I almost forgot—one more thing—and don't laugh." Fannie dug in her purse and pulled out a small box.

Unsure of where Fannie was going with this, Jean eyed her while she opened the box. Inside was a small plastic statue of a bearded man in a long robe.

"A Saint Joseph statue. He's the patron saint of real estate. You bury him on his head in the garden by the front steps while you say the doohickey prayer on the little instruction sheet. Real estate magic."

Spence and Jean laughed, but Fannie was dead serious.

"Okay, boss." She gave Fannie a salute.

After about four weeks, fifteen showings, three open houses, and a nod to St. Joe, Fannie called with the big news. The house was sold.

The only requests the buyers made were to keep Mycroft and leave the watercolor right on the dining room wall.

The watercolor rendering brought the house to life in meticulous detail: delicate gingerbread shingles, handmade spindles, and even the lush, Carolina jasmine along the wrought iron fence. On the roof's peak, doves and cardinals preened and fluttered in the warm, humid breeze. The bay windows showed their first two Maine Coon cats and Mycroft.

As much as they were anxious to leave, a piece of them would always remain behind in this neighborhood, and in this house. Mycroft, of course, wasn't part of the deal.

"Check out what I got," Jean announced, bumping a wide box against the jamb as she came through the back door.

"Honey, no more stuff *please!* We're almost all packed." Spence stopped the packing tape dispenser in mid-screech.

"This is the perfect solution to driving Mycroft out to Portland. A cabana. It'll fit in the backseat of the Volvo. I measured."

"A ca-what?" Spence was wearing out his last nerve. "That's a carrier for a ninety-pound dog."

"Right! He needs the room. We can't put him in a regular cat cage for six days. He'd get a muffin top. This will let him stretch out on a big blanket and have his food and water whenever he wants. We can put all his toys in here, and then pick the whole thing up and take him into the hotel at night. Like I said, it's perfect."

"Actually, not bad—you're right. How about you and Mycroft trade off driving, and I'll ride in the cabana."

"Deal! I'll roll you some kibble every hundred miles."

The last box was finally loaded on the van, the paperwork signed, and the kitchen counters had their final swipe with the cleaning rag. For each move over the years, she and Spence had stood and watched everything they owned drive away.

"What if the truck goes east, and we never see any of our stuff again?" she said without taking her eyes off the moving van.

"Yeah, I'd be pretty pissed if my copy of Green Day's *21st Century Breakdown* disappeared." Spence kissed her forehead.

They did one last nostalgic walk through the house. The emptiness echoed the remnants of laughing with neighbors, sparring over politics during holiday dinners, and also the wasted, sleepless nights worrying about work.

"You ready? Time to scoop up Mycroft and get the cabana on the road," Spence said, anxious, Jean knew, to beat the traffic.

"Let's breeze. I'll leave Fannie's present on the counter by the keys." She ran her hand across the top of the long box wrapped with a poufy satin bow. It contained a bright-yellow Coach handbag. Yes, Fannie earned her commission, but she was worth much more.

Mycroft settled in on his king-size cotton blanket after a few hours of squeaky discussion. He woke only to ask for a handful of his kibble and a squirt from the water bottle. Every day of the six-day trip became a little cooler, a little greener. With familiar ceremony, they carried the cabana into the hotel each night with Mycroft on full display to cooing guests. They were reduced to two servants transporting King Tut.

CHAPTER 2

Portland, Oregon

"Have you thought more about what you want to do, Jean?" Spence asked as they drove through the Columbia Gorge. "You've mentioned sewing and volunteering at the animal shelter, but do you think that's going to be enough?"

"For the first time, I can honestly say I don't know," Jean answered, looking out the window. "I want to do something tactile. I need to work with my hands. My brain is tired." She turned back to him. "Are you still set on starting a record store?"

"Art and music, baby. Two of life's food groups. Bill and I will take this year to sniff out the inventory. We need a business plan. Can you help us? We also thought about adding a coffee bar and book section."

"You should. Of course I'll help you guys. Don't get in over your heads, though. Start small and build up. I'm hoping the change of scenery inspires me too. Portland's much more conducive to being creative than Houston."

"Something will happen and then you'll be off and running."

"We're getting close, Spence. We're about ten minutes away."

Jean admired the park-like setting in their neighborhood. Every house was different; some were built in 1910, while others were custom-built in the early 1960s. The eclectic assortment was a reflection of the people who lived in them: retired couples walking their dogs, families with young children, and writers and artists working in solitude. The one consistent feature was the trees—hundreds of enormous evergreen trees. They filtered and cooled the air beneath their cone-laden branches.

Spence pulled into the driveway of their house in Milwaukie, a suburb bordering the southeast side of the city, to the welcome of a seventy degree breeze and bright, cloudless sunshine. September was an incredible time of year in Portland. Travel-weary and hungry, Jean opened the car door and drank in the clean pine aroma.

"Mmmm...Just like Christmas," she said, instantly energized by its magic. Their new life in Portland was an early Christmas present, and they anticipated a surprise inside.

Spence retrieved the key from the lockbox turned to her with a wide grin. "If the secret of this weather gets out, everybody will want to move here."

Mycroft lifted his head, eyes half closed, to greet the new woodsy aromas wafting over him through the open car doors. When the sunshine flickered on his face, he rolled on his back and drifted off to sleep. The squirrels scratched a barber-pole path around the huge tree trunks, but Mycroft wasn't interested.

Already making the to-do lists in her head, Jean surveyed the front of the house. Pine needles and broken branches covered the roof, and spiders seemed much too comfortable in the corners of the triangle-shaped, clerestory windows. They would need every minute of the two days before the moving truck arrived to get the place ready.

Spence fiddled with the lock. One of the large double doors swung open with a long groan. As they stepped across the threshold, their noses wrinkled.

"Oooh...eee, I know it's only been four months since the renters moved out, but it smells like 1963 in here!" Spence complained. "Let's leave the door wide open until we bring in Mycroft."

"We'll air it out. The house definitely needs a good cleaning—and a lot of paint," Jean said, calculating the number of gallons the walls would take.

"And a new front door." The door groaned as Spence swung it back and forth.

"I've been living in this house through the pictures for two years. Let's poke around."

"Hey! A gift basket." Spence nodded to the kitchen island.

Jean picked the card out of the cellophane wrap. "It's from Bill and Linda! I bet they called the property manager to let them in. There's salami, nuts, crackers, mustard and—oh baby—dark chocolate. Bill stuck a cigar in here for you too. Let's give them a call after we bring in the bags."

She ran her fingers over the granite countertop and grimaced at the months of dust layered over the counters, light fixtures, and bamboo floors. Everything looked gauzy under the veil of grit.

"Perfect." Spence gave her a long hug in the echo of the empty space.

Even through all the grime, the house held potential. The only source of light at the front was through the original basket-weave glass in the dramatic triangular windows. Those clerestory windows would sparkle and dance like morning sunshine on lake water when they were cleaned. The back of the house was all glass. The step-down living room, with its cedar-beam ceiling, had floor-to-ceiling windows. An unobstructed view of a patio with a rock-walled, tiered backyard filled the house with light. They could walk in the front door and keep on going, right into the arms of the season outside. She imagined a lush garden of bright-red, orange, and purple native plants. They would replace the current view of the dead branches, tall weeds, and neglected perennials.

"How about a big bird bath under the tree?" he said, pointing to the base of the eighty-foot cedar at the edge of the patio.

She nodded her agreement. "Okay—enough dreaming. Time to bring in Mycroft from the car. He's going to love it here. He can sit on his butt and watch *Animal Planet* out the window."

With the screens in and the sliding doors open, the house breathed with relief. Nearly all the glass doors opened as if gliding on butter, except one. The lock was broken on the one off the small upstairs bedroom, which they intended to use as their walk-in closet. A replacement latch from 1963 wouldn't be easy to find. That little project would have to wait since the one door wouldn't be opened, anyway. For now, the lock could be minimally secured if pulled up with a wrench.

Jean took a break from the boxes to meet Linda Flannery downtown for lunch. Spence spent the day with Linda's husband, Bill, in search of album finds in the Hawthorne District. They had been close as a foursome for over twenty-five years, even through all the moves Jean and Spence made since leaving Portland.

The first to arrive at Jake's Grill, Jean perused the long menu from the corner booth in the window. She longed for girlfriend conversation over fresh fish. Houston's definition of fresh fish resembled a bottom-feeding Gulf bug. And friendship? Well, she had known pleasant enough people but never clicked with anyone as she had Linda. Jean's face lit up when Linda slipped into the booth and beamed at her. She looked exactly the same, only better, with more wisdom in her eyes. She still wore Indian print dresses and went without fussy makeup, and her long, brown hair tickled her waist. They grabbed hands and all the years filled themselves in within moments. The meal became superfluous.

"What would you do with a year off to do anything you wanted?" Jean asked, truly seeking inspiration. Normally, Spence was the one who struggled, while she plowed forward with complete conviction. Now, she was the one floundering.

Linda was thoughtful for a moment. "I would love to learn sign language," Linda said—right out of the air. She sounded committed too.

Jean's eyes welled. "I want to be passionate again. All I did was work. Sewing is a fun hobby, but—" She squeezed Linda's hands across the table. "I want to do something really important."

"But you've done a lot—achieved so much. I don't know anyone else who could have survived so many mergers and acquisitions in the wicked, wicked entertainment business."

"Selling fun can be no fun. No, I've made a lot of money for people. 'Art Isn't Easy', as Stephen Sondheim wrote."

"Why don't you start small and volunteer? You made all of those flannel pet blankets for Best Friends Animal Sanctuary one year. They loved it, and so did you. Think about it. Or, maybe we can help Bill and Spence run the store."

"*That* I can't imagine." Jean laughed at the thought. "Those two have their own way of looking at the world. I'm sure they'll do just fine. I'm going to help them with their business plan, though. Spreadsheets are calling me back. The guys are hopeless at reining in the numbers. Budgets aren't exactly on the top of their list of priorities."

"Dive into that fabric you have in the closet. It'll be therapeutic. Don't go backwards, okay?"

That was a suggestion Jean wanted to take.

On the way home from lunch, Jean stopped by Powell's Books to cruise through the stacks for ideas on mid-century designs. She'd start by making a modern Christmas tree skirt and pillows for the loveseats in the living room. As she turned from the cash register, she spotted a book on sign language and smiled. *Linda has her priorities in order.*

Linda's words rang in her ears as she drove home. *Think about it.* She turned off the CD playing Bryan Ferry's cover of "Simple Twist of Fate." What would life be like without Vivaldi's *Four Seasons* or the blues of B. B. King? Tex-Mex dinners on Friday nights wouldn't be the same without the Beatles and Ella Fitzgerald. Life would change if she couldn't hear, see, speak, touch, or smell the pine air. Each one of these gifts was so important, and she took them for granted every day. Linda was right. She listened to the quiet in the car as she wound down River Road. Even the engine noise seemed like an intrusion.

As Jean crawled into to bed, she set her design book on the night-stand, took off her reading glasses, and turned to Spence. She held up her hand and bent her two middle fingers, leaving only her pinky, forefinger, and thumb. He smiled, kissed her good night, and mir-rored the gesture, saying aloud, "I love you too."

"I looked that up on the Internet when I got home. How did you know what that meant?" she asked.

"A girl in college taught me. She was deaf."

"A girlfriend?"

"No, just a classmate. But I think she had a crush on me. I was trying to explain to her what music sounded like—not an easy thing to do. It worked a little too well because she did that hand motion. Communicating with someone who's deaf leaves everything open to interpretation. I had to *show* her I wasn't interested. Uncomfortable dilemma. I'll never forget the experience."

"Huh . . ." She switched off the light.

The goose-down pillows seemed softer in the dark. She imagined herself blind. Her senses took over as she listened to Spence's streams of breath in and out. They slowed as he drifted off to sleep. Every sound was magnified, even the rustle of the sheets. She rested her hand on Spence's head and felt his heat radiate up through his hair to warm her fingers. Mycroft's rump was a solid lump against her stomach as he slept peacefully between them. Mycroft synchronized his breaths with the rise and fall of her own against his back. She moved her hand in a dark trail to Mycroft's head and grazed the delicate feathers of his ears. She stroked the smooth fur over his closed eyes, down to the short, bristly hairs on top of his nose, and up the strong cheek-bones of his broad face. Mycroft rolled on his back at her touch and let out a long, slow moan. The fur on his chest was silky. She worked her fingers to the warm, supple skin underneath. It even felt pink. Her fingers slowed as she drifted off to the lazy rumble of his purr vibrating her hand.

Touch is magic.

CHAPTER 3

The Dinner Party

Jean and Spence hosted their first dinner party in the new house with Phil and Patty, their former neighbors from their years on Nineteenth Street in the Irvington neighborhood. They arrived in a blaze of old stories. A free-spirited couple with an outrageous sense of humor, they both moved through life a little off from center. Phil was passionate. He collected vintage anything with a Christmas theme. Patty loved hockey. The four of them reminisced, laughed, and toasted themselves. Nothing had changed, but everything was different and new. The sobering moment of the evening, though, was when Spence poured wine at dinner. Phil refused and announced he'd been struggling with diabetes. One thing had indeed changed.

"When did you find out, Phil?" Spence said, trying to imagine not having a rich cabernet to accompany his Friday night cigar.

"Looking like Santa Claus has its drawbacks. Quite a shock to change my diet—for Patty too, since she's the cook."

"Phil doesn't drink," Patty chimed in, "but he makes up for no happy hour by going to estate sales. Now he buys twice as much."

The conversation quickly turned to Phil's passion: collecting vintage Christmas items at estate sales. Phil was a pro. He had a relationship with every big dealer in town and got the inside scoop on how to find heirlooms of the best quality.

"Oh, you have no idea," Phil laughed. "We moved to West Linn just so we could get a bigger house to hold everything. You remember only the basement being full in our old house. I still have all of that, but now the garage is packed with lawn decorations, and the den's completely lined with those pipe-cleaner table-top trees. Three of the bedrooms are stuffed with lighted reindeers and nativity scenes." Phil rolled his eyes, aware of his hobby's silly appearance, but there wasn't even a hint of guilt in his voice. "We're going to retire on the proceeds in a few years. I want to sell it all as a single collection, maybe at auction, for a million dollars. Now's not the time, though—everybody's way too cheap, and the market stinks. I'm not giving my treasures away."

"C'mon, Phil, you said the same thing when we used to live here. What—over twenty years ago?" Spence teased. "You'll never be able to let go. You're a hoarder."

Spence remembered being introduced to the collection. He had to shimmy through Phil and Patty's basement, side-stepping along the rows and rows of old ornaments, bubble-light sets, figurines, kugels, and lead tinsel, all in their original boxes. His particular passion was Shiny Brite bulbs from the 1940s. They were stacked from the floor to the rafters. Phil even looked like Santa Claus with his bushy gray beard, barrel chest, and sweet smile.

"I can put my powers to good." Phil gazed around the living room. "Jean, replace some of your stuff. These lamps are too traditional. You need more fun in a house like this. Go wild! Let's do a few estate sales and get vintage teak furniture and big, gaudy ceramic lamps in bright colors. I see them everywhere. And sixties ornaments that would look fab on your Christmas tree this year. You can borrow them."

"Okay, I'll bite," Jean said, sitting up straight. "Let's go to an estate sale. Even if I don't buy anything, you'll be fun to watch in action."

Spence eyed Jean and shook his head. Of course she'd love to spend the day with Phil, rummaging through somebody else's stuff in search of new treasures. An episode of the *Phil and Jean Show* itched to make a premiere.

"If you come home with any more of those pipe-cleaner trees and Santa candles, I'm cancelling Christmas," Patty said.

"Okay, we don't want that. Phil, you can't buy anything, but there are two things you can help me find: A bird bath for the yard and a chest to put at the foot of the bed to hold blankets—just something old and beat up, not valuable or anything. I'll sand and paint it a fun color to match the bedspread I'm going to make."

As they wound down the evening, Phil vowed to search for just the right estate sale to attend. "I'll do some sniffing, and I'll call you as soon as I find one."

Jean grinned, raised her hands over her head, and shouted, "Yea!" as Phil and Patty went out the door.

Spence stood in the entryway, glaring at her with his arms crossed.

CHAPTER 4

Letting Go

The September morning was cool and crisp as Raleigh Coulter pulled his silver Porsche 911 to the curb in front of his mother's bungalow on Northeast Nineteenth Street. The old Irvington neighborhood looked pretty good these days, but Mary's house hadn't kept up with the beautiful neighboring restorations. Maybe a good thing, in his opinion. As one of the oldest and most popular of Portland's historic districts, Irvington had regularly seen skyrocketing housing prices and managed to hold steady through the numerous economic dips. Untouched Craftsman bungalows reigned as prized jewels to young professional couples and house flippers.

Raleigh shut off the engine and sat in silence as he gazed at the front yard, seeing himself at the age of seven. He'd played in the leaves every fall from that maple tree. It was twice the size now. Forty-three years ago there wasn't an invisible line between having everything and nothing. Those days sounded pretty good at this moment. *But this feels pretty good too*, he thought as he rubbed his fingers over the steering wheel's hand-stitched leather. He didn't regret springing for this beauty when the stock tip went so well last fall. He didn't regret it—even now.

The thrill of turning inside tips into big cash with OPM—other people's money—couldn't be matched. As a broker, tips were his lifeblood, along with putting his clients into funds with high commissions. This time, though, he'd gotten caught with some bum information from that bastard, Nash Winthrop, his roommate at Yale back in the eighties. How could his buddy screw him over so badly? A bet on the market moves now proved to be a poison-filled garden. He'd eaten the shiny apple named VEY Steel Company. Instead of getting a thrill from the stress, his life was crumbling with desperation. He could lose everything.

Nash's information about VEY Steel's pending merger announcement seemed solid enough, so he'd purchased the stock as it plummeted on a disappointing quarterly earnings report. The company made themselves a great target for some quick cash, since the stock would soar once the news of the acquisition broke in the media. The hundred and fifty grand he'd borrowed from his mother's investment fund could have churned into a quick three hundred. Buy the shares at the bottom; sell them for double the price. He planned to pay the money back—his mother being none the wiser. Now, he had nothing to show for it except a mountain of debt.

Raleigh recalled the moment two days ago when he found out this deal turned rotten. His body went numb when his buddy called to say VEY Steel's negotiations fell apart. The merger evaporated. The only people flying high in this deal were the lawyers, stuffing themselves on the flock of lawsuits. Every day the stock tumbled widened the gap of what he owed to his mother's account. Now he had to find cash, or get new clients—a lot of new clients—into the Dromov Fund. Dromov paid him ten grand for every new client. He'd invested a good portion of his mother's money in the fund too. The statements looked stellar; returning the 18 percent interest as promised. But Dromov hadn't returned his calls. *Strange*. This whole process with his mother had to be sped up, or he'd need to find another deal. His mother seemed like a safer bet, if he could only convince her to liquidate her house and move into a senior living complex.

At least Mary allowed him to help manage her finances—she'd

agreed to add his name on her checking account. She wanted to simplify her life and didn't want to be bothered to pay bills, balance the checkbook, or even keep up with the array of medications for her litany of issues: high blood pressure and cholesterol, memory blips, and clotting problems. At eighty-six, Mary should feel lucky to still be ambulatory and have most of her faculties. He had to convince her to sell the house and all the stuff in it. *So much damned stuff.*

Time to glove up for round three of this conversation. Mary could be so unrealistic, and her reluctance to make a change was at her, and his, expense. What if she fell? Besides, Mary had what she needed to live comfortably. The hefty chunk she'd received from the mill after his dad was killed in the accident kept her in tall cotton. It was all going to be his at some point, anyway. Not too long.

"Show time," he muttered, thumping the steering wheel with the rhythm of his words. He ran his fingers through his wavy gray hair in his rearview mirror. The deep tan from his golf trip to Palm Springs last month made his olive eyes dance. Not bad for turning fifty-five this year. He swayed more important people than his mother every day. He could do this. Too bad he couldn't sway his wife when she walked out for some doctor five years ago.

His anxiety eased with the gentle, muffled thump of quality as he shut the car door. God, he loved the sound: *phoomph.*

As Raleigh sauntered up the steps to his mother's Craftsman bungalow, he admired the shine he'd been able to achieve on his black Ferragamo loafers. The reflection of a bird shot behind the shadow of his head as it crossed the top of the leather. The thing better not relieve itself on his freshly pressed suit.

The thumb lever on the brass handle depressed without resistance. He pushed open the heavy, solid-oak front door. *When will she ever learn to lock this door? Anyone can walk in here. Mary is so trusting.*

"Hey, Mom, it's me," Raleigh called out.

"I'll be right down. Give me a minute," Mary answered from one of the bedrooms at the top of the stairs. He heard the floorboards creak, and then the groan of the lid on the old chest in her bedroom.

What is she doing?

"Take your time. You should keep the front door locked."

Grateful to have a few minutes alone, he did a quick scan around the downstairs rooms. As the second owners of the 1921 bungalow, Mary and Jim hadn't changed a thing when they moved here from Richmond, Virginia, in 1945. He put a mental price tag on a few of her things as he roamed. Until now, he never appreciated the artistic details of the stained-glass light fixtures and hand-hewn oak beams in this old house. He admired the original crystal knobs on the doors and the Stickley lamps in the living and dining rooms. The intimate sitting area adjacent to the entryway housed his father's collection of mystery novels. His parents would sit together by its little fireplace of elaborate tile work. Jim read while Mary worked on one of her bird needlepoints.

Raleigh flicked the dust on one of the leaded-glass lampshades to admire the kaleidoscope of rich colors. The motes swirled in the late-afternoon sunlight. He made a mental note to call an architectural salvage company. They might give him a good price on some of the decorative details. If he sold them separately from the house, the overall results would get a boost. They'd be licking their lips for this stuff, especially all of the old Craftsman chandeliers, sconces, and hardware. He'd substitute reproductions to replace the originals before the house was sold. *More creaks of the floorboards upstairs.*

Faded needlepoint squares of birds, trapped in their frames behind clouded glass, dotted the walls of the entire living room. "Birds flying nowhere," he muttered.

Mary always had a needlepoint going. Sure enough, on her favorite chair by the front window lay a half-finished one in its wooden hoop. He inspected the robin on the cream-colored linen, a needle hanging from its most recent stitch. He jerked around when Mary entered the room. The needle stuck in his fingertip as he gathered up the thread.

"Ow!" He pulled out the sharp steel and tossed the hoop on the chair.

"Hello, dear! Sorry for the wait. I couldn't find something upstairs," Mary said and stepped toward the kitchen. An odd look on her face. He wondered if she even remembered what she was searching for upstairs.

Mary had purposely taken her time to come down the stairs, he knew. So irritating to play this cat-and-mouse game with her. He sucked at the droplet of blood forming on his finger.

"I've made a decision, Raleigh." Mary pulled two coffee cups from the cupboard. "I'm sure you'll be very happy." Raleigh snapped up his head in anticipation of her next words. "I'm going to move a bit south of here and take an apartment at Milwaukie Manor. A few friends from my book club live there. The change will be good for me." Mary paused, as if contemplating the effect of her words. "I thought about what you said, and you're right. I should be more social. And the complex has a bus and driver whenever I need it. I hate to admit this, but I've had a bit of a mishap with the old Bird."

The first part of Mary's proclamation faded with those words. He'd counted on that sky-blue Thunderbird to be in perfect condition. The car hardly had any miles on it and would fetch a pretty penny from a collector. Mary and Jim had searched for just the right one back in 1963 as a celebration of his dad's promotion at the lumber mill. Of course the car had to be another damn bird.

"What happened? Are you okay?"

"I'm fine, but one of his back wings is a bit dented. Poor thing. No worries, he can still fly. I got a bit dizzy and backed into a post at the Fred Meyer. I think I should leave the driving to someone else."

"Why do you always have to personify everything as a bird? Now the car's a bird. God, Mom, the car doesn't need a vet—a body shop might help, though."

"Anything can be alive if it's part of my life and means something special to me. Not you, but me." Mary's defenses reared up unexpectedly.

"Forget it, Mom." *Don't get her riled.* "So, when do you want to move in to this place? Milwaukie Hill?"

"No, Milwaukie *Manor*, and I need to give them the move-in deposit by next week. Can you pay them, please? My book club friend, Helen, showed me around, and I think I'd really enjoy living there. They have everything I need, and the view of the river is spectacular. I talked with the sales office and signed on the spot when they told me there was a one-bedroom apartment available with a river view. So, I need to decide what I'm taking with me. I guess I'll sell the rest. Aren't there people who do that sort of thing?"

Raleigh heard it in her voice; she sounded overwhelmed. She tended to talk fast and ramble. "When did you decide, Mom? I didn't know anything about this. Did you check them out?" Mary's decision, without his approval, bubbled up his anger. "You have no idea if these people are reputable, or even how much it is. How much is it, by the way?" Raleigh questioned her, and also himself, about flip-flopping on the issue. He should be happy with this development.

"I think so," Mary said, not directly answering the question. "I have savings and Social Security, plus I should get quite a bit when the house is sold. The market's pretty healthy in this neighborhood. Some of my things are quite valuable."

"What were you looking for upstairs?"

A slight hesitation. "Some fabric—very special fabric. I wish I could remember because I want to take it with me. Eagles and osprey fly by my new apartment. I'm right on the Willamette River."

"Is the fabric valuable?"

"More than you can imagine, Raleigh. Yes, more than you can imagine. Very old."

"What's this thing look like? Maybe I can help you find it."

"Birds. Beautiful birds. They're magical...changed my life."

"What do you mean? Like really magical, or just to you?" He narrowed his eyes, waiting for an answer.

"Really magical. It's from Egypt. Thousands of years old—yes—thousands."

"Huh..."

Raleigh made another mental note to search the house. Maybe it was valuable. One of his clients, an art and antiques dealer in London, might be able to move the thing if he found it before she did. Egyptian artifacts were worth a fortune. He shook himself out of his thoughts.

"Don't worry. I'll handle the arrangements." Now in control, his enthusiasm resurfaced. "There's an estate sale company, Hawkins & Company, here on Broadway. They'll come in and value everything you want to sell. The owner is a client of mine. Judy Hawkins can handle all the details. I'm sure she'd be happy to help."

Raleigh couldn't have hoped to make this much progress. If he moved on this quickly, Judy might conduct the estate sale in the next two weeks, and then the house could be listed.

"I can take possession of the apartment next week if you make the deposit right away," Mary said and poured coffee in two mugs.

"No problem. Why don't you sort through the house over the next few days and mark what you want to take with you. I'll go by Milwaukie Hill and make the deposit this afternoon, and then you can move in by Saturday." His mood brightened. "Mom, I gotta go. I'll make some calls and get back to you this afternoon." Raleigh moved toward the front door.

"Milwaukie Manor. And you didn't even drink your—"

As he walked out the door, he left Mary standing in the doorway of the kitchen holding two mugs.

Mary Coulter stood at the window and took a sip of her coffee. Her heart sank when the tires of her son's fancy car ran over the already-dead squirrel in the road. Slow down. A good man would have at least swerved to go around the poor soul.

She might be old, but she knew about good men. Her adopted father, Doc, was a good man. Jess, her family's workman, was a good man. James Coulter, her dear husband, who died too soon, an exemplary man. Her only son wasn't. Hard to admit, but sadly true.

Mary turned and gave herself an imaginary pat on the back.

Informing Raleigh of her decision to move to Milwaukie Manor propelled her forward. She had resisted for so long due to Raleigh's relentless hounding for her to sell the house. It had become difficult to maintain, and everything in it reminded her of a different life. Time for a fresh start. The last chapter of this life couldn't start soon enough. Besides, the family would always be there with her, with or without all these things, as long as she found the fabric..

Anxious to get back upstairs, she'd need every minute of daylight to look for the fabric and sort through the closets. Each step on the narrow staircase brought her closer to the next stage of her life. Only she could tackle this project, a parting wave to so many of her treasures. But one treasure meant more to her than anything: the delicately wrapped and tied square of precious fabric. It changed everything from ordinary to magic.

All of these trinkets, which held so much value to her over the years, quickly became insignificant when she couldn't find the one thing she wanted most. Frustrating. She could have sworn the chest held the fabric. Little details came to her with crystal clarity; important issues evaporated and stumped her. Somewhere, probably in plain sight...*but where?* "C'mon old gal, let's get started," she whispered with shaky confidence. "Raleigh is *not* going to get his greedy hands on it. He doesn't deserve to have something so precious."

The chest in her bedroom was empty when she pulled out the wedding ring quilt to take with her to Milwaukie Manor. Now she rummaged through the hall closet and began to remove boxes, stacking them in haphazard piles on the floor. Cartons of delicate, lead-glazed Christmas ornaments tinkled as she carried them to the guestroom and set them on the bureau. Her hands tingled. Many of them belonged to Miss Charlotte's family. All were carefully rewrapped with meticulous care and packed in their original boxes each New Year's Day as part of the ceremony of dismantling the tree. Doc's wife died before he adopted Mary, but Charlotte remained a loving specter in the old house in Richmond; her ghost mother. The smells and sounds of those holidays engulfed her: the scrumptious aromas from Birdie's secret recipes, the ring of caroling voices at the front door, and the stifled giggles when Doc attempted "Good King Wenceslas" over the years. All of these moments, like the ornaments inside, were preserved in delicate tissue. She and Jim cherished the tradition every year until his death in 1969, a terrible year.

The hall closet beckoned. Mary reached inside and gasped. A rectangular white box, tied with faded pink ribbon, sat on the worn hardwood floor. The bow, smashed flat, held the weight of so many Christmas celebrations. She wouldn't, she couldn't, open this box. She carried it to the guestroom as though a priceless addition to the Crown Jewels. Sitting on the edge of the bed and placing the box in her lap, she pictured with perfect clarity what was inside. A cut of this bow would be a sacrilege. Her hand tingled as she ran her fingers along the ribbon. The day when Doc first handed her this box filled her with light. The cluttered room faded to that hot summer of 1931, the year she became part of Doc's life.

So hungry. The lamp in the living room window urged her forward to the house on the corner with the big porch. The dark would descend soon. Mary slapped at the mosquitoes buzzing around her plump legs, emerging for their nightly feast. *Go up the walkway.* A quest to feel anything soft, cool, and not biting her. Her feet sore, sleep could be a mother. She couldn't make sense, at six years of age, of not having her father, or anybody, now.

She'd wandered all through the afternoon in the hot sun, since the terrible thing had happened this morning. Daddy told her to wait on the sidewalk. He said he was thirsty and would be right back. The commotion had terrified her. He lay so still in the road when he flew out of the swinging door covered in blood. The sound of the door banging against the wooden wall scared her anew.

Big, burly men descended, one after the other, to kick and beat her daddy. She screamed at them, but in all the commotion, no one paid any mind to the dark-haired little girl at the edge of the sidewalk. Fear took over her senses. The men smelled bad, like sweat and dirt. Mary retreated to the recesses of the store next door, her blue blanket tucked under her arm. Daddy wouldn't move. She sat in the corner while a crowd formed around him. The policemen came. She and Daddy always hid from policemen. They took him away. As she wandered down the sidewalk, people stared at her as they went by and whispered.

Hours later, she watched the large colored woman clean the front porch window of the big house on the corner. The woman turned as she wiped the glass and glanced at her. She had a kind face and a big white apron. The woman opened the front door and rushed inside the house, like she was scared of something. Then she came back out and lumbered down the steps. Mary didn't know if she should run into her arms or away to the shadows. In the end, she remained frozen in the heat.

"Child, what you doin' out here? Where's your momma and daddy?" the woman whispered, looking around with wide eyes. "Law, there's a story here. You better come on in the house."

The colored woman picked her up. Her arms, so strong, were warm and soft. Her flower-print house dress, damp with sweat, smelled earthy. Mary touched the patch of bumpy pink skin on one of the woman's dark arms. Releasing her muscles from their wary stance, she buried her head in the woman's chest and tried to wrap her short legs around her big waist.

"Doc! Jess! We got company comin'!" the woman called out. She did a half walk, half run through the front door, down the hall, and into the kitchen.

The inside of the house went by in a blur. No one had ever called her "company" before. When they arrived in the kitchen, the back screen door squeaked open. In walked a tall, burly colored man and a well-dressed white man with deep-brown eyes. The white man's wild gray hair reached out in a hundred different directions. They descended on her like a new-found puppy.

"My name is Doc, this here is Birdie, and he's Jess," the white man said. He pointed to each of them in turn and ended with a poke to her tummy. "And who might you be?" He stooped to inspect her from behind his glasses; his string tie tickled her scalp. He placed his hands on her each side of her face, cupping her cheeks. Soft hands.

"Mary," she responded in a barely audible whisper. "Daddy's gone on the sidewalk."

"Well, goodness gracious, Miss Mary. You just call me Doc."

Doc released her face and placed his hand on her forehead, poked around her neck, and thumped on her back. He picked up each foot and inspected her toes. Tapping her mosquito-bitten legs, he said, "I bet those itch." Doc turned and whispered to the others. "Good Lord! She appears to be all right but needs to have something hardy to eat, a thorough bath, and a clean bed for the night. Please, Birdie—as quickly as possible. I'll make a baking soda paste and chip some ice to put on those bites."

"Yes, Doc. Jess, you start the water for the bath upstairs. The chicken won't be done for an hour yet. I figure she ought to be a-sleep by then, but this girl needs some meat on her bones," Birdie said. "I'll get her some milk and a cheese sandwich. Law, we got to talk about this tonight, Doc."

A whirlwind of newness passed through an evening. She had never known such a soft bed; piles of blankets engulfed her. After Birdie shut the door, the bedroom was cast in a ghostly blue glow from the moon. It looked different too, kind of sparkly from behind the rippled glass. The cheese sandwich and milk had filled the void in her stomach. She replayed the whole evening. The warm water in the big white tub washed over her from the metal cup in Birdie's hand, clinking every time she dipped it in the water. She'd reached out her wet fingers to pat Birdie's squishy face and giggled at her large, deep-chocolate eyes. Birdie's eyelashes curled upward and waved at her. She batted them up and down and smiled wide, showing the gap in her two front teeth.

"Go down! Birdie, make it go away," she shouted, watching the dirty water of the horrible day swirl down the drain. It left behind a strip of grainy dirt in the tub.

"I'll get it later, little Miss Mary. Let's get you to bed," Birdie said, toweling her off. She waited at the commode and wrapped her in a blanket. "We don't got little girl clothes around here, but you keep this quilt around you. Miss Charlotte's quilt." *Who was Miss Charlotte?*

The sweet scent of freshly washed sheets, dried in the afternoon sunshine, lured her into a world she'd never known before. Her dirty square of blanket had been tucked under her pillow. Whispers from the kitchen drifted up the stairwell, accompanied by the aroma of the roasting chicken in the oven. She didn't know, at that moment, a lifeboat had been launched downstairs in the kitchen for her.

Mary pulled back the covers and wrapped Miss Charlotte's quilt around her. She padded to the stairs and lowered herself on the third step. She peeked through the balustrades. The words wafted to her on a savory current.

"Doc, what we gonna do? Don't seem like that little girl up there got anybody in this whole world takin' care a her. Breaks my heart, jus' breaks my heart," Birdie choked. "We got to help her. She really is the sweetest thing. Took her bath right nice and gone in the pot on her own. She give me no fuss about going into bed at all, not at all."

"You know, Birdie is sure right," Jess chimed in. "No different than findin' Wiley cryin' under the porch on Christmas; 1911 it was. Somebody try to throw him away too. A good omen. I think she be your little girl right about now." Jess touched Birdie's arm.

Doc buried his head in his hands. "Yes, Charlotte would have it no other way," he said, lifting his gaze to Birdie and Jess. "She's *our* little girl. Mary needs a family, if she doesn't already have one. We certainly have more than our fair share in this old house. Birdie? Jess? You're all I've got now." His face transformed from one of pain to exuberant determination. "You are a wise man, Jess. This girl has landed on our doorstep for a reason. I'm calling Judge Robert right now. He can surely find out what happened. And if she does need a family, he can make that happen too."

Doc turned the crank on the phone and asked the operator to connect him to Judge Robert's office. Birdie reached out her hand to Jess as if they heard the words on the other end of the line through Doc's face.

"Good evening, Robert—Doc here. A situation has arisen and I need your help. A little girl wandered into our home about half an hour ago. We need to find out what happened and her prospects. Yes, we'll keep her here. Please see what you can find out and we'll meet tomorrow. Thank you, my friend." Doc set the phone on the wall cradle and turned to face Birdie and Jess.

After a moment of quiet, Doc slapped both hands on the table. His eyes popped wide, as if he'd made too much noise.

"Birdie, let's eat. The smell of that bird has knocked all sense out of me."

The next morning, Mary opened her eyes and gazed out the window. She didn't move a muscle as three blue jays jumped from branch to branch in the dogwood tree outside, each framed in its own separate pane of wood and glass. She'd never seen anything so beautiful. Soft colors of cream, pale pink, and sky blue fluttered and hopped in the breeze. At the foot of the bed laid her old dress, now expertly cleaned and empty of the little girl who had worn it yesterday. She slipped it on and admired the reflection in the mirror of the walnut dressing table. Still empty of yesterday's girl. Balanced on tiptoe, she celebrated her shiny mahogany curls as she teetered back and forth. She padded down the stairs, her tiny bare feet slapping on the wooden steps toward the savory aroma of bacon and eggs. The clank of dishes celebrated her arrival into the kitchen.

"Well look at you—full a sunshine you are! I got your dress pretty again while you sleepin'." Nearly all of Birdie's bright-white teeth showed when she smiled. "Your plate's ready for you. I been keepin' it hot in the oven. Careful now—don't need to start the day with burned-up fingers," Birdie cautioned, holding the plate with a tea towel. "Doc says you eatin' in the fancy dining room tonight. Pretty special. You is big news around here today, yes you is!"

Mary gobbled down her breakfast and lifted the plate to lick the last of the egg yolk. She set it back on the table when Birdie shook her head in disapproval. Birdie shooed her outside to help Jess in the garden.

"The beans need to part ways with these vines here, Miss Mary," Jess said, showing her how to identify the ripe ones. He broke one in half and handed one end to her; the other he put in his mouth. "And that's how you pick 'em. Birdie makes good green beans. They crunchy now, but they melt in your mouth by supper time."

She'd never seen so much food. As she held the aluminum bowl in arms, Mary expounded about her daddy's antics and relayed made-up stories of the mother she never knew, who had died giving her birth.

"You had all that happen to you—and you ain't even sad? Certainly somethin'. You know, I sometime get sad, 'cause I'm so happy. What you think about that?" Jess tucked the bowl in the crook of one arm and held her hand. They strolled together toward the kitchen.

"Doc says I can watch the bird bath before supper," she said, leading Jess up the back porch stairs and running into the parlor.

Doc waved at her as he rounded the corner to the kitchen where Birdie seasoned the roast. "Well, I've got some chores of my own to do this afternoon, Birdie. I'll be back in an hour or two, but Mary can have something if she gets hungry again. Remember, supper in the dining room tonight!" he said and pointed his finger in the air. "You take care of that little angel while I'm gone, though I doubt she'll move from window seat in the parlor until I get back. She's waiting for the show in the bird bath. I told her they wouldn't come until after supper, but she couldn't be persuaded." Doc smiled and tipped his hat at Birdie on the way out the door.

"Nice to see you so happy, Doc. Supper be ready when you get back." Mary heard Birdie laugh behind him after the screen door banged closed. "I think Doc's got a surprise you, Miss Mary, when he get home!" Birdie called out.

Doc's Model-A chugged into the garage outside. Mary slid off the window seat. Time had passed, maybe an hour or two, but she'd lost track with the parade of colorful birds, all kinds of birds, preening and flapping their wings in the bird bath. She ran to the kitchen as the screen door stretched open.

Being careful to not bump the big white box in his arms, Doc announced, "Miss Belle's Dress Shop was a success, Birdie! And my meeting with Judge Robert was a hopeful one."

Mary stood on tiptoe and thumped the box with the bouncy pink ribbon. "I could see underneath their wings, Doc! And they looked right at me. Not even afraid," she squealed.

"What you got there, Doc?" Birdie asked, drying her hands. "What Judge Robert say?"

"Now you just hold your horses, Mary. All in due time." Doc said, raising the box out of reach.

Birdie pulled out the kitchen chair and motioned for Mary to sit in front of a bowl of peaches. The fruit was only a distraction; she couldn't take her eyes off that white box.

"Life is a mystery, Birdie." Doc set his hat on the hook by the door. "You never know what it'll hand us from day to day. I can't say too much more at the moment in front of present company, but Robert is looking into this girl's situation. We'll know soon. Her misfortune may very well be our gain—of a little girl."

"Well, well, this is some big news. And so is that box." Birdie turned to Mary and wiped the dribble of peach juice from her chin. "C'mon, let's get Jess and all go in the parlor. I think I'm excited as you to know what's in there."

Taking Birdie's hand, Mary padded to the front room and

hopped on the window seat. She waited, swinging her legs back and forth in anticipation. The white box seemed to grow even larger as Doc came toward her. He tapped the top and said:

"Mary, you're special, and now you're going to look special." He turned to Birdie and Jess. "Am I being foolish to get my hopes up at seventy-one?"

"Naw, I wouldn't say that word come to mind," Jess said, his expression tender as he leaned against the archway with his arms folded. "Maybe wonderful, but not foolish."

"You might need some help with the ribbon. I can tell you right now, Doc didn't tie it. And he won't be gettin' it undone neither," Birdie said, sitting next to Mary on the window seat. "You take one end; I'll take the other."

The bow sailed to the floor in a cascade of pink satin streamers. When Birdie lifted the lid, the suction fluttered the puffy tissue inside.

"Go on now, see what's under there," Doc said, fingering his watch in his vest pocket and peering over his wire-rimmed glasses.

Almost fearful, Mary pulled back the tissue. Everything looked white: the box, the tissue, and the cloud of soft fabric inside. Little bursts of bright colors radiated from a sea of white.

"Now that's a dress fit for a princess!" Doc announced, rubbing his chin. "And, Charlotte, I dare say, might have picked this out herself." He winked at Birdie. "Why, I think she did."

Mary extended her hand to touch the billowy white fabric. What mesmerized her most were the petite hand-embroidered humming-birds. They appeared to flutter around the waist. Each one was individual in its design; all the colors of the rainbow gleamed from beneath their delicate wings. It was as if the little birds stretched and sucked at tiny sugar-water feeders hidden in the seam. She touched each one, baptizing them with their imaginary names. *So alive. Like magic.*

"Oh, Doc, you have earned your wings today," Birdie said, her eyes glistening. "You done real good. How'd you know how to get a little girl dress?"

"Mmm...make no mistake about it, Charlotte still whispers in my ear." Doc raised his eyes, as if sharing a private moment. "Even got those little socks with daisies on them to go with it."

"Pretty fancy, yes it is." Jess gave Doc a nod that said: *Well done.*

Birdie helped Mary into the spectacular dress before the special meal in the dining room. Twirling in the mirror, the daisies blurred around her tiny ankles. She bounded down the stairs.

And then she dribbled gravy down the front of her beautiful dress. Three distinct, dark-brown blops descended on the gleaming white satin. Birdie came to her rescue with a damp cloth sprinkled with baking soda, uttering soothing words as she dabbed. Even Birdie couldn't make those spots fully disappear.

Doc consoled her after supper by assigning a name to each little hummingbird on her dress as she spun within the loose loop of his embrace. She stopped only for Doc to call out each one: "Jo Jo! Eric! Susie! Mary! Birdie! Jess! Wiley! And Charlotte, the prettiest one of all."

As she twirled, Mary imagined the little birds releasing themselves from her dress and flying around the room in a swirling line. She pulled herself from Doc's arms and ran to the window, pressing her hands on the glass. The colorful little birds settled in the bird bath in waves. The most magical day of her young life.

Mary sighed and stood from the bed with the box balanced in both hands. The corners on the lid were crushed; the faded ribbon tied and re-tied countless times. With the vision filling her from the inside, she placed the box on top of the Christmas decorations on the bureau. The dress should make another little girl feel special. Move on to the bedroom closets in her and Jim's room.

With trepidation, Mary opened Jim's closet door, the door across from his side of their bed. The faint, familiar scent of freshly cut wood washed over her—the scent of Jim. She pulled her hand across the line of flannel shirts, starched work shirts, sport coats, and trousers. After Jim's tragic death at the mill so many years ago, the strength never came to separate herself from this closet. He might come home as long as his clothes were here in this private space.

Raleigh believed it morbid to leave this closet intact. He urged her to donate Jim's clothes to charity. He would never understand what they meant to her. She ran her fingers along the sleeve of a red and black flannel shirt, its overwashed softness equivalent to smoothing Jim's blond hair while he slept.

Doc lived long enough to give her away to Jim. Doc loved him, as if his own son, and remained enthusiastic about their union. She and Jim stayed in the old Richmond house with Doc and Birdie for only a few weeks before she passed Doc into immortality. Jess became immortal with the fabric after having a stroke six months earlier, right after she met Jim.

Mary fanned through the jackets. Her fingers lingered on the black waistcoat with the satin piping; the one at the end of the aisle in 1945, with the man she loved inside. Lives ended and began again; her own beginning for the third time.

"Are you ready, my darling?" Doc asked as he stood with Mary in the intimate vestibule at the back of the old clapboard church.

The announcement of Mary and Jim's wedding swept the chatter circles of Richmond. Many of the congregation who had shown up held no invitation. Everyone wanted to witness Doc give away the little girl who was lucky enough to have found him.

Mary gazed at Doc with her vibrant olives eyes, eager for the new life awaiting her in Oregon after the wedding. Her mahogany hair, swept into an artful twist, framed her youthful face under the short, sheer veil. Two images stood in front of Doc: a little girl with mosquito bites, and a grown woman of twenty to the man who waited for her at the altar.

The open side doors of the church ushered in the warm, early-summer breeze. The rush of air fluttered Mary's veil. A mourning dove sailed along the current and perched on the sill of the high window at the entrance.

"Well, there's Charlotte now, nearly late, I'd say." Doc turned to her after following the bird's path. "Here, my dear," he said, searching her eyes, "this, from Charlotte's jewelry box, will complete the ensemble. Her personal choice." He held out his hand to reveal a hair comb topped with a sparkling hummingbird. The outstretched wings, encrusted with tiny diamonds, radiated a rainbow of opalescent colors in the sun streaming through the church window. The delicate eye contained a small sapphire. Doc pulled up her veil and placed the comb in her hair. "Old, blue, and borrowed, all in one. Charlotte will one day want it back. She told me so this morning."

"I'll cherish this always," Mary said, his words soaring past her. "I certainly am ready, Daddy. Let's go slow. I want to savor every moment." She took a breath to hold back tears.

The organ started the notes of Mary's favorite hymn, "All Things Bright and Beautiful." There had been no question this would be her wedding march, the first hymn she'd ever heard when Doc took her to church for the first time. She wrapped her arm under his elbow.

The distinctive sound of Birdie's whimper from the first pew made her choke a bit. Birdie needed three eyes today to accommodate her tears: one for Jess; the second for Charlotte; and a third for the little girl by Doc's side. But they were here; always here with her. Maybe Birdie would need a fourth one for Wiley, who Mary spotted running ahead of them down the aisle. His sparkling tail was a dead giveaway. Not everyone could see him, but she did.

Mary first met Jim Coulter when he arrived at Doc's office to have a deep cut on his arm stitched up. One of his workers at the lumber mill slipped his grip on a board when Jim walked by and gashed his left arm in the process. Mary and Doc stood ready to take care of him. She had dutifully filled Charlotte's shoes to manage the medical practice and waited at the front desk for Doc's new patient. Her face flushed when the tall, blond man, with eyes the color of glacier water, emerged through the screen door. The man's ripped and blood-stained sleeve disappeared when he said his name. Despite his pain, Jim took the time to comment on the beauty of her needlepoint as she greeted him at the reception desk. Mary was sure, right then and there, she would marry him. After six months of courting, the scar had completely healed with a proposal of marriage.

How nervous she had been before she and Doc left for the church. He stood behind her as she gazed at her reflection in the mirror in the front hallway.

"Is there a special sign of a good man?" she asked.

Doc's hooded, deep-brown eyes relaxed. A moment of quiet suspended between them as he considered a response to a question of such importance. He set his hands on her shoulders.

"Yes, my dear. A man's true measure can be seen in his com-munication with all creatures, great and small, when he thinks no one is looking. Tells you all you need to know."

Mary carried his words as a measuring tape reaching into infinity. *How could anyone ever measure up to Doc?*

Jim received a lucrative offer to run the Richmond company's new lumber mill in Portland, Oregon, but he and Mary wouldn't leave for two months after the wedding. The extended start date gave them time to help Birdie with Doc. Every day was a gift.

"Mary, why don't you have a sit? I need to talk with you 'bout somethin'," Birdie said one morning as she washed Jim's coffee mug after he'd left for the mill.

Mary refilled her own cup and locked her gaze on Birdie, curious about the serious tone in her voice. "What's going on? Is everything all right?" Birdie had an odd expression on her face too.

"Doc didn't get up for breakfast this mornin'." Birdie pulled a chair from the table. She sat and wrapped her thick, dark fingers around Mary's and squeezed. "You gonna help him rise much, much higher today, Miss Mary. Today is Doc's day."

What is she talking about?

"He's waitin' for you to come up those stairs and help him." Birdie turned her hand over and tapped her palm three times with her forefinger. Mary's throat started a slow burn as Birdie's words took shape. "C'mon, I show you."

Remaining silent, Mary followed Birdie up the stairs to Doc's bedroom. Every step crushed her with trepidation. She stepped through the doorway, her gaze settling on the still form under the covers. Relief washed over her as the quilt rose and fell with each of Doc's breaths. Mary's gaze trailed from him to a richly colored piece of fabric spread out on the foot of the bed.

Aware of their presence, Doc gave Birdie's hand a soft squeeze. She pressed her wide lips together, almost a smile, and nodded for Mary to look at the birds in the fabric.

"Oh Birdie...it's...I have no words. Why haven't I ever seen this before?" she said, breathless.

"This ain't the kind of secret you go hennin' about at parties, Miss Mary. Go on, set your hands on the birds—think about your life with Doc."

Not knowing what would happen but trusting Birdie, Mary set her hands on two of the three shimmering pheasants. Their eyes glistened, aware, and ready for instruction. She'd never seen anything so beautiful—*so alive*. The reflective, thick wings began to vibrate beneath her hands; moving, lifting, and gaining strength. Heat radiated up her arms and raced through her body like an electric current. The rippling faded and then disappeared. A succession of Doc's, Birdie's, Jess's, and Jim's embraces enveloped her. Mary followed Birdie's gaze, already trained to the window in anticipation of what she would see.

A rainbow of colors radiated from the three pheasants as they materialized in the old poplar tree outside of Doc's bedroom window. They meticulously preened and prepared for flight. Each enormous bird perched on a separate branch, bowing under the weight. She gasped at the sight. One after another, the majestic birds lifted their heavy wings and flew high above the tree. The leaves waved from the force. She turned back to the fabric. Empty. Only the swirl of green vines remained.

Leaning across Birdie, Mary instinctively placed her hands on each side of Doc's face, as was his first touch to her own cheeks fourteen years ago. She closed her eyes and smiled when Birdie rested her hand on her shoulder. When she opened them, the tree was empty—Doc gone. She couldn't move, couldn't let go.

"I had no idea," she whispered. Birdie pulled her back, and Mary had to force herself to release her hands from Doc's face.

"You jus' done a good thing, yes, a good thing. Doc's not gone." Birdie patted her cheek. "C'mon down to the kitchen, I'll make us some tea. You and me will have a talk. I'm gettin' on in years myself, so I think you ought to know. I promised Doc I'd tell you when the time right. The time is right, baby girl."

"I'll be down in a few minutes, Birdie."

"When you ready. I got to call Judge Robert's office to take care of the arrangements. They been waitin' for me. The whole town's comin' out for Doc, yes they will." Birdie clicked the heavy door closed behind her.

Holding on to the time alone with Doc, Mary gazed at the man who had changed her life, a man who had changed so many people's lives. Her limbs, anchors as she struggled to stand, wouldn't move. The magic of this day was the culmination of her life in this old house. Everything and everyone in it—magic.

Birdie hung up the phone as Mary entered the kitchen. "Well... the whole town knowin' now. She gonna be one busy operator, Miss Busy Fingers."

Mary picked up a piece of shortbread from the bright-green ceramic plate on the kitchen table and poured herself some tea from the matching pot.

"Birdie, where on earth did that fabric come from?" she asked, blowing into a green mug.

"Given to Doc by Miss Charlotte's daddy. Doc told me and Jess everything he knew after Wiley passed," Birdie said. She sat and patted the table. "Come over here and sit."

Mary sat took a bite of the shortbread. She closed her eyes, still in a daze. "Birdie, I don't want to leave you here alone...not after this." She waved her hand in a swirly pattern.

"I'm jus' fine. This house is home. I got the garden, and I got Jess, Doc, Miss Charlotte, and that bossy Mr. Wiley with me always. Still a family in this old house to take care of, Miss Mary. They're here with me, and you and Mr. Jim be back to visit. I know you will." Birdie went quiet before continuing. "Can I tell you I love that man like he's my own daddy? Confounds me, but I'm only a sight younger than he is, only a sight younger. Ain't it funny about time? So young when Jess and me came here—and Doc seemed old—wise. But he only twenty-one, Miss Mary, about as old as you is today. Now I'm old myself, and it jus' don't seem old to me. Should be about what you know in life, not all those numbers."

"You are so right, Birdie. Until today, I didn't know anything."

"I was Doc's very patient." Birdie tapped her forefinger on the linoleum table. "That's how me and Jess come to live here. Only seventeen." Birdie showed Mary the raised pink scar on her right forearm. "See this? Burned up my arm when the curtains caught fire in the house me and Jess workin' in. Reverend Payne at Fourth Baptist Church brought us here, so Doc could fix me up. The old Whitfield House burned to the ground that day." Birdie let out a low, sad chuckle. "Doc still paintin' his sign out front when we pulled up in a horse and carriage. A mighty fine doctor. Every stitch was a wish he made come true for good folks around here."

Mary squeezed Birdie's arm, almost feeling the heat of the old burn scar beneath her fingers. She'd never tire of hearing the story. The bell at the front door startled her.

"Be right back—coroner here." Birdie stood and did her half walk, half run to the entryway. Mary leaned sideways to gaze down the hall. Birdie held the door open for the stretcher.

Mary sat quiet while the coroner and ambulance staff took Doc out for transport to the funeral home. The whole process lasted less than ten minutes. *That man they just carried out wasn't Doc at all.*

Birdie returned to the kitchen, lowered herself in the chair, and gave her a sad smile. Mary wiped her eyes, a feeble attempt to hide she'd been crying.

"Miss Mary, I need to tell you about the birds while we got some quiet time—before Mr. Coulter get home. You be carin' for them when my time comes. Doc made me promise, and I will honor his wishes, I will." Birdie stood and poured more hot water over the tea strainer. "Miss Charlotte was the daughter of Simon Gamble, a fancy benefactor here in Richmond. Charlotte's daddy be a dreamer, a big dreamer. He put up money to dig up those old tombs over in Egypt."

Mary reached for Birdie's hand and never let go as she told the story.

The tall, oak doors groaned open as the petite black maid ushered Edwin Seymore into Simon Gamble's study. He didn't want to do this, but he couldn't pay back his debt. This last excavation trip to Egypt, financed entirely by Mr. Gamble, had been a disaster when his months of work yielded minimal results. He was no Ernesto Schiaparelli. What made him think he could lead his own expedition without his mentor? This time he'd come back empty-handed and broke. Mr. Gamble would soon discover the five thousand dollars invested would not be repaid. Edwin hoped the man would accept what he had to offer in return.

Mr. Gamble had complete trust in him to bring back treasures from the ancient world, one of the only men to have believed in him. He had almost hoped Mr. Gamble wouldn't outlive him, so he didn't have to see the disappointment on his face. The old man was seventy now but, ever the businessman, requested this meeting.

The maid, in her starched white dress, motioned for him to take a seat in the study. "Mr. Gamble be with you shortly, sir. Can I get you a cup of tea?"

"Yes, wonderful. Tea would be wonderful," Edwin muttered, self-conscious, and ran his hand through his wild hair to make himself somewhat presentable.

Edwin's gaze scanned around the room. The deep tock of the heavy clock in the front entry rhythmically punctured the stillness. Bookcases of aged oak wood lined the walls. Leather-bound books and papers filled the glass-fronted cabinets. The woody scent of family history and lemon-oil polish lingered in the still air. He took a deep breath. *What would it be like to live in such a house?* The hand-woven carpet, surely a prize from someone else's treasure hunt, sprawled with intricate elegance. The colors in the floral design glowed with vibrant red, deep indigo and rich ocher as pure as gold coins.

With the wrapped bundle on his lap, Edwin brushed the frayed fibers of the tied twine. Never a more exciting discovery than Queen Nefertari's tomb in 1904. As a member of Schiaparelli's original excavation team, he'd marveled at the tomb's size; chamber after chamber of spectacular art covered every inch of the walls. He'd never forget the hundreds of little gold stars painted on the dark, domed ceilings. Remnant chunks of the polished red granite sarcophagus remained littered on the dirt floor, the rest long gone at the hands of ancient plunderers. Nefertari's tomb had been one of the most important discoveries in the modern world. This one secret artifact, the one he'd hidden away for nearly ten years, would more than cover his debt.

His most treasured possession. How could he let go? He took it out of safekeeping every so often just to look at the exquisite birds. They had become his family. *Otherworldly* was the first word he'd uttered when he opened the urn. He surrendered the urn from a niche between two rock-cut benches in the burial chamber but not the fabric found inside. He tucked the treasure away and never said a word to anyone. It seemed a sacrilege for the fabric now to become a bargaining chip. No choice.

Nearly an old man himself, Edwin doubted he had another expedition left in him. This last one had taken its toll: the heat, dust storms, and exhaustion, more than he could bear. The relentless cough he'd developed upon his return wouldn't go away.

"Tea, sir. Mr. Gamble on his way downstairs." The maid set the silver tray on the corner of the expansive oak desk.

The surface of the desk contained only a stand with a silver and onyx pen gleaming under the glow of a green-shaded lamp. Edwin expected stacks of papers, legal contracts, anything to indicate Mr. Gamble's businesses flourished. Only that lonely pen.

"Thank you, Emma—very well." The familiar deep voice came from the doorway behind him. His stomach lurched in response. The maid rushed to stand behind Mr. Gamble's empty leather chair at his desk, ready to assist him.

Edwin envisioned Mr. Gamble as when they last met two years ago; a statue of wealth and prosperity, barrel-chested in his custom-tailored, navy-blue suit of the finest wool. He tried to swallow his shock when he faced the man of today. Mr. Gamble's hair, now powdery white, had thinned to reveal the shine of his scalp. His spotted, bony hand gripped the handle of a varnished wooden cane. His eyes shadowed and watery.

"Indeed, very nice to see you again," Edwin said and set the wrapped bundle on the empty leather chair next to him. He shook the man's hand, embarrassed by the condition of his own. His fingernails, caked with dirt, had yellowed from years of smoking unfiltered cigarettes. He smoked three on the way to this cavernous old house. Mr. Gamble surely took notice.

"Edwin, my good man, what bountiful treasure stories can you impart today? Sit, sit, please," Mr. Gamble said, trying to brighten his voice. The maroon leather groaned against the brass rivets when he lowered himself to the plush chair and hung the cane on the corner of the desk. "Don't be shocked in the change in me, my friend. Cancer is bad business—steals your dreams. I would trade all of this to spend one day in your shoes, to have seen what you have seen. I'm afraid I must be content to live those dreams through your stories. No matter what you've found, or not found, I believe my faith in you has not been misplaced."

Mr. Gamble laced and unlaced his fingers as he talked. He nodded to the maid, who anticipated his signal. She took three steps forward and expertly poured the tea.

"Thank you, Emma."

Edwin relaxed as the delicate china cup and saucer were set in front of him. This vital, immortal giant wasn't larger than life. Mr. Gamble was only a man, a fragile man. No ambush of a scolding session planned here as he feared, but surely the last time he would have the privilege to meet with him. Mr. Gamble's checkbook was filled with regrets and unfulfilled dreams, a desire to roam the world unattached, to get his hands dirty and have mud caked under his fingernails.

Yes, Mr. Gamble will have the chance to be an explorer.

"My time is short today, Edwin, as I am tired, tired of this...Quite regrettable."

Tired of what? His life of privilege? His illness?

"My lovely daughter, Charlotte, married a fine man," Mr. Gamble continued, gazing at an unexplored corner of the room. "They will be here shortly for supper, but it's a covert way to check on me. If not for Doc, I wouldn't be alive today. That's the honest-to-God truth. He's a mighty good doctor."

Edwin shook his head in agreement but his mind wandered. "Sir, I need to tell you this last trip did not yield the results I'd hoped." He hesitated and then continued. "I can't return the money you invested in me. But I can present to you an artifact from the Nefertari tomb expedition. My only asset."

Retrieving the bundle from the seat of the side chair, Edwin placed it in front of Mr. Gamble. "If you would accept this as payment for what I owe you, I would surely be grateful," he said, eager for a reaction but also sad to never lay eyes on the cloth again.

The saucer shuddered against the wood as Mr. Gamble pushed the teacup aside. He pulled on one end of the tie; the twine fell away. The paper quivered as he revealed the fabric, neatly folded in thirds.

"What is this? Never have I laid eyes on such an object."

"Open the folds. Please."

Mr. Gamble's face changed from quizzical to complete reverence when the full images of the three pheasants filled his view. Edwin's own face changed to a broad smile as he studied the man's expression. Thick silence floated and swirled around the study.

"See? The discovery of a priceless treasure. You made that happen. Thousands of years and no one's seen it—only you and me. We now have a deep secret between us."

Mr. Gamble wiped his eyes with his monogrammed handkerchief and pulled out the top drawer of his desk. He lifted out a leather-bound book and plucked the smooth silver and onyx pen from the stand. Opening the book to the front page, he began to write. He ripped the paper along the top perforation, from left to right. Once free, he held it out to Edwin. The ends fluttered like a little bird learning to reuse its broken wings as Edwin picked the paper from the fingers of its gilded cage. The reflective, gold-embossed vine around the perimeter glowed under the light of the desk lamp.

"You can't fail unless you stop trying, son."

Still staring at the paper, Edwin opened his mouth to say something, but nothing would come out.

"This evening, I will present this lovely fabric to my son-in-law, Doc, as a gift. I can never thank him enough for the extension of time to experience something such as this. I thank you, too, Edwin."

The maid moved toward the tall doors of the study, a gesture that suggested the meeting was over. He stood to take his leave and shook Mr. Gamble's hand. She escorted him to the imposing front door. The etched glass threw shimmery colors on the shiny marble floor. The door clicked shut behind him.

Edwin leaned against the colossal white column of the stately brick porch. The check for twenty thousand dollars, written in wobbly penmanship, quivered as he stared at it. Today he savored the thought of being the richest man in Richmond, not from of the paper in his hand but because he had done what the richest man in town had always wanted to do, and couldn't.

"Payment against a debt?" Mary asked. Her mouth gaped as she waited for more information.

"Charlotte's daddy passed that night after he gave the fabric to Doc. Told him and Miss Charlotte how he got it—after dinner it was. They'd jus' cleared away the dessert dishes. Mr. Gamble give the bundle to Doc to thank him for takin' such good care a him." Birdie smiled as she relived the whole story. "And when Doc laid the fabric out and put his hands on it—feelin' it and all—it started movin'. Yes, ma'am—it started movin'."

"Did the birds disappear like today?" She leaned forward; hanging on Birdie's every word.

"Yes, they did, right in front of Miss Charlotte and Doc in the dining room. Those three big birds appeared in the yard outside the window, the same ones in that fabric—the very same." Birdie thumped her forefinger on the linoleum table top. "Doc said he almost had the heart palpitation. He got hot all over and knew Mr. Gamble was goin'—he just *knew*."

"Birdie, did he die *because* of the fabric?"

"Oh no. That's not what it do. Let me keep going. Well, Miss Charlotte went to the window and couldn't stop lookin' at them birds." Birdie shook her head and took a sip of her tea. She wrinkled her nose. "Gone cold. Those birds raised up in the air, one after the other. Right then, Mr. Gamble fell right outta his chair. Doc run to him. Miss Charlotte run to him too, but Doc had all that magic goin' on. He grabbed the old man and held him like a baby till he's gone...Like a baby. And you know those birds come back, come right back as you seen them today, they did...uh-huh. Those birds helped him to die...and live on...forever."

"I feel so privileged, Birdie. Does anyone else know about this?"

"No, ma'am, you and me...all's left now. The whole family and Wiley are here with me 'cause of that fabric, immortal and all. Still got that magic in me too. Come out when I touch things—" Birdie stopped. They stared at each other when the car door shut on the station wagon outside.

Mary glanced at her watch—already four o'clock. Jim was home from the mill.

Birdie shook her head to stay quiet. They both waited in silence until the screen door squeaked open.

"Afternoon! How you two doing? How's Doc?" Jim asked, as he kissed Mary's forehead.

"He's gone, Jim. This morning—after you left, he passed." Mary stood to embrace him and eyed Birdie. "I'm sorry I didn't call you. It's been a day. But Doc will always be with us."

Jim squeezed his eyes. His tears, locked behind his stoic exterior, broke through as soon as Mary wrapped her arms around his waist. "God, I loved that man," Jim choked.

The chair scraped the floor as Birdie stood and patted Jim on the shoulder. "He not gone. Right here with us, he is. Pour yourself a whiskey, Mr. Jim—make it a double—and then I'll get some supper in you two. All done now, all done." Birdie lumbered to the refrigerator. She pulled out a plate of cold fried chicken. "Remember, baby girl, you got one more trip to make back here after you get out to Portland."

Mary lifted her head from Jim's shoulder and locked eyes with Birdie, who gave her a toothy smile. Her gaze shifted to the kitchen doorway. Doc leaned against the jamb with his arms crossed, nodding in agreement. He never looked better.

Mary didn't know how long she'd been sitting on her bed, remembering the turn of events the day Doc passed into immortality. She and Jim had flown back to Richmond, her first trip on an airplane, to help Birdie pass only three years later. She'd kept her word. They left the furniture for the renters to use and only took the most personal and valuable pieces; the fabric among them. An old painting, a boy dancing, she regretted leaving behind—beautiful in Doc's room.

Jim put the fabric away when they got home; the last time she'd seen it. If only that magical treasure had preserved Jim's life. He'd be with her now, always by her side. But the accident took him by the time she got the call. In the chest, but she couldn't remember. She hadn't used the fabric for anyone since Birdie. Decades ago. *Under something...under something.*

"Move forward, Mary," she said out loud. "It'll come to you." She slapped her knees. She had to pack her things to be ready to leave on Saturday. Besides, Birdie always said things couldn't be found when she was looking for them.

CHAPTER 5
Transition

Raleigh called Judy Hawkins's number on his cell phone as he drove down Northeast Nineteenth toward Knott Street. After the third ring, she picked up.

"Hawkins & Company, Judy speaking." Her tone was all business.

"It's Raleigh Coulter. I hope your calendar is clear over the next two weeks. My mother is moving into a senior community in a few days, and her house is an antiques gold mine. She wants to sell nearly everything," he said, his words a propeller on a plane out of this mess. "Can you meet me there on Monday? She'll be moving out this Saturday."

"Whoa, slow down, cowboy!" Judy said, rustling what he guessed were the pages of her appointment book. "I'd be delighted to help you. I've got a big sale this coming weekend and a ton of paperwork to do on Monday, but I could come by at around four in the afternoon. Will that work?"

"Yes, that'll be fine."

Perfect. I'll have all day Sunday, and almost the whole next week, in the house by myself.

Raleigh parked the rental truck in Mary's driveway the following Saturday morning.

"She'd better not have too much stuff," Raleigh muttered, climbing the stairs to his mother's bungalow. As he stepped on the wide porch, his cell phone rang its tinny version of Robert Palmer's "Big Time." He stopped, checked the number, and sighed before answering.

"Hey, Nash." He coughed up the name like a bad meal. "Calling to give me another fabulous tip?"

"No, we've got a problem," Nash said, his voice shaky and paranoid. "The company found out about me giving you the merger information. They called in the FBI. There's a witch hunt going on around here. I'm screwed, and so are you."

"How do they know you talked to me?" His heart rate moved up to police chase.

"Somebody whistled. Must have overheard me talking. Phone numbers dialed on the company phones are recorded. Put on your game face, man."

"Dammit! Why did you call me from the office?" He smacked the phone and hung up. He took a deep breath and composed himself to face his mother. She'd better have everything ready to go.

Raleigh shoved the last of his mother's boxes into the rental truck and slammed the door. He didn't need one this big, since Mary wasn't taking much to Milwaukie Manor.

"I'm proud of you, Mom," Raleigh said, still distracted by Nash's phone call but genuinely impressed. "I didn't think you'd ever be able to separate yourself like this."

"I won't have room for much in a one-bedroom apartment." Mary sounded worn out as she gazed around the first floor. Her eyes locked on the patio door. "One more thing—the patio set will need to come with me. Can you get the table and chairs on the truck while I do one last walk around? Then we'll go."

Raleigh blew out a breath in frustration. He'd hoped they were done. "All right, but that's enough. By the way, did you find that old fabric?"

"Unfortunately, I didn't," Mary sighed. "I'm just sick. I don't want it sold. Promise you'll bring it to me."

"Mom, why don't you wait in the truck? I'll lock up and get the patio furniture. C'mon, let's go."

The fabric is still in the house.

Mary stepped through the door of her new apartment and padded straight past the small kitchen to the expansive picture window in the dining area. She stared at the Willamette River, an oasis in her desert. The cozy, one-bedroom space had only what she needed—no more, no less. She opened the back door next to the window and stepped outside. This view would give her the energy to sprint to the finish line. She took a deep breath; the air was cool and crisp. The Willamette surged through the evergreens, with fiery explosions of burnt-orange, gold, cayenne, and magenta splashing the hills. From this vantage point, her decision to make the move was cinched; today she celebrated.

The few pieces of furniture she'd kept and her personal belongings were right behind her. The staff at Milwaukie Manor was gracious enough to help Raleigh unload the truck. This first evening outside with a cup of tea before walking over to the dining facility would be heaven. The week's elaborate menu was included in her welcome packet, a far cry from her usual frozen dinners and green salads. First, she wanted to bundle up and sit outside. She might spot one of the majestic birds of prey fly by to give her an equally warm welcome.

Raleigh and a staff person appeared with the patio set and then disappeared without a word about Mary's new home.

"Everything's in, Mom. I'm going to take off to return the truck," Raleigh called out.

"Thanks for everything. I hope the sale goes well next week. Before you leave, can you open the box marked Kitchen and pull out my tea pot?"

"Sure. Then I have to go."

Mary listened to Raleigh rummage through the boxes. Finally, the front door closed him out of her new world. The atmosphere instantly changed to quiet and peaceful. The cool breeze pushed her to the kitchen to fill the teapot. As the water started to rumble, she picked up the wall phone and dialed Helen's number.

"Good afternoon, Mary here. Guess who's arrived." She heard in her own voice a giddiness, as though embarking on an exotic vacation.

"That's wonderful. Do you need some help unpacking?" Helen said, eager to support her friend's transition.

"I do thank you for the offer. I'll work my way through the boxes in time, but let's have dinner together this evening."

"Excellent idea! I'll call Evelyn to meet us. I can reserve the round table by the back window. The view is terrific. How about five thirty?"

"Perfect." Mary hung up the phone and smiled at having friends around her. *Could one of them possibly help her to immortality if she found the fabric?*

Mary pulled a mug out of the kitchen box and poured the steaming water over the tea bag. She wrapped herself in her fleece jacket and returned to the patio. As she took a sip, the graceful wings appeared. *A hawk or an eagle?* The bird followed the course of the river, its wingspan stretching wider. She could barely see the limp fish in its powerful claws. The enormous osprey glided by her patio, silent and focused on its deadly mission. She fixed her gaze, unblinking, until it was out of sight. Yes, this was how she wanted to spend every evening for the rest of this life. The world could wreak its havoc without her.

She glanced at her watch. She padded back to the kitchen and set her mug in the sink. There was still time to take a leisurely stroll over for a meal in the company of friends.

The next day, Raleigh cruised through the Irvington house to assess what was left. He identified a few items Judy Hawkins would be particularly excited about when she arrived tomorrow: the original Craftsman sofa and chairs, oak and stained-glass lamps, old Christmas decorations, and his grandmother's china service that Mary used only on holidays. He fingered over the faded bindings of the first edition books; sure they'd bring in a bundle. His father's passion for the crime mysteries of Dashiell Hammett and Arthur Conan Doyle would certainly draw book collectors with big wallets. He should push Judy for estimates when he showed her those particular books.

The walls of the living room were lined with shadowed squares where Mary's framed needlepoint birds had hung. The original wallpaper was a vibrant, but simple, Arts and Crafts pattern in swirls of cream, tangerine, and sage green. The exposed paper had become dingy over the years. All of it would need to be removed and the walls painted a neutral color.

Raleigh moved to the kitchen; he couldn't believe Mary had never replaced anything in her cabinets. The canister of Calumet baking powder was the same one from when he was in high school. The petrified glop of gingerbread batter on the side was still there, dark brown and hard as a rock. The spices hadn't been used in quite some time. In fact, he doubted she cooked much at all. He'd have to call a professional cleaning company when the sale was over.

The scratched pattern on the stairs guided his climb to the guestroom and his mother's bedroom. He stopped at the top step to catch his breath. He'd need to resume his workouts at the gym.

Raleigh peered through the doorways of the two upstairs bedrooms. The second floor was in even worse disarray than the first. Starting in the guestroom, he scanned the boxes stacked on the bed. His gaze traveled over to the stack of Christmas ornaments on the bureau. They'd be a big draw for collectors. His eyes zeroed in on the large box with crushed corners, still tied with faded pink ribbon. Odd for this particular one to remain unopened since his mother had made the effort to pull it out of the closet. He yanked on the bow. Knotted too tight.

I wonder. Unable to find a pair of scissors, he dashed to the kitchen and rummaged through the drawers. He pulled out a small paring knife and ran back up the stairs, two at a time. He puffed to catch his breath. The ribbon released with a *pop*. He threw it on the floor. When he lifted the lid, the tissue shuddered. Brightly colored hummingbirds peeked out of the folds. *Pay dirt.*

"Wait a minute—" He pulled back the wrinkled paper. The little birds were attached to a small dress. "Are you kidding me? What the hell was she doing with that?" He tossed the dress in the box and turned to rummage through the closet: blankets, sheets, extra towels, and old winter coats. *Nothing.*

He moved to his mother's bedroom. Mary's nightstand offered only wadded tissues, a magnifying glass, bobby pins, a bottle of aspirin, and a packet of sewing needles. Strange for Mary to take his father's empty nightstand with her and leave her own behind.

The bureau still contained his father's socks, T-shirts, an old Timex watch, and a set of nail clippers. He'd have to arrange for the donation of all this stuff if they didn't sell. He slammed the last drawer shut and turned. His gaze locked on the chest in the corner.

The hinges gave a long squeal. Raleigh remembered hearing that annoying sound every night of his childhood when his mother removed the old quilt. She must have taken it with her to Milwaukie Manor. The chest was empty. He dropped the lid so hard one of the hinge screws popped out and rolled on the floor. He stomped out of the room.

On Monday afternoon, Judy Hawkins pulled up to Mary Coulter's house. She was a precise woman—not overly stylish but precise. In her sixties and slender, Judy was ready for business. Niceties were locked in the glove compartment of her spanking-new Jaguar XK. She wore a mid-length, dark-brown wool skirt and a camel-colored cashmere sweater draped over the shoulders of her matching silk blouse. Her tortoiseshell bifocals balanced on her thin, pointed nose. Judy peered over her glasses as she climbed the steps and held out her hand when she reached the porch.

"Everything goes," Raleigh said. "Mary removed what she wanted to keep for her new apartment."

"Well, that certainly makes things easier for my team," Judy replied, ticking off the first question on her list.

"Oh. The Thunderbird in the driveway doesn't go in the sale. I'm selling that separately."

"Fair enough."

Raleigh led Judy through the downstairs room by room. "All the furniture is authentic. My mother took the loveseat and one of the chairs but left the rest." He hoped Judy would be impressed by the original Stickley pieces.

"You can get top dollar for these, Raleigh. Craftsman furniture is hot. I know three—maybe four—people who are rabid collectors of anything Arts and Crafts. The Rookwood vases on the fireplace mantel are wonderful—big money on those. I'd say two to three thousand each." Judy turned the vase over to authenticate the maker's mark. "I may want to sell them on the Internet. No dickering." She moved to the nook off the entryway and perused the bookcases on each end, which held his father's mystery novels. "I wouldn't go less than two hundred on any of these books; some are worth way more. The Conan Doyle and Dashiell Hammett first editions are especially valuable. My book collectors will want to snatch those up when I call them."

Pleased with the response so far, he led Judy to the kitchen. He opened the pantry door and asked, "Should I empty these cabinets before the sale?" He picked up the can of baking powder. "See this? Doesn't that take you back to the sixties?"

"Oh no, leave everything. You wouldn't believe what people will buy, especially the vintage stuff with original labels." Judy pulled out her clipboard from her brown leather satchel and made several notes.

As they worked their way up the stairs, Judy's thick heels on her leather pumps hammered out each step toward the guest bedroom. She picked and poked through the ornaments. "I have about three collectors who will snap up these in a heartbeat. One of them is a real stitch—name's Phil. He buys everything he can get his hands on. I'll mark them up a bit higher since Phil's a negotiator."

Judy glanced at the bed and spotted the white box. She set her satchel on the floor, picked up the dress, and held it out with both hands.

"This is lovely. You can tell all of these birds are hand-stitched. It would be worth much more, though, without those stains. Too bad, but somebody will buy it." Judy laid the dress back in the box.

"Are you ready for something bizarre? Let's go to my mother's bedroom." He led her across the hall. In mocking ceremony, Raleigh opened the closet and ran his hand over his father's clothes like teeth on a comb. "Can you believe this?"

"Don't worry; they'll sell." Judy made another a note on her clipboard. "A vintage shop will come in and mow through these. Unfortunately, I see this kind of thing a lot. Some people just can't let go."

"What about this old chest? Came from my grandmother," he said, expecting her to be impressed.

Opening the lid, Judy inspected the wood joints and fingered the inside edge. "Old—nothing special. The bottom piece of wood's been replaced. The hinge is broken. I'd put a hundred bucks on it—and that would be the top end."

Raleigh's expression fell. Now he had another reason to hate that chest.

Judy completed her preview of the rest of the house with military efficiency. Once at the front door, she said, "Tomorrow I'll send over a team to do a detailed inventory of everything, including all the tools in the basement. You have some nice things here, Raleigh. I think we should do well. The weather is supposed to hold, and if it warms up, we'll have a good turnout. Once the inventory is complete, I'll e-mail you the contract with an itemized list. Send it back by Wednesday. On Thursday, we'll stage the house and then price every-thing on Friday. I'll be here for the sale on Saturday. We'll start at 10:00 a.m. sharp. By the way, that Dromov Fund you got me in is returning nicely."

Judy's voice pelted him like a pea-shooter pointed at his face. Relief washed through him when his cell phone rang.

"Okay. Good to hear. I'll wait for your e-mail."

As Judy marched back to her car, he glanced at the message on the screen: One new voice mail. He punched in his access code and listened. In his mind, he dropped to his knees.

"This is agent Jon Segert with the Portland office of the FBI. I would like to set up a time to meet with you regarding your trading activity on VEY Steel. Please call me back, as soon as possible, at—"

Raleigh hit DELETE.

CHAPTER 6

The Estate Sale

The phone didn't ring often, but when it did, a workman was usually on the other end of the line. Jean hadn't reached out to many of their friends since they'd been back in Portland. She and Spence wanted to complete a few more projects on the house first. But after dinner with Phil and Patty, Jean waited, not so patiently, for a call from Phil. The thrill of a hunt for something—anything—would break the calm. The phone rang.

"Can you get that, Jean? I'm setting up new files in the den," Spence called out.

She rushed down the stairs, leaving the project of organizing her sewing notions in the guestroom closet. Picking up the phone in anticipation of good news, Jean sighed when she heard the automated voice ask if she'd planned for "final expenses."

"Are you kidding me? Don't do me in yet." She hit the END button a little too hard. Halfway up the stairs, the phone rang again. Jean eyed the digital readout. *Go to voicemail?* Unable to ignore the ring, she raced back down the stairs and checked the caller ID...Phil. Her adrenaline surged.

"I found an estate sale for us this coming Saturday," Phil sang. "And are you ready? This one's on our old street. Remember the yellow bungalow, one block from our houses?"

"Oh, yeah. Spence and I used to run by that woman's house."

"That's the one! Judy Hawkins called me this morning. She said there would be a ton of Christmas stuff, so I definitely want to go."

"Outstanding! I'm all over this."

"Judy wouldn't have called if it wasn't going to be good. I've saved her butt on more than one occasion. I help her salt her sales with some of my extra ornaments to beef up her inventory. She owes me."

"Should I meet you? Do you want to ride together? What time?" *Right now?* She didn't know if she could wait until Saturday.

"How about I pick you up at nine? Opens at ten. I'll bring my big, fat SUV. You're going to buy a ton of stuff. Plus, parking will be horrendous."

"Fabulous! I want to be the first ones in the door." She hung up the phone and did a twisty dance in the kitchen. "Yeah baby...yeah baby...going to an estate sale, baby!"

Jean pictured the exact house Phil was referring to, in vivid detail. She and Spence used to jog by that charming bungalow every day in her younger and suppler years. She could picture the elderly woman who smiled and waved to her each morning on her way down the street. She was meticulous about cleaning out her bird bath when the weather was nice, always neatly dressed, and wore her peppery hair in a French twist. She probably got decked out to go to the grocery store. Finally seeing the inside of the house would be a treat.

"Phil and I are going to an estate sale on Saturday, Spence!" she shouted as she ran back up the stairs.

"Uh-oh. Trouble. Don't buy anything!"

She leaned over the upstairs railing. "You wouldn't say that if there were tons of albums!"

"Check if they have any. You can buy those. That's all."

"Uh-huh..."

Buoyed by the prospect of finding a chest for their bedroom, she pulled out the bolt of thick fabric to start on their new bedspread. As she unwound the tube, she hoped the old woman in the yellow bungalow was still alive. She'd never known her name, but figured she must have been in her mid-sixties twenty years ago.

Jean fanned out the leading edge of the fabric over the guest bed and ran her hand across the raised pattern. She couldn't wait to start sleeping under the rounded squares of deep brown, ginger, persimmon, and sage. She and Spence would soon wake up under the multiple textures, rich colors, and soft feel of everything new in their life. A pleasure to cut and sew. Time to get started.

On Saturday, the Portland fall color was in full glory, especially in Irvington where the resident trees had seen more history than the rest of the city. Jean and Phil cruised around the block a couple of times to view their old houses.

"Your house needs a paint job, but the lawn looks good. Ours is as cute as ever," Phil said. "I hope they never mess with the gingerbread trim."

"Couldn't touch these now. I wish we could have kept the house after we moved. Can't go back and change things." She craned her neck to peer inside her and Spence's old house as they went by.

"So how are you doing with the whole 'not working' thing?"

"My body has stress memory; like an old friend I'm learning to live without. I thought this would be easy, but no go. I need something to happen—anything to keep from getting bored. That's worse than being stressed out."

"You need time. Think like me. Today is the day."

"If we have that kind of time, then let's get coffee," Jean said and started to laugh.

After stopping to pick up a cinnamon roll and two tall coffees, she and Phil parked in front of the yellow Craftsman bungalow. They got out and leaned against Phil's Land Cruiser. The canopy of the old trees gave up the fall season, one leaf at a time.

"This sticky bun is going to raise hell with your diabetes." She took a big bite and handed the roll back to him.

"Hon, I do a lot of things I shouldn't do." Phil's gaze zeroed in on a BMW pulling up to the curb on the opposite side of the street. "See that guy? I know him—he's a dealer. Shark like you wouldn't believe."

"And we're here so early because—" She took a sip of her coffee and spotted the shabbily dressed man in the BMW. She figured he was probably none too happy to see Phil here either.

"You have to get here early to make the clean sweep of the inventory. If you spot something, even if you don't think you'll buy it, hold on tight." Phil licked the sticky off his fingers. "Is your heart pumping yet?"

"Kind of, but I don't know if the thumping is from excitement or the cinnamon roll. We're vultures."

"Peck or get pecked, sweetie. If you're not careful, you'll end up like that fat, flat squirrel in the road." Phil pointed to the asphalt behind them. "I'll bet Judy's checking out how many cars are here early. She's buzzing around the house like a figure skater on steroids and changing all the prices because people are waiting. Yes, ma'am, a good one like this doesn't come along too often anymore." Phil polished off the last of the cinnamon roll and brushed his gray beard of remnant flecks of sugar glaze.

"I feel like chum. How long until we can go in?" Jean watched Phil's face calculate his strategy with the intensity of a Navy SEAL as he licked his fingers.

"We've got about five minutes, and then we'll work our way to the porch to queue up." A twinge of espionage twinkled in his eyes. "If you had to dig for one good thing to say for Judy, she's always on time."

They waited. The fiery leaves of the maple tree drifted to the ground in the front yard. As her gaze followed a leaf's path, she spotted the bird bath.

"Phil—the bird bath's still here! I want it. How can I keep anybody else from buying it?" Jean whipped her head around and grabbed his shoulders. "I want that bird bath!"

"You can't just go up and take it, Jean." Phil's voice jiggled with her shake. "Against the rules. When we get inside we'll ask how much it is." He grimaced at the front yard. "You know, we'll lose some valuable time if we're held up with that door stop. Okay, I get it—it's all about *you* today. All right, I'll go in and tell Judy you want to buy the friggin' bird bath. I hate that thing already."

"I don't care what the price is. The calla lilies around the rim are fantastic. Let's go!"

"You're too excited. For God's sake, Jean—act blasé." Phil rolled his eyes and adjusted his red bandana.

Game on.

Jean and Phil were the second and third people through the door. She stopped in her tracks at the small fireplace in a sitting area just to the right of the front door. The intimate space was only big enough for two chairs; its entrance was flanked by tiger-striped oak columns. Old books lined the built-in bookcases on each end. A raised border rimmed the handmade aqua tiles around the fireplace. She ran her finger over the spines and pulled out a first edition of Dashiell Hammett's *The Maltese Falcon*. She knew Spence would go crazy for this one, especially with the original dust jacket. She'd save it for Christmas. The book was in excellent condition for four hundred dollars, a good deal. She tucked it under her arm and checked out the competition.

Phil reported back that Judy would reserve the bird bath for Jean, and then he was off through the living room at lightning speed to the dining room. He called out to her as she stared at the two Stickley chairs in the little sitting area. The deep indent on only one of the cushions gave her pause.

"Jean, look at these dishes. Too bad you're into modern now, or I'd make you buy them."

Jean pulled herself away and wandered into the dining room to join Phil. The wide-planked oak floor creaked under her footsteps. She picked up one of the plates to admire the soft yellow roses and reflective gold vine circling the rim.

"These are beautiful. People don't entertain this way anymore. In another life, I would have snapped these up."

"Let's go upstairs. The Christmas stuff must be in the bedrooms."

Jean climbed the scratched stairs to follow Phil into one of the two bedrooms. Like a raccoon, Phil was immediately drawn to the boxes of Shiny Brite Christmas ornaments stacked on the bureau. Satisfied he'd found his prize, he grinned at her.

"These are fabulous! I'm taking them all. You can tell they're super old." Phil pulled out one of the delicate glass ornaments and held it up to the light. He twirled the cobalt-blue globe, inspecting the surface for cracks. "If you pull up the hanger tops and see uneven edges like this underneath, that's a sure sign they're hand-blown. The color is fantastic. I'd say they're from about 1880 to 1900. Yeah, I'm all over *these*. Jump, jive, and Judy!"

"Patty's going to love seeing those come in the house." Jean turned to the brass bed, which practically filled the small bedroom, and gasped at a little girl's dress fanned out across the bedspread.

"I'll sneak them in when she goes to the store. She'll never know."

"Check out this dress, Phil. The hummingbirds are so sweet."

"Way too small for you, honey," Phil chortled and continued to inspect the ornaments.

Jean ran her hand down the length of the little dress and fingered the wispy, transparent layer of sheer fabric that seemed to float over the luminescent white satin underneath. *Weightless and so much movement.* Her face fell when she noticed the three brownish spots on the bodice under the soft satin piping around the neckline.

"Wow, I'd cry my eyes out if I spilled something on this dress," she said, holding up the dress to show Phil.

"I can just imagine you in that. Put a bow in your hair and smoke a cigarette, then you'd turn into Bette Davis as Baby Jane."

Jean laughed, but she had so much compassion for the little girl who wore this adorable dress. She must have been devastated to deface something so fantastic. Jean imagined herself twirling around and around in front of a mirror with the delicate folds of the skirt lifting into the air, the hummingbirds chasing each other.

The dress pulled at her. Jean succumbed. She folded and tucked it under the tissue, secured the lid, and retied the ribbon. She slipped the box under her arm. "I'm moving to the bedroom across the way."

"I have a few more to go through in here."

Ambling across the short hall, Jean stuck her head in the doorway of the master bedroom. The room was fairly small but had two closet doors instead of one. No bed. She hoped the old lady was still using it somewhere.

In the corner, where surely a second nightstand once stood, was a chest. She floated toward it, as if magnetized. She smoothed her hand over the lid. The sticker on the corner indicated one hundred dollars. The pine wood was stained dark with a crackly finish. Vacant worm holes dotted the legs; the edges were marred and dinged. She lifted the wobbly lid; the hinges groaned in protest, but revealed nothing inside. The interior smelled woodsy sweet and earthy. If the price could be negotiated down to seventy-five, she'd buy it. There would be no guilt in painting the chest a fun color. She needed to drag Phil away from the ornaments to get a second opinion.

Jean placed the white box and book on the floor. Phil would give her grief if he found out she was going to buy the dress. She hadn't even checked the price.

"Hey, Phil! C'mere! I need your opinion on something."

Phil joined her with the stack of ornament boxes in his arms. He never took one eye off them after he set them on the floor.

"What do you think of this chest?" she asked, squeezing her bottom lip with her fingers.

"Girl, this is just trash. So ugly. You buy this and I'll divorce you."

"I know, but imagine the wood sanded and painted in a rich magenta with an eggshell sheen." She swept her hand across the chest, like one of the striking models in front of a shiny red Ferrari at a car show.

"Uh-hmmm. Whatever. Don't pay over twenty-five."

"I'm going down to negotiate. Hang on to your bandana."

"Oh, God—I'm ruined." Phil rolled his eyes.

Jean stuck out her tongue and picked up the white box, balancing the book on top. She rehearsed her negotiation as she teetered down the stairs.

"Hi, I'm Jean." She planted herself in front of Judy's table in the entry way. "I was looking at the chest up in the master bedroom. It's kind of rough. Would you take seventy?"

Judy acted overly busy and fingered through the cash box. "The chest is an antique. We've had a few others interested."

Act blasé. "That may be, but I have cash. I'll buy the chest right now for seventy. I'm also the one who wants the bird bath. And I'll take this book and this little dress with the stains on the front." She thumped the box for emphasis. "The two heavy pieces—I'll take them off your hands. Phil will be happy to help me move them." *Bundle everything for one lower price.* She'd learned the strategy on a television show. She set the box and book on the card table, dug through her purse, and pulled out her wallet.

"All four for three twenty-five and they're sold. The bird bath is dirty." She presented Judy with a wide smile and waved the cash at her as if the wad were on fire.

"Okay, how about this: five twenty-five for all four," Judy countered, continuing to fidget with the stack of receipts. She glanced at the wad.

"Five hundred and we have a deal," she came back. Too quick. *Dammit!*

After a moment of silence, Judy shook her head. "Five twenty-five—that's it. Somebody else has asked about the bird bath. I told them it was already sold to you."

Thank God Phil's not here. I think I just got screwed.

Judy wrote up the receipt as Phil lumbered down the stairs with the entire pile of Christmas ornament boxes. Sweat poured from beneath his red bandana. He looked more like *Sauna* Claus delivering Christmas presents in Brazil...in the summer. Jean beamed at him and ran over to take a few before they slid off from the top of the stack. Phil consummated a deal on the ornaments for half the marked price.

I got pecked and left for the buzzards.

With the white box and book tucked under her arm, Jean follow-ed Phil to the truck. She closed the door and ran up the steps, two at a time, and stood next to the bird bath. Phil plodded after her as she heaved the bowl and lugged the top piece to the truck. He stayed behind and twisted the base, swearing as he tried to release it from the ground.

"God, Jean! You're busting my hump." Phil smacked his hands together to shake off the dirt. "Too heavy...and dirty."

"Just wait. Let's go back inside to get the chest in the upstairs bedroom. I bought it." She wiped her hands on her jeans and gave Phil a guilty grin, already anticipating his reaction.

"Are you kidding me?"

They laughed their way through the crook of the stairs as they wrestled with the chest. Twice she had to rest on the steps to catch her breath because they couldn't stop breaking up.

"You and me, bud, need to start working out."

"No, you have to work out." Phil said wiped the sweat off his face. "I should be in the truck, smoking a cigarette, watching you drag this damn thing out of here. I'm making you buy lunch."

While Spence and Bill met with a prospective client who wanted to sell his record collection, Jean took her time hosing off the dirt from the bird bath. She moved the base to different spots under the tree and darted inside after each adjustment to inspect the view. Once satisfied, she filled the bowl with fresh water and admired the relief of the vines snaking up the base to meet the calla lilies lying the rim.

Back inside the house, Jean took a sip from her water bottle and eyed the chest. Maybe Spence wouldn't hate it, but he certainly wasn't going to be thrilled. Buyer's remorse crept up on her. Phil's assessment was right. She pulled several strips of paint samples from the banded stack and placed them in a random pattern on the lid. Sanded and painted, she might feel better about the purchase.

The lid wiggled and groaned. The hinge was missing a screw. *Why hadn't I seen that at the estate sale?* She trotted to the tool chest in the garage and dug out a screwdriver and a couple of screws. She grabbed the can of WD40. The last thing she wanted was for Spence to hear the chest squeak. The noise would drive him crazy.

Once secured and silenced, she opened and closed the lid several times. Something seemed odd. The bottom was set higher than normal. She stuck her hand inside and pressed on the wood. Some give, which also seemed odd for a solid-wood chest. She studied the sides. The bottom piece was only floating inside, unattached. Her radar sounded.

In her white socks, she sprinted back to the garage to retrieve a putty knife. She searched through the toolbox, envisioning all kinds of treasures underneath the wood. She tried not to get excited, but the suspense was like matching up the first three numbers on a lottery ticket. Back in the living room, she leaned into the chest and pried at the edges. It finally released. She lifted out the plywood piece and saw a square bundle of faded brown paper, knotted with frayed hemp twine.

"Oh my God! Something is in here."

The weight surprised her as she lifted the bundle and set it on the living room rug. One more time, Jean did a tiptoe trot to the mudroom to get her scissors from her sewing basket.

Poising the scissors around the twine, she made two cuts. She turned the bundle over to find the folded seam. Keeping the paper intact seemed like a good idea...just in case. She pulled open the paper as if what was inside might bite. Her breath caught in her throat: a flower garden of colors swirled in front of her. A folded piece of spectacular fabric.

She opened the three folds and stared in awe. Mycroft rubbed against her. As he moved around her to investigate, his back arched and his tail puffed like a stiff bottle brush. He sniffed the fabric, stalked in a slow crab walk, and sat. He stared, staying close by her side.

"Now, you stay away from this, big boy." She smoothed his fur and continued to stare at the fabric. Mycroft leaned forward and nosed the edges. His bright-green eyes on full alert.

The rumble of the garage door broke her trance. Spence. She glanced at her watch, shocked it was already five thirty. To hide the surprise, she folded the fabric in the paper and set the bundle inside the chest. Mycroft raced up the steps.

"Hi, honey! Yes, yes, Mycroft, I love you too!"

Jean grinned with all the tools littered around her. She must have looked like a school kid in shop class.

"You've been busy."

"Oh, I've been busy all right. C'mere—you won't believe what I found."

Spence joined her in the living room and grimaced at the chest. "This is lovely, honey. I hope you're not thinking of keeping this in the house."

"I know, right? But I don't think it was a knucklehead purchase. Take a gander at what was inside."

Spence sat on the hassock as she pulled the bundle from the chest. She unfolded the fabric and, with careful ceremony, turned it to face Spence.

"Oh my God!"

"Can you believe this? I said the same thing too."

The fabric was approximately eighteen inches square. The red-plumed heads of three large pheasant-like birds were turned toward their viewer, their eyes alert, questioning. The reflective quality of the material gave the illusion their eyes were real. The feathers graduated in a luminescent spray of sparkling turquoise, bright gold, rich pumpkin, and chestnut brown. Deep-green vines, with delicate white flowers, swirled around the rich vanilla background. Jean crawled on the floor to view it from different angles. Spence continued to stare, speechless.

"Spence, I know fabric. This isn't like anything I've seen before. No fuzz from fraying thread...and no real weave. It just *is*. Feel it. Smooth and heavy. Weird, huh?" She fingered only the borders to avoid touching the images.

"Do you think it's old? Where did this come from?" Spence leaned over to touch the corners.

"I don't know. I'm going to try and find out. I'm calling the estate sale lady at Hawkins & Company first thing on Monday. I want to talk to the old woman who owned that house, if she's still alive." She refolded the fabric in the original paper and set the bundle back in the chest. "Oh, wait. Check this out." She pointed out the window at the bird bath.

"Wow, I love it! Those birds in that fabric could take a drink. Perfect! Hey, and I've got good news too." Spence bounded up to the kitchen and retrieved a bag. "Bill and I found a collection we're going to buy. I brought some choice ones home. I got some vintage Wes Montgomery, John Coltrane, and—drum roll, please—the original soundtrack from *Goldfinger*." He pulled out the album, slid the vinyl disc from its sleeve, and blew around the edge. He placed the record on the turntable and lowered the needle. Through the crackle and pop, Shirley Bassey's penetrating, powerful voice belted out the first song on side one.

CHAPTER 7

Life Isn't What We Thought It Was

Jean's eyes flew open at five o'clock on Sunday morning. Lying in bed, she stared at the fir trees through the sliding glass door. She smiled as she thought about last night's party for two. Having played all five of Spence's new albums, they'd sipped wine, fantasized about the fabric, and imagined the possibilities. The fabric got pulled out and put away at least three times.

As the evening wound down, they laughed about their favorite show, *Antiques Roadshow*, a public television program of experts who estimated the worth of attic treasures from all over the country. She and Spence played out what the show's appraisers might say about the fabric. Their favorite part of the program highlighted obscure objects with estimates far beyond what anyone could have imagined.

"What would they say if we took this to the *Roadshow*? 'Ma'am, you have a national treasure...cha-ching!' Should I weep or just start run-ning around the studio whooping?" Spence laughed as she practiced her emotional reactions.

Now, she slipped out of the comforter and padded to the bath-room, unprepared for the early morning chill. She needed coffee, and also a few minutes to herself to inspect the fabric with more sober eyes. Jean shook her head at Mycroft; on his back, smashed up against Spence's leg and snoring. Once the smell of fresh brew wafted up the stairs, Spence would get up and so would Mycroft.

Jean flipped on the coffee maker. While it chugged and steamed, she stepped down to the living room and pulled back the three sets of drapes to enjoy a complete view of the backyard garden—and so the light would be good for another examination of the fabric. She unfolded it and went back to the kitchen. The coffee wasn't quite done, but no-drip machines existed for impatient souls with a hangover. She poured herself a cup and set an empty one on the counter for Spence.

The first peeks of sunlight cast soft shafts through the backyard and into the living room. As if making a planned journey, one of them found its destination and bounced off the reflective fabric. The light danced on the feathers, causing the birds' eyes to glint. She took her first sip, convinced they were admiring her too. She retrieved her Droid. Perfect for taking a few pictures.

As she snapped photos from different angles, the floor squeaked. Spence and Mycroft plodded down the stairs. They both stood in a daze, each with their hair going in several directions. Mycroft blinked awake, and Spence yawned. He filled his coffee cup and joined her in the living room.

"Hey, hi! I'm a bit fuzzy this morning. I had a lot of fun last night—how about you?" Spence glanced at the albums strewn on the floor around the stereo. "I can't believe I didn't put those away before we went to bed."

"Way too much fun." She took another swig of her coffee, her eyes fixed on the fabric. "The light plays games on it."

"I think you're about to get obsessed with that thing."

"I know we kidded around last night, but there's a quality I can't explain. It's so ethereal. I've got to find out more."

Throughout the morning, they completed their chores. She cleaned up the house. Spence mowed the backyard and replaced the water in the bird bath. The fabric remained flat on the hassock. She couldn't resist stopping to admire it every time she went by. Mycroft guarded, as if he had ownership. She broke away to do the laundry in the garage and met up with Spence as he put away the lawnmower.

"Let's make some lunch, or we can go to GG's Deli," Spence suggested.

As they walked inside, Jean noticed Mycroft had was changed position and crouched on the fabric—no, half crouched.

"Honey, pull him off there. He'll get his fur all over it."

A loud *bang* on the window made them both jump.

"What was that?" she asked. "No, wait—look at Mycroft. His face is weird." She touched Spence's arm to prevent him from moving. Curious, they both stood on the top step and studied the cat.

"He's trying to lay an egg or something. His back feet are scooting around, and his eyes are closed," Spence whispered.

Mycroft opened his eyes wide, jumped off the fabric, and ran to the three living room windows. He ran past them and bounded up the stairs. Alarmed, they followed him.

Mycroft bounded back down the stairs. He slid to a stop at the glass door to the patio off the dining room. Jean ran behind him. Mycroft launched himself over the threshold.

"What the heck was *that* about? He's fine now."

"Umm...look at this." Spence stared at the fabric as if a sink hole had opened up.

"Spence! Where are the birds? Where are...the...birds?" The fabric was empty. Only the flowering vines remained.

Their gaze rose in unison to the bird bath in the backyard. Around the rim of stone calla lilies perched three enormous pheasants, stretching their wings and dipping their beaks into the sparkling fresh water to take a drink. An exact match to the birds in the fabric. The long spikes of their tail feathers touched the ground. One launched its heavy wings into the air, followed by the second and then the third. They ran to the window. The birds' iridescent bodies rose higher and higher, past the tops of towering fir trees and into the sun. They shielded their eyes from the glare and followed the birds' path until they disappeared.

"Spence..." she whispered, gawking out the window.

"No...not possible."

Jean turned to check on Mycroft. Her legs dragged concrete; a quest to do something normal, to make sure the world still spun on its axis.

On the patio, Mycroft crouched in the same position as on the fabric. Something was underneath him. He sprung up when she opened the sliding glass door. A dead robin lay on the patio, blood pooled around its head.

CHAPTER 8

Mycroft

The house changed after Jean brought the wood box into the living room. Mycroft didn't know if he liked the box, but it was different. The scent was like nothing else in the house. This air was strange. Not Jean's or Spence's clothes, his toys, the rugs, or his condo in front of the window.

Jean was focused on something inside it. *What is she doing?* He hopped down the steps and stopped; an aroma so sweet, so rich and inviting wafted over him. He studied her. Jean had something in her hands. Unable to resist, he sauntered to her and rubbed against her back. A flower scent, and she was all his.

A wave of alarm flowed through him, from head to tail, as he wound to the front of her. The birds on the floor stared back at him, willing him forward. *Are they predator or prey?* He sniffed the piece of cloth and distinctly heard his name. Other voices. His concentration broke when Jean warned him to stay away. The birds wanted him close. His body relaxed. They weren't a threat. Something good.

The garage door opened. Spence would be coming inside any minute. He must tell Spence about this new development.

Mycroft bounded to the mudroom to wait. *Open...Open...Come up the stairs.* As soon as Spence came in the door, he tried to slow him down to listen. Something amazing had happened while he was away. Finally he threw himself on the floor in front of Spence's feet. Worked every time.

"Yes, yes, Mycroft, I love you too," Spence cooed.

More discussion than normal. Even Spence was excited about the birds in the house. After dinner, he listened to Jean to Spence fawn over his fabric from his perch on the living room stairs.

Don't hurt my birds.

Mycroft didn't mind the music being played in the evening, but this was louder than usual, past his normal bedtime. Sleepy, his belly full, he slinked up to bed. He needed quiet. Think.

He slept soundly next to Spence's leg. Warm and solid. Thinking about the birds made him want to be near the birds. He opened his eyes and studied Spence's upside-down face, willing him to wake up. The aroma of coffee might speed this process along.

"Good morning, big boy," Spence whispered and stroked the soft spot under his chin. "What's Mommy doing? I bet she's playing with the birds. What do you think?"

Let's go see my birds.

Mycroft led Spence down the stairs and into the kitchen. He stopped at the bottom. His name being called, but Jean wasn't talking. The voice wasn't her voice. More like little bells ringing.

Mycroft, your enemy is your friend.

Confused, he trotted to Jean for comfort. The *pop* of the lid on the can got his attention. After breakfast, he'd sit by the birds until they told him what to do.

He returned to the living room and hopped on the couch. He stared. The birds' eyes shifted toward the sound of the lawnmower outside. Curious. A sense of calm lured him forward.

Mycroft inched closer, raised his paw, and set his pads on one of the birds in the fabric. He pulled back, waiting for a reaction. Three sets of eyes moved in unison to gaze back at him, blinking. A tail feather ruffled up. He set his paw down to still it. A wing bulged. A feather popped out.

Stepping on the fabric, Mycroft lowered himself over the birds. They stirred beneath his belly. His paws rose up and down as the wings emerged. The warmth ran up his paws, into his chest, and raced through his body to his tail. He closed his eyes and absorbed their instructions.

Yes, I will help.

Jean and Spence coming inside.

Bang!

He must hurry. It would happen soon. *Where?* He jumped from the fabric and ran to the windows in the living room. *Not here.*

Bedroom! He ran past Jean and Spence. They called after him. *Not here.*

His patio! He bounded down the stairs, two at a time, and raced to the sliding glass door in the dining room. Jean ran behind him.

Open...open...the door...Please hurry!

As Jean opened it, Mycroft launched himself over the threshold. He searched the walkway and spotted the robin thrashing in pain; blood oozed from its beak.

Mycroft inched to the robin and lowered his body over it. Yes, the bird needed his soft, warm fur, to comfort, to cease the agony. He purred a deep rumble. Soothe. Mycroft closed his eyes to focus.

Go, little bird...Fly again...where you belong.

CHAPTER 9

Milwaukie Manor

Mary smiled at Helen and Evelyn across the table, their newly established spot when they dined together in the evening. She placed her white linen napkin in her lap, smoothed out the folds, and announced, "Well, my things were sold yesterday."

"Oh, Mary...so hard." Helen said and reached for her hand.

Evelyn nodded in agreement. "Are you all right?"

"The anticipation was harder than the sale actually happening. I had the opportunity to go through everything before I left the house last week. I relived so many special moments in my life. Wonderful things happened to me, which was more important than to have collected wonderful things."

The trio toasted each other through the tasty meal of brisket and fresh vegetables from the community's organic garden.

Back at her apartment, Mary smoothed her sheets into place and unfolded the wedding ring quilt at the bottom of the bed. Charlotte's old quilt, her nighttime companion, had been with her since that first night in Doc's house. She regretted, now, leaving behind the antique chest. Her hands froze in mid-fold.

"The chest!" she said aloud. "The bottom comes out."

Mary reached for the phone on the nightstand. She hit nine for an outside line and called Raleigh's cell number. Mixing up the digits, she hung up and tried again. His phone rang as if under water. She wrinkled her nose. So hard to understand his voice, and the ugly tune annoyed her. Raleigh disconnected his home service to exclusively use his cell phone. At least he answered when she called.

"Raleigh, your mother here."

"Mom, I know who you are. Is everything okay?"

"I want my chest back. The one I had at the bottom of the bed."

"The chest's been sold. I have no idea where it is. You should have taken it with you when you had the chance."

"Don't argue with me. I remembered something as I was making the bed. I want that chest."

"All right." Raleigh sighed. "I'll call Judy Hawkins to see if I can find out any information. Be prepared to pay more than what it sold for. That's *if* we can track down the buyer."

"Please, Raleigh. Do what you need to do. This is important."

"Dammit," Raleigh shouted and tossed his phone on the kitchen counter. *Here we go.* Of course Mary would try and claw back her stuff and make his life miserable. This probably wouldn't be the last panicky call he'd get in the coming weeks. Call Judy Hawkins in the morning. No—maybe he shouldn't, and tell Mary he did. Tell her Judy didn't know who bought the chest. Yes, a much better plan. If he stood on his head to get the chest back, the floodgates would open. But Mary had sounded funny, a little too desperate. Something about the edge in her voice. Nothing was inside that ugly chest. Mary had taken the quilt with her. *What's going on?*

Raleigh considered the situation for a few minutes. Mary must be having one of her moments.

CHAPTER 10

Game On...Again

Monday morning the birds were back in the fabric as if nothing had happened. *Am I crazy?* Jean tried to distract herself with puttering. Spence had experienced them fly too. *Are we both insane?* She cleaned up the dishes, wiped the counters, and helped Spence change the sheets. Normally the bed would have been changed on Sunday, but yesterday's events had interrupted their routine.

The clock on the coffee maker flashed 9:45; the microwave showed 9:46. The morning financial news might provide some distraction for fourteen or fifteen minutes. Spence attempted to bury himself in the *Oregonian* in the living room. When she peeked around the corner from the kitchen, he was staring into the backyard. The pendulum on his mother's farmhouse clock in the dining room ticked for a three-minute eternity. Ten bongs. She made herself wait one additional minute.

At 10:01, she turned off the television and called the number for Hawkins & Company. She tapped the pen on her list pad, waiting for Judy Hawkins to answer. Ink marks dotted the cat cartoon at the top of the paper that said: *Time and cats wait for no one.* On the fourth ring, she anticipated the start of a voicemail greeting and jumped when Judy's voice came on the line.

"Hawkins & Company, Judy speaking." Judy sounded like she had already regretted picking up the phone.

"Good morning. This is Jean Collins. I bought a chest this past Saturday at your sale on Northeast Nineteenth Street."

"Yes, I remember you. No returns. All sales are final."

"No, I love the chest," she said, closing her eyes. *Patience.* "I'm calling to get the number of the woman who owned it. I'd like to find out more of the family history."

"We don't give out personal information, and I don't have the owner's number, anyway." Judy sighed. "She's moved to a retirement community, somewhere by the river in Milwaukie. I've been dealing with her son."

"Can I call her son then?" she pressed. At least she had con-firmation the old woman was alive. Jean was hoping for that not only to get information about the fabric but because she had a soft spot for the woman in her and Spence's previous life in Portland.

"Well, I guess that's okay." She could tell Judy wanted to get her off the line. "Here's his cell phone number. His name is Raleigh Coulter."

Jean jotted the information on her list pad. As she recited the number back, she realized she was talking into dead air. Judy had already hung up.

"Unbelievable!" She stared at the phone, appalled.

Jean set her mug in the microwave and punched in twenty seconds. The digital indicator counted down as she pondered her next move. The oven dinged. She picked up the phone.

Raleigh stared at the computer screen in his high-rise office down-town, watching the day's trade price tick downward on VEY Steel. He flinched when his cell phone rang. He glanced at the little clock in the upper-right corner...10:17 a.m. He checked the caller ID to make sure it wasn't that FBI clown. A local number he didn't recognize.

Curious, he answered and scribbled a reminder to set up a separate ring tone for the FBI guy.

"Raleigh Coulter." He kept his voice firm. Intimidation worked well to cut short any superfluous conversation.

"Hello, Mr. Coulter. My name is Jean Collins. I purchased your mother's chest at her estate sale this past Saturday."

"Okay...yeah?" Raleigh sat up straight.

"Judy Hawkins gave me your number this morning. I'm calling because I'd like to find out a little more about where the chest came from—you know—the history."

"Well...it's old." This was too much of a coincidence. His mother calling about the chest in a panic last night and now this woman who bought it is calling? Something must have been inside. "How about I come by? What's your address? I'll tell you what I know."

"Uh...no, that's okay. I don't want to trouble you. Not a big deal. Really."

Raleigh winced. Coming on a little too strong. "No trouble at all...*really*," he said, mimicking her in an attempt to soothe. This woman had found something.

Click.

He stared at his phone.

Raleigh gabbed a Post-it note and wrote down the number for the woman who had just called him. *Did she say her name was Jean?* He turned to his computer and opened a new window in his browser. He typed the phone number into the online white pages and selected the reverse look-up option. *Bingo!* The address for a Spencer and Jean Collins. The accompanying map pinpointed their house to be off River Road in Milwaukie. He moved the cursor around. The Collinses' were less than a mile from Milwaukie Manor.

"Well, what do you know..."

He shut down the computer and grabbed his keys to the Porsche. Time to visit his mother.

After the conversation with Raleigh Coulter, Jean went into the living room to sit with Spence.

"What happened? Your side of the call sounded pretty scratchy," Spence said.

"It was a mistake to call this Raleigh guy. I don't trust his motives."

"You're the one who called him, sweetie. How can he have a motive?"

"Weird. I think he knew I found something in that chest. I just got a bad vibe and hung up on him." Embarrassed now, explaining the call to Spence, she questioned her rude reaction to the phone conversation.

"Well...why don't we bypass this guy altogether and find the woman ourselves? We can go straight to the source. It shouldn't be too hard. Tax records on the address should tell you her name."

"Brilliant! The estate sale lady said she's in a retirement community right here on the river in Milwaukie. Pretty easy to narrow down."

She dashed to the computer in the den. Drumming her nails on the desk, the links to the real estate tax records came up. After a few minutes, she called out, "I found her! You're a genius."

Spence peered over her shoulder. "Hello, Mary Coulter."

Jean proceeded to map the area on Google Earth. She wrote the names of four retirement communities dotted along the route. Most of them she'd already recognized while running errands.

"All I have to do is call these places and ask for Mary. We might be able to speak with her today."

"What do we do with the fabric in the meantime? We can't keep it out like this."

She studied the beam in the ceiling. "Let's put it in the trunk of the car. That way, if we leave the house it goes with us. While we're home, it's safe in the garage, and Mycroft won't get all freaked out again. I'll keep the car locked and alarmed."

"Uh...okay...I guess."

CHAPTER 11

Sniffing Out the Details

Raleigh slowed the Porsche as he approached the Collinses' house. All of the triangular clerestory windows on the front were patterned glass.

"You can't see in," he muttered. "Pretty cool."

Some windows acted as one-way shields, but from keeping such a close eye on his mother's neighborhood, he knew old windows. The Collinses couldn't see out either.

The house looked to be one story, but the back revealed the peak of a second level. Tiny pine cones littered the driveway and swirled in circles when the wind kicked up.

A car approached in the rearview mirror. Spooked, Raleigh continued around the block, circled, and pulled in front of the house next door. He idled in park and formulated a plan.

The same car he'd seen in the rearview, a black Crown Victoria, drove toward him from the opposite direction. The man inside stared at him as he passed.

"Huh..."

Focus on the house. He had to get inside. The fabric was in there. This Jean character wouldn't tell him anything if he knocked. But if the Collinses left, he might find a way in. He pulled away from the curb. Before he took any risks, he needed more information out of

Mary.

He pulled into Milwaukie Manor and parked in a spot marked Visitors Only. The sloped path led him to his mother's apartment. He opened the screen door and tapped the knocker. No answer. He banged a little harder.

"Raleigh," Mary said as she strolled up the sidewalk behind him, carrying a canvas tote bag. "You should have called. I was over at the library building."

"In the neighborhood, so I thought I'd drop by."

"Come in, come in. I have everything nearly unpacked. Did you find out who has the chest yet?" Mary set the canvas bag on the living room chair. She padded to the kitchen. "Tea? Coffee?"

"No, I can't stay. I don't have any new information. I tried to call Judy this morning but had to leave a message. Why do you want the chest back so badly? Did you find that fabric you were looking for?" He tried to sound casual.

"No...I miss the chest more than I thought I would, that's all. The quilt was always kept in there, and now I don't have a place to store it. There's not a lot of extra room in here." Mary pulled a mug out of the cabinet, avoiding eye contact. "How'd I do at the estate sale?"

"You did all right. I'm waiting for Judy to send me a full reconciliation and a check. I talked with her last night, and she thought the sale was well-attended."

"Didn't you ask her about the chest?"

"Uh...no...I mean, she called me before you called last night."

"Do you want to sit outside with me? Lovely day."

"No, I gotta go."

"Bye, dear." Mary reached for the phone.

The screen on its base flashed a red one, indicating she had a new voice mail. He hesitated. Should he wait? He decided against it. The screen door hissed behind him.

Raleigh drove back to the Collinses' house. He pulled to the house next door and turned off the ignition. The plan for reconciling the estate sale rolled around in his head. If he doubled the sales commission percentage and lowered some of the prices on the reconciliation, he could keep the difference before making the deposit into his mother's account. He'd have to remind Judy to make the check out to him, not to Mary. The rest could be made up when the house was sold.

Bored with the lack of any activity around the Collinses' house, the grumble in his stomach reminded him of the time. Pick up lunch and come back. If he could catch them leave, then he'd survey the scene, and possibly find an easy way to get inside. If not, he'd head back to his office downtown. This would definitely need some careful planning.

The process took less than fifteen minutes for Jean to locate Mary Coulter. After calling Homefront Estates, River Villas, and Bluffs on the Willamette with no luck, she scored with Milwaukie Manor. By that call she had her pitch down cold.

"Hi, my name is Jean Collins. I'm trying to reach a resident who just moved in—Mary Coulter. Can you to transfer me or give me her direct number?"

"Yes, certainly. I apologize, but I can't give out direct numbers without express permission from the resident. This policy ensures their privacy. But I can transfer you." The receptionist sounded polite and professional.

The line rang several times before voice mail picked up.

Damn! she thought but left a message. "Hello, Ms. Coulter. My name is Jean Collins. I purchased a chest from the estate sale at your house this past Saturday. My husband, Spencer, and I would love to visit you to find out more of the history behind it. We live close to Milwaukie Manor. Please give us a call as soon as you can." She recited their number and hung up. Jean was too nervous to say anything about the fabric. The woman may not even know it was inside the chest. She'd have to wait for a call back.

Jean folded the fabric in some fresh tissue and placed it in a white gift box.

"Spence, can you listen for the phone while I take the fabric out to the car? I'm waiting for Mary Coulter to call." She glanced at the chest still sitting in the living room.

"Sure thing," Spence called back from the den. He had been researching ancient fabric on the Internet all morning.

Jean walked the white box through the mudroom and out to the garage. She placed the fabric in the Volvo's trunk and pushed the lid closed. She blew out a breath, not realizing she'd been holding it. The door in the garage squealed when she opened it to the backyard. She'd have to remind Spence to put some WD40 on the hinges.

The back patio offered a savored moment of solitude to view the new landscaping. The sliding glass door buzzed with Spence's deep voice. She peered through the glass. Spence was on the phone. He waved her inside, continuing his conversation. She stepped inside and latched the sliding door behind her.

"We'll look forward to seeing you in an hour," Spence said, wrapping up the call. He nodded and mouthed, *Mary*.

"I can't believe she called. I was gone for just a second. What did she say?"

"We're going to talk when we meet at one. She sounds like a nice lady and was excited to hear from us."

"We'll have the fabric in the trunk, just in case."

As Jean made lunch, they talked about what to say to Mary. A false step in the world of family heirlooms could open up all kinds of problems—and wounds. In the end, they figured it best to take their cues from Mary. If she relayed anything weird or supernatural, then they'd spill.

Jon Segert was a fifteen-year veteran of the FBI in Portland. He tailed Raleigh Coulter in his black Crown Victoria down McLoughlin Avenue toward Milwaukie. Unbelievable how these yahoos flashed their misdeeds in fancy cars, custom suits, and shiny shoes. Raleigh's refusal to return his calls resulted in this: hauling his ass in the car and following him to get up in his business. All the guy had to do was to show up for the damned meeting. Raleigh had just moved up a spot in the short line to the big spanking room. Guys like Raleigh thought of themselves as above everyone else, so entitled, and not accountable because he was richer, smarter, and cockier. Jon would enjoy nailing this guy.

Since starting this investigation a few weeks ago, he had reviewed everything he found on Raleigh: social networking pages, financial records, trading activity, and phone calls with his buddy Nash Winthrop. The timing of his trades lined up, straight as an arrow, with his calls to Winthrop. His next step was to file a criminal complaint, so he could dive into Raleigh's e-mail and voicemail. Maybe, just maybe, he was a small fry in a supersize basket.

Jon spotted Raleigh pulling in front of a modern-looking house— *kind of a cool house*. He drove past the Porsche and stared straight into the car at Raleigh. He did it on purpose. Perps reacted the same way when they were feeling guilty and paranoid. Raleigh sat up a little too fast—alert, like prey.

Continuing to drive around the block, Jon pulled to the curb on the next street. Who owned that house? Were those people linked to Coulter? Jon took out his phone and entered the address.

"Spencer and Jean Collins—never heard of them." He made a note to access their tax records and credit history. *Follow the money.*

He put the Crown Victoria into drive and headed back to his new office near the Portland airport. As he drove up Highway 205, he called Raleigh's number and grinned as he left him another voice mail.

"Hey, buddy. You've avoided my calls and screwed with my schedule. You need to come in and talk with me. This is your last chance to call me back, or I'm filing a criminal complaint."

Jon disconnected and tossed his phone on the passenger seat.

Unleash the Kraken.

Raleigh straightened when the garage door rolled up. He rewrapped his sandwich and set it on the passenger seat. The Volvo wagon backed out with both of the Collinses inside.

"Sweet." He glanced at his watch: 12:50 p.m. They must be going out to lunch. The car turned right on River Road.

He unlatched the door and, at the last minute, set his cell phone on the driver's seat. He needed to focus.

No one around. Raleigh strolled up the driveway as if he belonged there. *Act casual.* The miniature pine cones crunched under his loafers as he moved toward the side gate next to the garage. Unlocked. Slipping inside, he crept along the cement walkway past the garbage bins and emerged into to the backyard.

The back of the house had two levels divided by a metal-railed balcony. The top level showed three sliding glass doors, one off each room; the bottom level had one sliding door and three floor-to-ceiling fixed windows. With his hands around his eyes, he peered into the living room.

"Cool. I kind of like these people," he muttered, scanning the room. The blond brick fireplace was the centerpiece of the sunken living room. Three wide, carpeted steps led to the open kitchen with a granite-topped island, a large dining area with vintage teak furniture, and an entryway with double front doors. The metal rail on the staircase matched the railing on the balcony outside.

"Bamboo floors...nice. Like a picture out of a *Sunset* magazine from the sixties."

He froze when he spotted his mother's chest next to the loveseat. What the hell was on top of it? *Is that a dog?* He scrunched his hands tighter around his eyes to reduce the glare. An enormous cat, with electric-green eyes, stared at him.

"Whoa—it's a cat—a monster cat," he said with his face still pressed against the window. The cat jumped off the chest, its back arched. Within inches on the other side of the glass, it stared a hole into him, interrogated him.

The monster cat put a wrinkle in his plan. He hated cats—didn't trust them—too unpredictable. Plus, he was still in his good suit from work.

The crunch under his feet reminded him to slow his steps as he moved along the walkway at the back of the garage. He stopped and took a step back. The knob beckoned to be turned. The door opened with a long squeal. He stepped inside, past the washer and dryer, and up the short staircase to try the door to the house. Locked.

He took a quick inventory. A tall ladder was propped up against the wall. *Useful for getting on the balcony.* He snatched up the can of WD40 from the top of the multi-drawer toolbox and carefully sprayed the hinges on the door. Silence would be important when he came in to get the ladder. They'd better not lock it.

He stepped out of the garage, slinked along the side walkway, and slipped out through the gate. Once back in the driveway, he straightened his tie and sauntered back to the sanctuary of his car. He checked his phone. A new voice mail flashed on the screen, the number taunting him.

"Dammit! Leave me the hell alone!" He had to listen to the message but not right now. His left foot shook as he depressed the clutch.

CHAPTER 12

Nice to Meet You, Mary Coulter

Spence took Jean's hand as the Volvo gained speed. They always had a lot at stake, no matter what they did, but never like this.

"Honey, calm down," he said, entwining her fingers.

"I thought I could handle anything. You watch this stuff in movies, but it doesn't happen in real life."

"We'll be fine. I think this is pretty amazing. I'm jazzed."

"Those birds. They challenge everything...everything, Spence." Her voice faded away as she gazed out the window, as if nothing went by.

"I'm trying to reassure you, so I reassure myself. No doubt, this is weird."

He and Jean rode in uneasy silence for the five-minute drive to Milwaukie Manor. When they reached the top of the hill, Spence put on his left turn signal and pulled into an open space marked Visitors Only. Jean leaned over and kissed him. She might be right. Jean was getting lost in the fabric, which meant he was getting lost too.

"Let's find out what this is all about," she said, reaching for the handle.

They followed the winding, manicured walkway toward the Willamette River and turned left to Mary's apartment. He opened the screen door and tapped the knocker twice. Jean wrinkled her nose and pointed to the label, No Solicitors Please. He heard Mary inside. *We're soliciting something, all right!*

"Hello, my new friends! Right on time," Mary said and ushered them into her apartment.

"Pleasure to meet you, Mary. I'm Spencer Collins and this is my wife, Jean. Please call me Spence." He extended his hand to Mary. Her skin was soft and warm.

In turn, Jean took Mary's hand. Spence watched her face instantly relax. "Jean Collins, Mary. Thank you for seeing us."

"Welcome. I'm so pleased to meet you both. Would you like some tea?"

Spence would rather been offered an espresso, or maybe a stiff shot of Maker's Mark. Too early. Instead, he said, "Sure, we'd love some tea."

"We can sit on the patio. Let's enjoy the last burst of beautiful weather before the rain sets in." Mary acted as if they'd always been friends.

She set out three mugs, lowered in the tea bags, and filled them with steaming water. Mary looked older and frailer, of course, than she had when he and Jean used to jog past her house, but he recognized her sweet face and admired her warm olive eyes. Mary still wore her hair in a French twist. As she moved around the kitchen, the sparkly hair comb caught his attention. It caught Jean's eye too. They both fixed on the twinkling diamonds in the wings of the hummingbird, like little laser lights.

Mary handed each of them mug. They streamed out to the patio and took seats facing the river.

"This is a stunning view. I'm sure you enjoy some spectacular wildlife from here," Jean said, scanning the vista.

"My dear, I've waited a long time for this view. Worked through a lifetime of joy and heartache to have this."

"You had some beautiful things in your house. Quite the estate sale." Spence tapped Jean's foot with his as a warning to tread carefully. Selling personal possessions might be a touchy subject for

Mary. She got the hint. "It must have been hard...letting go of your things."

"Yes, beautiful things, but I don't need them anymore. What did you find that you couldn't live without, besides the chest?"

"The bird bath. I want to plant calla lilies all around it in the spring. Oh—and the dress. I bought a darling little dress," Jean said and took a sip of her tea. "We don't even have any children, but the embroidered hummingbirds are so beautiful."

Spence shot a look at Jean and mouthed, *What?* She'd never mentioned buying a little dress at the estate sale.

Jean pressed her lips together and gave him a sheepish grin. Guilty as charged.

"That was my dress," Mary said, blowing into her mug. "My adopted father gave it to me when I was six. A long time ago. I'm eighty-six now."

Mary proceeded to tell them the whole story of how she got the dress, her upbringing with Doc, Birdie, and Jess, and her marriage to Jim. He and Jean listened, enraptured, for nearly an hour without interrupting her. Mary was a wonderful storyteller.

"Do you remember Jean and me jogging past your house many years ago?" Spence asked. "We lived about two blocks from you. We'd wave as we went by."

"I do remember!" Mary and Spence both smiled. Her expression changed to be more playful, a glint of mischief in her eyes. "Why are you here?"

"Well, as I mentioned when we talked on the phone this morning, we'd like to know more about the chest. It's...unusual."

"I don't think you two are here about the chest at all but for what you found inside." Mary's voice had no hint of suspicion, only amusement.

Spence locked his gaze on Jean. An entire conversation passed between them in the awkward silence. Jean's resolve crumbled in the emotion of the moment. Of course she'd dive into talking about the fabric after he urged her not to say anything.

"We experienced something yesterday," Jean said, trying to stop her throat from closing. "We found a piece of fabric, exquisite fabric, in the bottom of the chest. Can you tell us anything about it?"

"Oh yes, magical—quite magical." Mary paused, letting her words float over them like weightless snowflakes. "Ultimately, I would like the fabric and the chest back." Mary reached over and set her hand on Jean's. "Thankfully they found you two. Not everyone would seek out the previous owner—or even recognize the fabric's value."

Mary's delicate fingers made Jean's hand tingle. Wisdom didn't always come with age, but she was sure if the spots on Mary's thin skin were connected, they would reveal a treasure map. Spence's deep voice jolted her back into reality.

"Where did it come from?" Spence asked.

"I'll tell you. Someone, besides me, has to know I suppose. I'm the end of the line of the people who keep its secrets."

Mary talked for another hour about her family's history with the fabric. Her face took on a reverence when she relayed her own magical experiences.

"Doc helped everybody his whole life. He wasn't only a father to me; he was a special man to anyone who knew him. I was privileged to be the one to help him in the end." Mary paused and swallowed hard. "Passing Doc was my first experience with the fabric. I had no idea life held such secrets. My stepmother, Charlotte, and Wiley, Doc's dog, appeared to me as a child, but I thought they were ghosts; beings I made up. They were at my wedding, but I didn't say anything. Doc only hinted at their presence. But then, Birdie told me the story after we used the fabric together to pass Doc. I wasn't crazy, after all."

Jean's throat swelled with a slow burn as Mary talked. She glanced at Spence. He had his lips pressed together. The truth was more amazing than they ever dreamed.

"Birdie was ready...so ready," Mary continued. "Wiley material-ized next to her before the birds disappeared. She told me that dog slept at her side every night after she helped him pass back in 1928, before I came into the family."

"Birdie used the fabric on the dog?" Spence asked.

"Not just any dog, Spence. Wiley had a special presence in our house. Wiley became immortal after Birdie helped him pass with the fabric. There was a warm dip in the bedspread when she woke up every morning. He used to sleep in my bed, too, when I was a child. I helped Birdie myself, in 1948, just the way she asked me to." Mary tried to smile, but a tear escaped and raced down her cheek. Spence pulled a packet out of his pocket and handed her a tissue.

"How long did Birdie work for your family?" she asked.

"Birdie and Jess came to Doc and Charlotte in 1881. Birdie was Doc's very first patient. She had a severe burn on her arm from a house fire. They were just teenagers and ended up working for Doc for the rest of their human lives. Their own families were slaves and didn't survive to the end of Civil War. Birdie was the heart of that house for over sixty-seven years. She and Jess even took the family name of Gaines."

"And Jess?"

"Jess died the year Jim and I got married. He was the kindest man you'd ever want to meet. Big man, but so gentle. Still is. They're all there...in the house. But they don't show themselves to the renters who run it as an inn."

"Still there?" Spence asked, incredulous.

"Oh yes—Doc, Birdie, Jess, Wiley and even Charlotte. They're immortal. They live in the family home in Richmond." Mary smiled at Spence shaking his head.

"What happened to your husband?" Jean couldn't get enough of every one of Mary's rich words.

"Jim died in a mill accident without me at his side—killed in an instant. One of my deepest regrets. He just went to work one day and was gone. He wasn't supposed to die that way, all by himself, without me, without immortality. That was back in 1969. I've never been right since, but I did my best." Mary raised her eyes and scanned the autumn color along the river.

Odd for Mary never once mention her son, Raleigh, as she relayed the stories of her life. Given her own uncomfortable phone conversation with him, Jean's curiosity overflowed.

"Tell us about your son, Raleigh."

"Yes...well," Mary expression turned stern. Their tea had gone cool, but all three of them took a sip. "I'm afraid he succumbed to modern temptations. A cold soul, even as a young boy. I believe his problems started with the damned TV."

Jean and Spence grinned at each other. A cuss word from Mary seemed out of character. They understood, and they didn't understand, having both been raised with television.

"Greed is a terrible thing." Mary paused and let out a soft breath. "After a while, you stop appreciating what's all around you because you're too busy wanting things." Mary followed a bird's path as it settled on the top branch of a maple tree on the slope to the river and continued, "I'm afraid my Raleigh is a victim of this philosophy. I feel sorry for him, actually. He'll never know how magical life can be. Some people do nothing with everything, and others do everything with nothing." Mary went silent, signaling the end of the subject.

"Mary, we have no desire to profit from this fabric. And of course you can have it back. We want to know more about where it came from, and what it means. Would you let us do some research?"

"Some things should be left alone. So many sharks are out there when it comes to valuable artifacts, never mind magical ones."

"I don't know anyone I would trust either, except—" An idea sparked.

On one of their trips to London, she and Spence had spent considerable time at the Victoria and Albert Museum. Her obsession with all kinds of fabric design led her to spend hours with the antique tapestries and textiles. She had an informative and lengthy discussion with the curator, Graham Hollingsworth. She still had his card in their notebook from the trip.

"Spence, do you think Graham Hollingsworth at the V&A could help us? I completely trust him to give us the best advice. He's connected to everyone in the field."

"Maybe." Spence straightened. "He might at least point us in the right direction."

"I can put in a call to him as soon as we get home," Jean said. "If he wants to see the fabric, we should take it to London."

Spence clapped his hands together. "I'm totally up for a trip back to London. We need a break from house projects, anyway."

Jean turned to Mary for affirmation. Mary warmed to the idea. This would be an adventure Mary could share, vicariously, from the comfort of her patio.

"Do you want to see it?" Spence's eyes danced. "We brought the fabric with us. It's in the car." Without waiting for a response, Spence stood and disappeared through the patio door, jingling his keys.

Jean listened to the front door shut. Alone with Mary, she reached out and took her hand. The gesture was returned with a squeeze. Together they sat in silence and gazed out over the river, bonded by their shared secrets of the fabric.

"Oh, and before Spence comes in," she whispered, "I bought one of your husband's books. A Christmas present."

"Which one?"

"*The Maltese Falcon.*"

"One of Jim's favorites. Good choice."

Jean grinned, satisfied with her secret prize.

Spence emerged through the patio door with a white box in his hands. The biggest smile Jean had ever seen on his face greeted her as he set the box in front of Mary. He lifted the lid and presented the wrapped bundle. He pulled away the tissue, like a magician releasing doves as part of a magic trick, and unfolded the fabric. The pheasants' eyes sparkled, and their feathers radiated a light show of colors in the afternoon sun.

"Ta-da," Spence sang.

Mary released Jean's hand and raised her own to her cheek, staring at the fabric as a lifetime of memories washed over her face. Mary covered her eyes as her shoulders shook. Spence fished in his pocket and pulled out two rounds of tissues.

Jean wrapped her arms around Mary to comfort her, and herself.

"When the soul is ready, the birds fly from the fabric, and one becomes immortal. The magic lingers behind. Yes, take it to London," Mary whispered, reaching out to Spence. "Solve this mystery. You must do this for me."

"I should have brought more of these." Spence handed a tissue to Mary, and then one to Jean. "Geez. Not many men can make two beautiful women cry. And we're happy to bring over the chest. Our treat." Spence winked at Jean.

CHAPTER 13

The Squeak

Spence returned the fabric to the trunk, closed the lid, and joined Jean in the car. "What a lovely person," he said, backing out of the parking space. "A wild way to spend an afternoon, though. Like stepping into another world."

"Certainly was," Jean said, running her fingers through her hair. "What a story—amazing. She confirmed we're not crazy too. I never dreamed the magic involved immortality."

"What do you think she meant by—"

"'Do this for me?' Like wanting us to make her immortal?"

"Yeah. She's probably referring to our research of the fabric."

"Mmm-mmm."

On the drive home, he kept an eye on Jean's dreamy expression. He, too, was stunned at the thought of immortality. Live forever? Was that a good thing? Did she want to be immortal? A necessary discussion over a glass of wine and several albums. He started to hum "The Dark Side of the Moon," his deep voice filling the silence in the car.

The low shadows of sun blinked through the trees and across her face. Her expression told him her mind was compiling a list. Without turning from the window, she said, "Pink Floyd—should be the wild side of the moon."

"Excellent," he said, impressed by her ability to identify songs.

Jean glanced at her watch. "You know, I almost forgot—it's Monday. Linda and I are getting together for a girl's night dinner. I don't want to cancel on her this late. I'm supposed to pick her up at five thirty. I've got an hour."

"Don't cancel. I'll send Graham an e-mail—he might check messages after hours—and poke around about the cost of London flights while you're at dinner." A couple of hours to himself to privately process the turn of events sounded good. "Mycroft and I can have a bachelor's night. We'll be fine. Why don't you take the Mini Cooper? You shouldn't be driving this car around by yourself with the fabric in the trunk. Something could happen—to you."

"Are you sure? We need to talk about the day."

"No worries." He wanted her to be distracted from the fabric—for a little bit. After the conversation with Mary, Jean would get obsessed to the exclusion of everything else in her life. When she got focused, she was lost to him until she followed through, whatever it was. Now he could identify. He was obsessed too.

As they walked in the house, Mycroft flopped on the floor in front of Spence and rolled. Jean had already raced upstairs to get ready for her dinner with Linda.

Spence resumed his normal, late-afternoon duties of feeding Mycroft and taking out the garbage. The routines associated with daily life were strange and mundane when compared to the excitement of yesterday's events and today's information. *Magical.* Mary's words still resonated in his head.

Jean came down the stairs, adjusting her necklace and smoothing the collar of her black turtleneck sweater. She disappeared to the den to paw through the shelf of travel binders.

"I put the sheets in the dryer and took out the garbage," he called out from the kitchen. "Did you know you left the back door in the garage unlocked this morning? Honey, you have to be careful. And, thanks for getting rid of the squeak. It drove me crazy."

"I just found Graham's card," Jean called back. "I'll leave it on the keyboard of the computer." She stepped up to the kitchen and grabbed her purse and keys. "Sorry about the door; I'll be more careful."

"I left the side gate unlocked when I brought in the trash bins yesterday. We're all catawampus. No wonder."

"Call me if you hear anything from Graham." Jean gave him a hug.

"Have fun. Love you!"

"Love you! This feels so weird." Jean closed the door.

Jean backed the Mini Cooper out of the garage and stopped. She clicked the lock button on the Volvo key. The double flash of the taillights indicated the car alarm was armed.

She pulled into Linda's driveway and wrinkled her nose at Spence's comment. She didn't do anything about the squeak in the door at the back of the garage. It made a racket when she opened it to go in the yard. Weird. She'd have to remember to say something if Spence called. God, she didn't even remember putting the sheets in the laundry this morning.

Linda waved at her as she came out of the house. She plunked into the passenger seat of the Mini Cooper and threw her enormous fringed purse on the floor mat. "Bill's always looking for something as I'm about to walk out of the house. This time he couldn't find the remote. Since when is *History Detectives* an emergency?"

"Today...apparently."

Jean's muscles relaxed as they drove to the Mexican restaurant.

"Life is getting interesting, Linda," she said as the waiter brought them each a glass of wine. "You were right about diving into fabric. A game changer. Let's order. I'm starved."

"Do tell."

"Something good—completely new. Energizing. There's a whole world to discover when you're not stuck in an office. So, is Bill excited about the progress on the store?"

"Ecstatic. Bill's never been happier."

"I think they're committed to doing this. But we're going to take a quick break to go to London for a week."

"Wow! How did that come about?"

Jean's Droid strummed twice a few minutes before dinner arrived, signaling the arrival of two new e-mails. "I know this is rude, but I bet these e-mails will answer your question." Spence had copied her on his inquiry to Graham Hollingsworth at the museum. The second message was Graham's enthusiastic response. He wanted to meet with them this Friday at 4:30 p.m. He must be excited to answer their e-mail at two o'clock in the morning, London time. "One more minute, Linda." She called Spence. She held up her finger when Spence came on the line. "Hey, hi! I read Graham's response."

"I didn't expect anything back until tomorrow. I'm impressed." Spence said. "I'm looking at flights now. Pretty expensive if we go this week. Depends on how long you want to wait."

"Tell you what. Timing's more important. Check what's available for using my airline miles. I have tons. We'll need to leave Thursday to be there by Friday afternoon. I'll book the tickets when I get home. I'm dropping off Linda first."

"Sounds good."

"Oh wait, one more thing! I didn't do anything about the squeak on the door in the garage."

"Huh..."

"Gotta go. Love you!" She turned off her phone and slipped it in her purse.

"Everything okay?" Linda asked.

"We're going to London because we're having an expert analyze some fabric—really old fabric. Can you guys babysit Mycroft while we're gone?"

Linda stood in her driveway as Jean's Mini Cooper backed down the steep grade, the headlights diminishing as she reached the street. She recognized that tone in Jean's voice. Filled with conviction and completely different from when they had lunch at Jake's Grill. Something's up; more than just sewing and fabric. Must be important to draw Spence in so fast and spark an immediate trip to London. They were on a quest. She'd get Bill to call Spence.

CHAPTER 14

Nice to Meet You, Jean and Spencer Collins

Spence peered over Jean's shoulder while she booked the flight to London. They would leave Thursday, with a return the following Thursday. Normally the cost would be an issue, but this time they were willing to spend whatever necessary for the trip of a lifetime.

After marking *London* on the tab of a blank manila folder, he slipped the stapled flight and hotel confirmations inside, along with a copy of the e-mail from Graham Hollingsworth. The phone rang.

"Can you grab that? I'm in the middle of picking out seats," Jean said, clicking the computer keys.

He glanced at the phone. "It's Bill. You didn't say anything about this to Linda, did you?"

"No. Only that we were going to London to have a piece of old fabric researched. I asked if she and Bill could watch Mycroft."

"Here goes—" Spence answered the phone. "Hey Bill! No, everything's fine. We're going to London to research a piece of old fabric Jean found. This is her gig, but I can't resist a trip to London. I'm going to dig through some of those record stores on Portobello Road. Imports will sell over here. Yup, I'll keep you posted. Thanks for helping to watch Mycroft while we're gone. Jean will call with all the details."

Once Spence ended the call, he felt bad about being cagey with Bill. He'd always been completely truthful with him about every little thing. Bill was like the brother he never had, but this was too hot to talk about with anyone. They would fill him and Linda in on the whole story, but not until they had more information. He wouldn't even know what to say. He turned to Jean.

"How should we travel with the fabric? We can fold it in our carry-on bags, can't we?"

"Hmmm...I'll think of something."

She'll think of something.

The fabric would be fine in their carry-on bag, but Jean's wheels were spinning. She'd make this much more complicated.

On Tuesday morning, Jean blew out a breath of relief as she hung up the phone with Linda, whose antenna was on full alert. At least Mycroft would be fine. She studied her list and scratched off *Babysitter.* Next was *The Fabric.*

Travel with the fabric. She had visions of being stopped at customs—the fabric being confiscated. What if magic was like drugs and the dogs sniffed the scent? What if the magic actually happened in the airport? What if they suspected it was stolen? Wasn't Europe hyperaware of Nazi artifacts, and weren't the Nazis involved with magic? Or had she been watching too many movies?

Besides, they liked to travel light and took only carry-on bags for international travel. The bags would be fairly full with a week's clothes, anyway.

She pushed two pieces of bread in the toaster and sparked on an idea. *In plain sight!*

Jean flipped to a new page on her list pad and drew the outline of a jacket. If the back panel was cut from an oversize denim jacket, the fabric could be inserted in its place. She remembered seeing women wear similar elaborate jackets for the rodeo in Houston. A gaudy, but hip, fashion statement. Nobody could steal her jacket, if she was wearing it.

She ran up the stairs, two at a time, to the small third bedroom they'd converted to a walk-in closet. She didn't find anything she was willing to tear apart or big enough to fit the dimensions of the fabric. Her hand stopped on the denim jacket for one of the Broadway touring shows she'd helped to launch when they lived in Minneapolis. The embroidered show logo on the back practically sang out the magical opening number. *Another life.* She blew out a breath and walked out of the room. "Much more exciting," she muttered. This really was magic, and right now, she and Spence didn't want to share the experience with anyone. *Not that jacket.*

Only one place came to mind where she might find something suitable. Ray's Ragtime had a dizzying array of vintage clothing, from military camouflage to Don Ho–era Hawaiian shirts. They'd have an oversize denim jacket.

"Hey, Spence?" she called out over the upstairs railing. "Are you up for a trip downtown with me? I want to go to Ray's Ragtime."

Raleigh called in sick on Tuesday morning. After all, he was sick; sick and tired of his world collapsing around him. He brushed the blueberry muffin crumbs to the floor mat and took a sip of his coffee. He peered over the plastic lid and stared at the Collinses' house.

He could still back out; walk away. But after researching the value of Egyptian artifacts on the Internet, no doubt he had to get inside that house. The fabric was in there, and if it was from Egypt, then it was worth a fortune. Quick in, quick out. He wasn't a thief. The Collinses didn't buy the fabric. He only wanted to take back what was rightfully his. No need to get into some drawn-out hassle with that impossible woman.

This neighborhood was quiet during the work week. He questioned his decision to do this in broad daylight, but the heavily wooded backyard had a tall fence. Unlike other residential parts of Portland, houses here were situated on big lots.

Raleigh was careful to wear the right clothes this time: a hunter-green T-shirt, black jeans, and a black wool jacket. The foliage of the Collinses' yard would give him some level of camouflage. Never having put together a break-in outfit before, he was impressed when he examined himself in the mirror. Raleigh's gaze darted to the house. The garage door rolled up.

"Here we go," he muttered and put his coffee in the cup holder.

He tossed his phone in the glove compartment and wiped his mouth. The Collinses' Volvo turned on River Road. He opened the car door.

The crunch of tiny pine cones forced him to lengthen his strides up the driveway. He jiggled the side gate. Locked. He'd have to climb over the fence. Thankful he'd resumed his morning workouts, he rolled over the top and jumped to the concrete walkway. He crept along the garage wall, staying close. When he reached the end, he turned right and tried the knob on the back door of the garage. Locked. *Not so trusting.* The sliding glass door on the first floor appeared to be a den. He peered into the room and pulled on the handle. Locked.

He didn't want to do this, but he'd have to break one of the panes in the garage door. The ladder was against the wall, with only a small pane of thin glass between them. He had to get to the ladder to check the three sliding doors off the second-floor balcony. He took a deep breath and swung his left elbow into the lower right pane. The glass gave way, shattering in a tinkling cascade to the concrete floor inside. He stopped and listened. Maneuvering his hand through the jagged opening, he turned the lock button on the handle. It popped out. The door swung in without a sound.

"Good thinking on that one," he muttered.

He stepped past the washer and dryer and tried the inside door to the house. *Locked.* He moved back toward the ladder and pulled it forward, making sure not to smack the water heater as he leveled it out the back door. He rested the top rung against the metal rail of the balcony. *Piece of cake.*

Eight rungs taunted him on the ladder as he climbed. Grabbing the rail, he swung one leg over, and then the other. The decking creaked as he crept to the first sliding door. He cupped his hands to look beyond the mirrored image of the huge fir tree from the yard. A small bedroom, with only enough space to hold a double bed and nightstand. The sliding glass door was locked. He moved along the balcony. Another small room being used as a closet. A shelving system had been erected and clothes hung around the walls, with shoes lined underneath. He pulled the handle. A little give. He jiggled and lifted it. The latch released. As he glided the door to the side, the curtain billowed with the cold air being sucked inside. His adrenaline rushed.

The floor crunched and squeaked under the shag carpet with each step. He emerged to a catwalk hallway overlooking the first floor. He surveyed the view of the open kitchen, dining room, and entryway below. *Where was that damn cat?*

He stepped into the master bedroom. Pencil etchings of three cats, all the same, big-boned breed and elaborately framed, hung over the bed. The floor squeaked downstairs. The sound made the hairs on his neck stand up. *Where is the cat?*

The room, bright and open, was accentuated by a window wall with a sliding glass door to the balcony. The former closet had been converted to shelving, which held family pictures and scenes of the Collinses in front of various European landmarks. He backed out of the bedroom.

He slinked along the catwalk hallway to check the end bedroom, unnerved by floor's muffled crunch. The doors of the closet groaned and popped as they unfolded. Ten, maybe fifteen, large bolts of fabric lined the wall, flanked by vertical organizers stuffed with ribbon and sewing implements: Velcro, bags of buttons, smaller fabric remnants, and collapsed gift boxes. He didn't see anything with birds. Then he spotted a white box with an old book on top; they looked familiar. *That's one of my father's books!* He wanted to take it but changed his mind. He opened the box. *She bought that dress.* He set the book and box back in the closet. Check the chest downstairs.

As he started his descent, he froze with one foot in midair. He jerked his foot back to the top step, as if the next one held a carpet of hot coals. The cat. Glowing green eyes examined him from the bottom of the stairs.

"Hey, kitty, kitty," Raleigh cooed in a flat monotone. "You be a good kitty. I'm not going to hurt you."

The risers creaked as he took two steps down. The enormous cat seemed to grow even larger with one slow, silent step up. His heart hammered his ribs.

"C'mon kitty, I want to get by and check the chest. I'll be gone in a few minutes." He tried to keep his voice calm; the cat wasn't buying it.

The cat took another step; eyes fixed like a laser. They both ended up together on the landing of the L-shaped staircase, as if in a game of chicken. Raleigh launched himself down the stairs, past the cat—almost. The cat's claw caught the leg of his jeans. *That monster is pulling me back!*

Raleigh yanked his leg forward. The cat screamed and hissed in pain. With a low growl behind him, he darted to the living room.

As he rubbed the sting developing on his calf, he opened the chest. Empty. He pressed on the bottom. The supports on the sides indicated there had been another piece of wood. He spotted the insert leaning against the hassock. Something was in there. He contemplated his next move. A line of red smudges spotted the beige carpet. They appeared to circle rhythmically around him. The nape of his neck tingled. *Where was that cat?*

Raleigh glanced at the back of his pant leg. No blood. Uneasy, he turned to the den. The geometric pattern of the screen saver swirled on the computer monitor. It drew him to the corner desk. He wiggled the mouse. The desktop showed a picture of the Collinses with their arms around each other in front of some castle.

"So pleased to meet you both," he whispered, studying their faces.

He shook himself loose of the image and turned to the book-cases. An electric current raced through him. More red smears circled on the carpet around his feet, but no cat. He inspected his hands and wiped his nose. *Nothing. Where is it coming from?*

He surveyed the hundreds of books about rock music: bio-graphies, retrospectives on bands and pop culture, and auction catalogues. The bottom cabinets contained record albums, thousands of them. *These are worth a fortune.* He flipped through the collection, all in plastic sleeves. *A Beatles butcher cover. Rare. Don't get distracted.*

The den and living room held nothing. Raleigh turned and stepped up the three wide steps to the kitchen. A manila folder marked *London* drew his gaze to the granite island. Inside were an itinerary, a hotel confirmation, and a printout of an e-mail, and photos of the fabric.

Greetings, Mr. and Mrs. Collins,

I'm delighted to hear from you! And I do remember you very well. It is rare to find one as passionate about fabric as Mrs. Collins. The fabric you discovered sounds intriguing. Please forward pictures of it, as soon as possible, in advance of your arrival. I would like to start my research immediately. I will clear my schedule on Friday afternoon at 4:30 p.m. to host you when you arrive. We'll meet at the central information desk in the lobby of the front entrance, under the Chihuly glass chandelier. Safe travels!
Graham Hollingsworth
Curator, Textiles
Victoria and Albert Museum

"Uh-huh, here we go," he whispered. Now he had proof the fabric was in the Collinses' possession. It must be as valuable if they were going all the way to London.

Raleigh rummaged through the drawers in the island and found a notepad and a pen. He ripped the top sheet from the long, skinny list pad and noted the travel and meeting dates and times, the airline name and flight numbers, the hotel and address, and the meeting contact name. He sensed something. The hair on his neck prickled. The fanged hiss, inches from his face, sent an electrical charge up his spine. A vicious sound followed a clawed paw tearing across his left cheek. Bright-red blood sprayed across the manila folder.

"Ahhh! What the—"

A bushy orange tail disappeared from the counter. Blistering pain spread through his face. Panic radiated down his limbs.

Raleigh pressed his left cheek and sprinted through the mudroom, fumbling to unlock the back door. He missed his step on the stairs and banged into the side mirror on the Mini Cooper. Blood oozed between his fingers.

Adrenaline pumped at full speed as he pulled away the ladder from the railing with his blood-slicked hand. Warm blood tricked down his neck, soaking into his T-shirt. The ladder smacked the frame as he reeled it through the doorway. Wide-eyed, he scanned the dark space for a towel or a rag, anything to use to wipe down the rungs. He eyed the dryer door. With his clean hand he opened it and spotted a pile of freshly dried laundry. A purple hand towel on top. Careful to not get blood on anything else, he wiped the edge of the ladder. The clock was ticking. Just a paint stain. He rushed out the back door. A few leftover chunks of glass tinkled to the floor.

Keep it together. Get back to the car.

Raleigh sprinted past the side of the garage and unlocked the gate from the inside. He tried to act unassuming, slowing his pace back to the car. As he pressed his cheek with the purple towel, he dropped his keys on the pavement. The fob finally beeped. He slumped in the seat. His hand shook as he turned the keys in the ignition. The tires squealed as he pulled away. He threw the bloody towel on the passenger seat. Glancing back at the fence, he made sure the side gate was closed. When he turned his head, hot liquid ran down his cheek. After reaching the connection to McLoughlin Avenue, he gasped when he realized his mistake.

"I left the door open upstairs!"

His stomach bottomed-out again as the image of the blood on

the folder—his blood—filled his head. The island in the kitchen.

Jon Segert sat in his Crown Victoria, parked five houses away from the Collinses', and waited to spot Raleigh. The Collinses' tax records hadn't indicated anything out of order, but today Raleigh had parked three houses away, so maybe another resident was his connection.

Nope, here came Raleigh down the Collinses' driveway. He started the car. What was with the purple towel against his face? Did someone punch his lights out? He pressed the key on his phone to start the GPS on Raleigh's car. The red dot crept toward River Road.

"Dammit!" He banged the steering wheel and made a U-turn.

That's it. He had to wrap this up and get an answer on the criminal complaint. Once he got a warrant, he'd haul Raleigh in on Thursday morning.

CHAPTER 15

The Purple Hand Towel

Ray's Ragtime had been a jackpot. Spence smiled as Jean admired the denim jacket on the drive home from downtown. Her expression reflected the figuring and measuring going on in her head.

"Seems like a pretty wild idea," he said as they pulled into the garage.

"So James Bondy...right?" Jean stuffed the jacket into the plastic bag. "This won't take me long."

Spence stepped to the back of the garage to unlock the door for when he took out the garbage. Jean had her head buried in the trunk of the Volvo.

"Whoa! Honey! There's glass all over the floor back here. I think somebody broke in."

"What?" Jean smacked her head on the trunk lid. "Ow...dammit!"

"I'll check around the outside. Don't go inside yet." Spence bolted to the patio.

As he scanned the back of the house, his gaze rose to the second-floor balcony. Mycroft's head poked through the railing. The curtain in the closet room billowed behind him.

"Jean!"

The door to the house was unlocked.

"What the—this door was locked!" More angry than shocked, Jean marched to the kitchen. All quiet.

She set the white box and plastic bag on one of the leather counter chairs. A streak of bright red was splattered across the manila folder for their London trip. Still damp and shiny.

Spence called her name from above.

The muffled call from the closet room sent her bounding up the stairs. A rush of cold air hit her face. The sliding door was open, the curtain waving and snapping outside.

Spence shouted up at her, "Get Mycroft inside! He's on the balcony!"

"I've got him. Come in. Quick!"

Mycroft ran to her. She picked him up and swung him over her shoulder, burying her face in his fur. She brought him back inside and slid the door shut. The wrench was on the floor. *Why did we procrastinate about getting this door fixed?*

Mycroft rubbed against her arm while she struggled with the latch. She froze at the blood on his right paw.

"What happened, baby?"

In quipped meows, Mycroft recited the whole story. Jean draped Mycroft over her shoulder as she went downstairs. Spence met her in the kitchen. She pointed to the blood on the folder. "Let's walk around first to see if anything's missing."

"You shouldn't have come in by yourself," Spence said on full alert. "Let me check to make sure nobody's still here. Don't move."

She froze and waited, staring at the folder.

Spence came back and shrugged. "Everything's here. Nothing's missing that I can tell. Even the cash I left on the desk is still there."

Jean set Mycroft on the loveseat and followed the blood smudges in the living room, patterned in wide circles. They led to the den and under the desk.

"This must be from Mycroft's paw. I think he's torn a nail. Looks like he followed somebody around in here. Creepy." Spence picked up Mycroft and fluffed his fur, checked his head and neck, and pulled up his paw. "He appears to be all right. Yep, a torn claw, the middle one—It'll heal."

Jean pointed to the kitchen counter. "The London folder. *That's* not from Mycroft. *That* blood was airborne."

"I'm calling the police."

The doorbell rang a long bong. Jean squeezed one eye and peered through the peephole. Two Milwaukie police officers resembled uniformed Teletubbies in the glass bubble.

"Thank you for coming so fast," she said. "My husband, Spence, is in the garage."

"I'm Officer Steve Boardsen, and this is my partner, Jim Cook. You had a break-in?"

"Yes, let me show you what we found when we got home. We came in through the garage." Jean escorted them to the mudroom. "And this door was unlocked. I locked it myself a few hours ago."

Officer Boardsen made a note on his clipboard. They caught up with Spence sweeping up broken glass. The officers fanned around the garage.

"There's blood on the ladder over here." Officer Cook said, pointing to the dark stains in the grooves on two of the rungs. "Yours?"

"Definitely not."

"Someone tried to wipe it off. Don't touch anything for right now. Keep going."

"I'll show you what we found inside the house," Spence said. "We're going out of the country for a week, so this is more than a little upsetting."

After the officers searched the house, they returned to the living room. Spence and the two officers discussed the red splotches. Jean studied them from the kitchen while she held Mycroft over her shoulder and patted his back. She glanced at the counter and grimaced at the blood on the manila folder. Her anxiety increased by the minute about traveling out of the country in two days.

"If this was a run-of-the-mill break-in, your computer and flat-screen TV would be gone," Officer Boardsen said. "Somebody was after something specific."

"And don't forget that cash is still in the den. Has anything happened recently to prompt this?" Officer Cook asked.

A pregnant pause. Jean's gaze locked with Spence's. She shook her head, hesitant. "No...not really. The only new thing is that chest in the living room. I bought it on Saturday at an estate sale. Nothing special. In fact, my husband would've have been happy to carry it out for the jerk."

"I'd have helped him." Officer Boardsen smirked at Spence. "From what I can tell your cat attacked the guy and followed him around the house. The blood in the living room and den doesn't belong to the intruder. Those are paw prints. You can go ahead and clean those up."

"What about this blood on the folder and on the ladder?" Spence asked.

The officer raised his eyes from filling out the police report. "Let me take that folder with me. To be honest, don't hold your breath. Nothing appears to have been taken, and no one was hurt. Since you'll be out of town, though, we'll step up our patrol here for the next week. I doubt this guy will to try anything again. He'll be nursing a bad cut. And he certainly isn't going to line up for another Tango dance with your cat. This fellow is a pretty good watchdog." He rubbed the top of Mycroft's ears, squashing them. The gesture was tolerated, but not without an indignant stare.

"Mycroft was injured. Shouldn't that count for something?" Jean asked, defensive.

"He's a cat, ma'am, not a person," Officer Cook said. He took the empty folder from Spence. "Do you have a big plastic bag?"

Spence retrieved a gallon-size bag from the kitchen drawer and held it open for him to slide the folder inside.

"Can someone check on the house while you're gone? You should make sure that sliding door upstairs is locked tight. At least put a pole or a yard stick in the track on the inside. That's how the guy got in here," Officer Boardsen said with finality. He pulled a copy of the police report from his clipboard and handed it to Spence with his card. "In the meantime, call right away if anything else happens."

Jean sighed as she closed the front door. Violated. She didn't even want to think about what Mycroft had gone through. She immediately went to the cabinet under the kitchen sink and pulled out a can of foaming rug cleaner. The first priority was to scrub away Mycroft's pain.

"I'll call a glass repair place. Maybe they'll come tonight or to-morrow," Spence said.

With every swipe of the wet sponge, her anger expanded with the foam. "Spence, can you get me a towel in the dryer?" He didn't hear her. He was already talking with the glass company. "Damn!" She stood and stomped to the garage.

Jean rummaged through the clean laundry, searching for the purple hand towel. She brought the whole pile to the kitchen. Re-membering to call Linda about staying in the house, she picked up her Droid.

"Linda. Hi, it's Jean. You're not going to believe this. We had a break-in. Nothing was taken, but I have a huge favor to ask. Can you step up your visits with Mycroft while we're gone? I'm a little freaked out about leaving him alone during the day."

"Are you and Spence all right? Is Mycroft okay?"

"Yeah, we weren't home. Mycroft hurt his claw going after the guy who got in. I think he chased him out of here. The police didn't believe anyone would dare try again."

"Sure thing. In fact, I hope I run into the cretin. Bill will take him down. We can watch movies with Mycroft by the fire. And when you get back you *are* going to tell us what this trip is all about."

"Fabulous! We owe you big time! And, yes, we'll fill you in. Promise." Her mood lifted as she hung up the phone.

She folded the clothes. No purple hand towel. It should have been easy to spot.

"Huh...I'm positive I washed it."

CHAPTER 16

Get the Passports Out

The hydrogen peroxide fizzed and foamed in the splayed, three-inch gash on his left cheek. Raleigh winced and tilted his head to examine the cut in the bathroom mirror, hoping he didn't need stitches. The gash oozed blood and pulsed with heat. With a soaked cotton ball, he wiped the dried residue from his neck.

"That damned cat! I knew he'd be vicious," he seethed, searching the medicine cabinet for antibiotic ointment. A bottle of cough syrup smashed in the sink.

After taping a piece of gauze over his cheek, Raleigh stomped to the living room. He yanked his black jacket from the chair and dug through the pocket. He pulled out the crinkled paper and studied the notes, grimacing at the cartoon on the top that mocked him: A cat in pajamas with all its hair standing on end and tongue sticking out. Underneath were the words *Hot Flash* in a frenzied scrawl. The picture reflected his current mood.

Raleigh propped his notes next to his computer and booked a coach ticket on the same early-morning flight to London as the Collinses. He preferred to sit in first class but was determined to take every opportunity to get his hands on the fabric. This thing was too valuable to let out of his sight.

He opened his client list and noted the contact information for

Gerrod Barnes, Owner, Barnes & Company Fine Antiques, in Holland Park, not too far from the museum and near where the Collinses were staying in London. Gerrod split his time between New York and London and had amassed a fortune buying and selling antiques at auction. If he got the fabric off them, Gerrod might move it through one of his sales, but he needed to act fast. He dashed off an e-mail to request a meeting.

The Tumi carry-on bag thumped when he threw it on the bed. He packed a pair of navy wool pants, a couple of patterned sweaters, three white shirts, and a good pair of brown, tasseled loafers. He tossed in a plastic bag of toiletries with his passport.

The timing for this trip was perfect. He needed to get out of town, anyway; away from the office, the FBI, and his mother. *Mother.* He'd have to remember to call Mary to say he'd be out of town. She'd have to wait. The priority was to book himself into the Portland Airport Suites so there wouldn't be any issue with the early flight time. Tonight was for mapping out his plan and trying to sleep without thinking about the cat. His cheek started to bleed again.

Jon Segert hadn't unpacked his office from when his division moved, two months ago, to the new FBI building near Portland International Airport. A tall ficus tree stood in the corner; still with a ribbon tag that said, *Welcome to your new digs!* Curled leaves littered the carpet. He'd have to remind his assistant to throw some water on the dirt.

He didn't really care. There was one thing Jon needed in his office, and it was sitting right on his desk: the picture of his smiling wife, Meg, and his daughter, Amy, hugging each other in 2004. If only Amy could be ten years old forever. When he and Meg dropped off Amy last month at Bryant University in Rhode Island to start her first semester of college, the day was the hardest of his life. Driving away exceeded the stress of any criminal case over his fifteen-year career. His buddies on the police force in Rhode Island, where he grew up, would keep an eye on Amy for him. She wouldn't be able to take even a sip in one of those college dive bars without him getting a call.

As he studied the view from his third-story window, he pictured what Amy might be doing right now. She was probably laughing with new friends, dressing up for a date, and wearing those dangly earrings he'd never let her wear as a teenager.

His deep blue eyes pulled away from the manicured lawn along Airport Way. Brushing the top of his blond crew-cut back and forth with his hand, he sat at his desk and logged on to his computer. He'd gotten access to Coulter's accounts to provide more support for the warrant. Time for another check of his e-mail account. Something new may have come in since last night. A warrant on Raleigh would almost be like his wish coming true for Amy to be studying in her pajamas right now.

"Heeello!" he said in a sing-song voice, staring at the screen. "The stupid twit is trying to leave the country. Unbelievable!"

He printed out the confirmation e-mail from the airline and hotel. Raleigh had also sent an e-mail to an antiques dealer in London, somebody named Gerrod Barnes. Raleigh must be trying to sell something to cover his losses on the insider trading deal.

"Hey, Jenny!" He needed to nab his assistant before she went home for the day.

After a few minutes, she marched into his office with a folder.

"Did the warrant for Raleigh Coulter come through, yet?"

"Not yet—still waiting. I bet you'd like to see this," Jenny said, giving him a coy smile. "You know that couple, Jean and Spencer Collins, you had me doing some research on?"

"Yeah...?" He straightened at the mention of the Collinses' names. "Their house was broken into this afternoon. Here's a copy of the police report. Still warm."

"You're kidding! Come to daddy." He reached for the folder and scanned the report. "I don't have time to go over to their house tonight. Meg's got some friends coming over for dinner in an hour, but can you get a requisition signed for me to go to London tomorrow? Raleigh-boy is making a move." He handed Jenny a copy of the itinerary. "I need to be on that same exact flight—the 8:30 a.m. to Newark, going on to London Heathrow. With or without the warrant, I'll be on him like stink. I can't wrap this up if he's out of the country. While you're getting the arrangements done, I'll coordinate with my guys at Scotland Yard." Jon glanced at his watch and calculated the time difference. "Damn, I'll have to call them early tomorrow morning. Middle of the night over there right now."

"Well, aren't you the big man. Off to a dinner party and then flitting about in London to chase a bad guy?" Jenny grinned as she pushed the end of her nose up.

"Yeah. Whatever, Miss Moneypenny."

CHAPTER 17

The Jacket

On Wednesday morning, Jean woke up exhausted. She and Spence tossed and turned most of the night, jumping at every little sound. At least laying awake had given her time to work through her entire checklist: all packed; toiletries in their regulation bags; passports out of the safe and sitting on the kitchen counter; and the international adapters tucked in her purse, along with two sets of earplugs for the flight. Spence had cleaned the house while she packed. All she had left on her list for this morning was to take the chest over to Mary's and to sew the jacket, and she'd already planned every meticulous cut and stitch of how the seams would go together. Spence arranged to get the glass replaced in the garage by late afternoon.

After breakfast, Jean reviewed her notes and measurements. Time to start. As she inspected the back of the denim jacket, she couldn't help but stop and glance into the next room at the pheasants in the fabric. She would never tire of drinking in the rich colors of their feathers. The birds' eyes seemed to stare back at her. Unnerved, she tried not to think about it. Time was not on her side.

Jean spread out the jacket on the living room floor. Her hand trembled as she poised the scissors, the blades eager to make the first cut. Usually so comfortable when working on a sewing project, she was beyond nervous today. The seams separated with ease. The extra material cut from the back would be used to make strips to encase the fabric. Then she would loosely hand-baste the fabric to the strips. When completed, the jacket would resemble a picture frame, with the pheasants showcased inside. The basting thread could be snipped away for their meeting at the museum. The fabric—on her, next to her, near her skin.

The sewing machine whirred as she pulled the denim through its needle. She glanced up at the clock every few minutes while she sewed, trying not to step on the pedal too hard. After clipping the last errant thread, she held up the jacket. *Yes, this is going to work out fine.* With the sewing basket in hand, she joined Spence in the living room.

Spence was engrossed in a biography of Eric Clapton. He had the Beatles' *Revolver* spinning on the turntable. Jean admired the way Spence could relax before leaving on a major trip. Mycroft, asleep on the chair in front of the gas fireplace, enjoyed the soothing heat of the flames licking the pads of his sore paw.

The morning fire was toasty and welcoming to Jean too, a sharp contrast to the gray, cold rain tapping at the window. She plopped herself on the loveseat and stopped to gaze at the fabric on the hassock. She smiled at the irony of "Good Day Sunshine" bursting from the album.

"The pheasants watched me read," Spence said, glancing over his reading glasses. "I swear. About fifteen minutes ago, the eyes were looking that way toward Mycroft by the fire." Spence didn't seem to be fazed, only amused. "Now, they're zeroed in on you."

"Oh, c'mon. You're trying to freak me out."

"Then you be the judge. I'm not kidding."

Jean wrinkled her nose, unnerved by the comment. It took her over five minutes to thread the needle. Adjusting her bifocals, she willed her fingers to remain steady. She positioned the fabric on the first corner of the jacket. She paused, waiting to see if anything would happen.

Spence was playing with her. She held the fabric corner pieces together and pushed the needle into the denim. The sharp steel went through, but stopped at the fabric. She leaned over, dug in her sewing basket, and pulled out a metal thimble. She pushed again, a little harder. The steel broke off clean.

"What the hell?" She looked at both sides, re-threaded a new needle, and tried again. The new one broke off, right in the same place as the old.

"That fabric is trying to stick it to you, dear," Spence said, laughing.

Jean gazed out the window. The rain flicked at the orange leaves of the maple tree in the backyard. She listened to John Lennon's voice fill the room with the next song on the album. She tapped her fingers on the sleeve of the jacket to the beat of "And Your Bird Can Sing," smiling as the lyrics unfolded.

The song ended. She tried not to analyze *why* the needle wouldn't go through the fabric. She focused on two facts: the needle *couldn't* go through, and the eyes of the pheasants were definitely watching her in amusement. Spence was absolutely right. *Stick it!*

"Hmmm. You won't let me stick you, so I'll stick *on* you."

"What did you say?" Spence asked.

"I'll be right back."

Jean stood and set the jacket and fabric on the hassock. Spence's gaze trailed after her as she bounded up the stairs.

The folding doors of the guestroom closet opened with a groan. She poked in the cubbies of the hanging storage unit and pulled out several long strips of heavy-weight, stick-on Velcro. If she couldn't sew the fabric, then she'd secure it with Velcro.

Retrieving the jacket from the living room, she machine-sewed the grabbing side of the Velcro strips around the inside of the opening.

"Let's try this again."

"I hope it works." Spence waved his brown slippers in circles to the rhythm of "Tomorrow Never Knows," the last cut on the second side of the album "And when you're done, we need to take that chest over to Mary's apartment. Looks like the rain is letting up. We might get a break."

"No problem. Almost finished."

After pressing the sticky side of the Velcro around three edges of the fabric, she matched them to their grabby companions.

"Viola! Worked like a charm! I have to be careful, but this should be fine for sitting on the plane." She slipped her arms into the sleeves and flapped them up and down, turning in a slow circle in front of Spence.

Spence's face beamed at her each time she completed a turn. He picked up the remote and adjusted the volume of Lennon's beckoning, repeating chant at the end of the album. "Yes...a beginning."

She glided the birds in and out of his view.

CHAPTER 18

Ready to Go?

"I know I forgot something, Spence," Jean said as they drove up Highway 205 on their way to the airport. She glanced in the backseat at their carry-on luggage and ticked off her mental list. She couldn't think of anything she'd missed.

"Honey, you went through everything. Relax; we're going to London, not the moon," Spence said.

"Do you think Mycroft's okay?"

"He'll be fine. Linda will be at the house this afternoon. She'll spoil him more than we do. All he's going to do is eat, sleep, poop, and watch movies by the fire. Heaven."

"Okay, I know you're right." She wiggled in the jacket. *All quiet. Warm.* She checked in her purse to make sure her passport was readily available. "You have your passport?"

"Right here." Spence patted his breast pocket. "Let's park in short-term. It's more expensive, but we can make a hasty exit when we get back. The jetlag will be bad."

"Good thinking. We'll get to the terminal faster from here too."

Jean approached the ticket counter and stuck out their preprinted boarding passes and passports, avoiding eye contact. The agent took them and clicked the keys.

"You'll be on the same plane and have your same seats when you connect in Newark," the ticket agent said, pushing the documents back over the counter. "You'll be logging some serious time in those seats. By the way, I like your jacket."

"Thanks." Jean slipped her passport in her purse. As they stepped away, she pulled on Spence's sleeve. "Walk close behind me—people are noticing my jacket."

"Uh...yeah, ya think? What would you say if somebody went by with three real-looking pheasants on their back? And if they stared at you like that, you'd gawk too," Spence said, laughing. "Remember, wearing the fabric was your idea."

She wrinkled her nose—*he's right*. They proceeded toward the Terminal E security area and entered the shorter frequent-flyer line.

"At least we can get on the plane first. My priority status is still valid. It'll suck when it expires." She flashed on the day trip she'd made from Houston to Costa Mesa over one Christmas holiday, just so she could keep her Platinum status with the airline for another year. The flight attendant thought she was a nut to spend a whole day on an airplane with nowhere to go.

"Let's take advantage while we can." Spence jerked up his head to find the source of the screaming child in the security area. "Ugh. I hope that kid isn't on our plane."

As they stood in line, Jean turned when she got a tap on the shoulder. A large cosmetically altered woman with bleached-blond hair peered around Spence and smiled at her.

"God, I love your jacket! Where'd you get it? It's beautiful!"

"Thank you. I made it." Worried she might be leaning toward surliness, she tried smiling back with confidence. "I like it too." Jean flinched when her nose picked up a strong whiff of synthetic vanilla and gardenia. As she stepped forward to the TSA agent, a vision popped in her head: she was standing there naked.

Self-conscious before, now she was freaking out. After their passports and boarding passes were checked, the agent waved them forward. Hopefully, the black mark he put next her name wasn't a sign.

The gray bin containing her purse and shoes disappeared behind her carry-on bag on the conveyer belt. She took a step toward the electronic archway.

"Ma'am, you need to take off your jacket," the TSA agent said, nodding his head toward the moving belt.

Oh, please, no. She slipped her arms from the sleeves and placed the jacket in another gray bin. It glided into the X-ray machine. She felt like a marshmallow being squeezed through the head of a needle as she stepped into the archway in her stocking feet. She waited on the other side for Spence to follow her.

"Bag check!" shouted a voice from behind the machine.

Molten panic rose in her throat. She swallowed hard to tamp it down. Two TSA agents pointed at the screen, whispering to each other. Spence stood in front of the archway with a what-the-hell look on his face. The security agent waved him forward.

Jean waited, not saying a word, as the TSA agent snatched up the jacket. He walked the length of the chute to a separate table. She padded after him with her shoes, purse, and carry-on bag jumbled in her arms. She mouthed back at Spence, "I don't know. Wait."

Spence gave her a thumbs-up of support.

Horrified, Jean watched the agent hold up the jacket, squeeze each sleeve, and turn it inside out. He paused to inspect the fabric insert. Finally, he handed it to her.

"Sorry, ma'am, the back of the jacket was solid white on the X-ray. Normally, clothing is transparent."

"No problem," she said, oversmiling. "I'm glad you guys check everything." She inspected the fabric, slipped on the jacket, and swung her purse over her shoulder.

She sat in a folding chair, eying Spence as she adjusted the heel of her shoe. She mouthed, "Oh...my...God!" She turned to show him the back of the jacket. "Is it okay?"

"A-okay."

With clipped steps in front of Spence, she started the trek to Terminal E. A thousand eyes stared at her jacket as she walked past gate one through four.

Raleigh jerked awake when the hotel alarm clock buzzed at five fifteen. He pushed in the button to stop the annoying assault and flopped back down on the bed. He touched his left cheek. The gash was more swollen and sore this morning, but at least the bleeding had stopped. Reddish-brown smudges stained the pillow.

He shaved, being careful to avoid the open cut. After showering, he applied a fresh, antiseptic-laden bandage. Blood trickled down his cheek.

"I hate that damn cat. I ought to wring its neck."

A better option was to check out of the hotel and drive to the airport as fast as possible. He wanted to get to the gate before the Collinses arrived for the flight. After verifying the plane's departure was on time, Raleigh settled the bill on his credit card and darted to the car.

The bloody, purple towel glared at him from the passenger seat. His cheek pulsed from the image. He stuffed it under the driver's seat and threw in his bag.

Raleigh pulled the Porsche into a space in the long-term parking lot and jumped on the shuttle. The short-term option made his car more noticeable. He stood at the front door of the bus, ready to rush out before the driver could guilt him out of a tip. He stepped to the counter for the ticket agent to verify his passport. The woman stared at the bandage. All chit-chat ceased. He wanted to rip off the gauze to see her reaction. Instead, his stare challenged her to ask.

Rounding the corner from the ticket counter, Raleigh rolled his eyes at the security line. It snaked well into the retail area. As he joined the queue, a toddler in front of him threw itself down in a temper tantrum. This kid had better not be on the flight to Newark, or worse yet, continuing on to London. Its mother tried to quiet the little beast and neglected to move forward. The gap widened in front of her.

"Ma'am, can you move up, *please*. I need to make my flight," he snapped, unable to contain his frustration.

The woman glared at him and dragged her screaming child along the carpet. She wrestled with a stroller and scooted a diaper bag with her foot like a soccer ball.

The drumbeat in Raleigh's chest accelerated as the line moved toward the TSA agent. He approached the podium and handed over his passport and boarding pass. The agent made a slash next to his name, matched his face to the photo, and pointed to one of scanning stations. *Did that TSA guy nod to somebody in the ceiling?* Maybe he was being paranoid. Raleigh grabbed a plastic bin for his shoes and coat, and set his carry-on bag on the conveyer belt. His stomach squeezed when he turned to the electronic archway. He was waved through.

"What happened to your face?" the TSA agent said behind him.

Raleigh froze, and then glanced over his shoulder.

"I had a mole removed yesterday." He snatched up his coat, bag, and shoes, right as they emerged from the X-ray machine.

He stopped in at the minimart to buy a box of large square bandages and a tube of antibiotic ointment.

"That looks nasty," the cashier said, and handed him back his change.

"So do you." He turned and continued the downward path of the concourse to Gate E-5.

"Yep, that's him." Jon Segert pointed to the image on the video monitor in the security office of the airport

"Had his passport checked about twenty-five minutes ago," the supervising officer said, handing Jon the passenger list for the Newark flight.

Jon leaned on the counter and studied the list. His finger ran down the length the page; the names Jean and Spencer Collins jumped out at him. The printout indicated they'd already checked in to seats A and B, row twenty-three. "A 767, right?—and a two-three-two seat configuration? Who's in seat C—across the aisle from this couple?" he asked, tapping the Collinses' names on the paper. "Can you move some butts around to get me in that seat all the way through to Heathrow? Coulter's got the aisle, two rows ahead in row twenty-one—perfect." He folded the passenger list and slipped it into his breast pocket.

"A solo female has the C seat in row twenty-three. Her name is Susan Foster," the female police officer said, glancing up from the screen. She clicked the keys and printed out a new boarding pass. "The gate agent will intercept Ms. Foster before you board."

"One more thing." Jon pulled out a business card and wrote on the back. "Here's a license number for a late-model silver Porsche 911. Let me know if you find this car in any of the parking lots here at the airport. I can send one of our agents over to check it out while I'm gone."

"Sure thing," the supervising officer said and shook Jon's hand. "You're all set. I cleared your gun with the airline and also with the security agent at the Terminal E scanning area. Use the employees-only entrance."

Jon nodded, waved to the group, and slipped his new boarding pass in his breast pocket with the passenger list. On his way down the hall, he stopped to check his reflection in the two-way mirror. A little gray in the temples of his short, precision-cut blonde hair. A few more crow's feet spread from his deep blue eyes. Not bad for turning fifty this year. He pulled out his phone and speed-dialed the office.

"Yeah, Jenny, can you coordinate the guys when you get a call from the Port of Portland Police here at the airport? They're going to search for Coulter's car in the lots. We'll need to send someone over if they find it." He heard the scratch of Jenny taking notes. "I'll be out of touch until I land in Newark."

Jon ended the call and took one last glance in the mirrored window. "I'm getting too old for this crap."

He hit the elevator button three times in rapid succession.

Jon sipped his coffee from a paper cup at the opposite end of the gate area from Raleigh Coulter. *What's with the bandage on Coulter's face? The purple hand towel.* He opened his *USA Today* and pretended to read the front page. He kept his gaze on the concourse and immediately recognized Jean and Spencer Collins. A fairly accurate likeness to their passports and driver's license pictures. They scanned the area to select two seats together. *Wow, some jacket.* He admired the birds on the back when Jean turned to set her carry-on bag under the seat. Something wasn't right about those things; kind of spooky. The birds seemed to be gazing around at the people, checking them out.

The Collinses were nervous. Raleigh? They didn't acknowledge him. Raleigh glanced over at the Collinses; they seemed unaware. Coulter knew them, but Jean and Spencer didn't know him.

The gate agent plucked the hand microphone from the wall behind the counter. "Will Susan Foster please come to the counter at E-5? Susan Foster, report the gate agent at E-5."

A brown-haired, plump woman in her forties pounded out her steps to the counter. From her ill-fitting pantsuit, wheeled laptop case, and the chip on her shoulder, Jon figured Ms. Foster had been passed over for a promotion more than once. The woman's strident voice escalated in volume.

"I specifically picked *that* seat. You people need to put me to first class!"

Jon smirked, folded his paper, and strolled to the counter. Best to upgrade her. He signaled the gate agent to join him by the rear window wall, showed her his badge, and lowered his voice. She smiled back and nodded. Susan Foster waited, tapping her freshly polished acrylic nails.

"Not a problem, Ms. Foster, we have a seat for you in first class." After a few click of the keys, the woman snatched up her fresh boarding pass and beamed with a self-congratulatory smile.

The gate agent's stare bored a hole into Jon's back as he returned to his seat. He slowed as he passed Raleigh. A spot of blood. The police report mentioned a cat. Nice cat.

It was time to engage the Collinses in conversation.

Spence guided Jean toward the two open seats at the far end of the gate area across from a nice-looking, clean-cut man reading a *USA Today*. He wanted to get distance between them and that guy with the bandage on his face. The blood was disgusting. The man with the newspaper got up, talked to the gate agent, and returned to his seat across from him and Jean.

He nudged Jean's shoulder and made a stinky-cheese face. With narrowed eyes, Spence nodded to a haggard-looking woman as she approached the gate. She dragged a stroller and an exhausted, whining child behind her. He grimaced when she hoisted a diaper bag over her shoulder with a hissed string of profanity.

"If they connect on our plane to London, I'm ejecting myself out over Greenland. Did you bring some earplugs?"

"Lower your voice. Yes, I brought them, but let me double-check." Jean chuckled and rummaged through her purse.

The guy with the newspaper laughed, obviously overhearing his snarky banter.

"Sorry," Spence said, embarrassed. "It's not that I hate kids. Just on planes."

"You two off to New York?" the man asked.

"No, we're connecting in Newark on our way to London."

"Pleasure trip, I hope."

"Actually, we're doing some research, but we're counting on mostly pleasure." He turned toward the Jetway as the gate agent secured the door open with the kickstand. "We're getting ready to—"

Before Spence finished his comment, the man folded his *USA Today*, stood, and grabbed his bag without saying a word. He bolted through the doorway and disappeared.

"Geez...that guy must have überincredible platinum status, or I stink."

"Honey, there's no such thing as überincredible platinum." Jean gave his knee three quick pats. "And you smell *delicioso*."

Jean shimmied by the guy with the bandage on his face as they boarded the plane. Not only did the wound give her the creeps but the look he gave her did too. At row twenty-three, she turned and handed Spence the shoulder strap of her carry-on bag. She paused, deciding whether to keep the jacket on or take it off. Leave it on. She ducked to the window seat, knowing Spence wanted the aisle.

"No beauty queen and the little monster," Spence said, scanning the aisles as he slid in beside her. "I'm keeping my fingers crossed."

"Me too. But guess who just came out of the cockpit: Mr. Überplatinum."

"What's that about?"

Mr. Überplatinum grew even more über as he moved toward their row. "I don't know, but I think we need to be careful what we say."

As he came closer to their seats, the man glanced down as he passed the guy with the bandage. He stopped at the seat across from them.

"Hi, again." The man placed the folded newspaper and a water bottle in the seat pocket.

"Hey, hi," Spence said. "You must rate. How'd you get on the plane so early?"

"Oh, you could say I work for the airline. It's a small perk that comes with the brutal schedule." He offered his hand to Spence. "I'm Jon, by the way, no H."

"Nice to meet you, Jon-with-no-H. I'm Spence, and this is my wife, Jean."

"I'm taking this plane to London too." Jon studied her and smiled. "I guess we'll become friends over the next fourteen hours."

Jean reached her hand over Spence's lap to give Jon's a shake. *Firm. Official.* He didn't have his carry-on. If Jon were such a muckety-muck with the airline, then why wasn't he in first class? *Curious.*

CHAPTER 19

Watching in the Air

J on could tell a lot about people from their handshake. Spence and Jean were decent, genuine and trusting. If he had to interrogate them, they'd sing like canaries in spring. Jean looked him straight on with those aqua eyes. She was cautious and analytical but honest for sure. Her rimmed irises almost glowed with the morning light streaming through the oval window of the plane. Spence's sense of humor was a kick, and he had soulful brown eyes. A fun guy; comfortable with himself.

He had plenty of time to talk up the Collinses during the flight and listen to their conversation. For now, he'd sit back and watch the top third of Coulter's salt-and-pepper head two rows in front of him.

The whine of the engines increased as they retreated from the Jetway. This was going to be one of his more interesting trips: He was about to fly 6,500 miles with a perp and two keys to the case. And they weren't going anywhere.

As the plane pulled away from the gate, Raleigh jerked up his head. He'd forgotten to call his mother. He turned on his phone and waited for the signal to connect. He punched in Mary's number. He ducked forward as the too-efficient flight attendant raced past him. A wave of heavy, sweet perfume swirled behind her. He sneezed just as Mary's voice mail made its announcement.

"Hi, Mom. I had a sudden business trip come up. I'm on my way to London this morning and should be gone for a week—" A tap on his shoulder. The flight attendant stood over him. Her diamond wedding ring flashed a warning shot in the sun as her left hand rested on the seat in front of him.

"Sir, you have to power down—right now. And please pull your seat all the way forward."

Raleigh shook his head in defiance and continued with his voice mail. "Mom, we're taking off. I gotta go. I'll call you when I get to London."

Raleigh gave the attendant a sarcastic smile. He rummaged in the seat pocket for an unused napkin but didn't find one. The flight attendant darted to the galley, strapped herself in the jump seat, and glared at him. Frustrated, he wiped his nose with the back of his hand.

The plane rolled toward the runway. Raleigh glanced over his left shoulder. The Collinses chatted with the guy across the aisle. Instinct made him touch the gauze on his left cheek; wet and throbbing. When they reached cruising altitude, he'd have to pull his bag from the overhead bin so he could change the bandage.

Raleigh flipped through the airline magazine without looking at the pages. The guy the Collinses were talking with seemed familiar, but he couldn't place where he'd seen him before. Something about him was weird while sitting at the gate. The repeating pattern on the upholstery blurred as the plane lifted. Rollercoaster stomach. Behind him, Spencer Collins laughed.

"You know, I call Ringo the grateful Beatle," Spence proclaimed when the subject of the Beatles came up. "In my opinion, he was so-so, just an okay drummer. But there was so much talent in the rest of the band even Ringo's drumming couldn't cover it up." Spence shook his head. "He's rolling in the dough now."

Jon laughed out loud, agreeing wholeheartedly, as they lifted off the runway. He liked this guy. Refreshing for Spence to reach for Jean's hand while he talked, squeezing it tighter as the plane banked left and made a wide ninety-degree turn to the north. Spence's two greatest strengths were his knowledge of rock music and Jean; Jon's own were rock music and Meg.

"I'm a big Rolling Stones fan myself," Jon added.

"Well, did you know Keith Richards used a five-string tuning on "Brown Sugar"? I read that in his biography. That's why nobody can replicate his particular sound with six strings. The sound Keith gets is magic."

As the plane leveled off, the seat belt sign chimed. Still listening to Spence, Jon's gaze darted to Raleigh, who stood and opened the overhead bin to retrieve his bag. After pulling out a box of bandages and ointment of some kind, he moved forward to the restroom.

"What do you think happened to that guy's cheek? I bet there's a story to go with that bandage," Spence said and tipped his head toward Raleigh.

"I don't know. Maybe a cat tore up his face." He paused, waiting for a reaction. Spence opened and closed his mouth, as if he wanted to say something but changed his mind. "Excuse me a moment, drank too much coffee this morning."

Jon stepped into the restroom on the opposite side of the plane, closed the door, and stared in the mirror. He waited. He wanted to see Raleigh's face after he returned to his seat.

Jean held Spence's hand too tight. "Sorry."

"All good." Spence wiped the sweat on the knee of his jeans. "That was weird—what Jon said about that guy's face."

"Yeah...weird. Jon's an okay guy, though. I think I'm going to be listening to hours of rock trivia. Let me know when you're ready to hit the bathroom, and I'll go too."

"I'll wait until those two come out and then get up."

The bandage guy pressed at the fresh gauze on his left cheek as he returned to his seat. Jean poked Spence's knee and pointed to the open restroom. She followed him. The bandage guy gasped when she passed his seat. She turned in the galley space to get a glimpse of him. He seemed shaken.

Jon nodded to her as he exited the opposite restroom. He paused at the bandage guy's seat.

She tapped her toes and flexed her knees, studying both men as she waited for Spence to come out.

You've got to be kidding. The guy with the bandage got up and came toward her. He stopped and stood so close she could feel his heat. A wave of nausea rolled over her when his expensive cologne crowded the air in the small space. He eyed the back of her jacket. Her lungs seemed incapable of anything but shallow breaths.

"Nice jacket. Where did you get it?"

"Uh...a gift. That one's open on the other side." She pointed to the restroom Jon had vacated. "I'll wait here for my husband."

"Yeah, okay." The bandage guy took another drink of her jacket and sauntered to the other side. He glanced back one more time before the label flipped to Occupied.

Jean turned her gaze to the aisle, surprised that Jon had been staring at her. Their eyes locked. She raised her brows, smiled, and shrugged her shoulders. She flinched as someone, or something, bumped her back.

"Oh, I'm sorry—" Nothing. She whipped her head around as Spence emerged from the restroom. "You won't believe this," she said under her breath.

"What?" he whispered, searching her eyes.

"I'll tell you when I get back to the seat."

Jean latched the door and leaned against the sink. She turned in the mirror. She sucked in a breath. *The birds are changing.* They seemed dull; two of them were disappearing. The middle one was definitely bigger than the others. The wings on the center bird were a deeper brown; the bright colors were streaked with white, beige, and black.

As she washed her hands, she studied her face and flexed out the tension by stretching her mouth open several times. *Check the jacket again.* The two other birds were faint shadows. The middle one had grown larger in only a few minutes; the vivid colors had changed to more solid shades of black, brown, gray, and cream. Its features were pointed. The plane bumped with turbulence. She grabbed the counter to keep her balance. The seatbelt sign illuminated. Taking a deep breath, she slid the knob on the door.

"Ladies and gentlemen, please make sure your seat belts are securely fastened. We'll be going through a patch of bumpy air ahead," the flight attendant announced.

Jean lasered her eyes at Spence the entire way back to her seat.

Something happened. Jon could see it on Raleigh's face as he came down the aisle and grabbed the seat to lower himself; on full alert. Jean watched Raleigh—and also him.

Jon sat stock still as Jean walked stiff-legged by Raleigh's seat. Yes, Raleigh seemed to be extremely interested in her jacket—and Jean was highly uncomfortable. Why did she turn around so fast before she went in the restroom? She acted like someone bumped into her. Nobody was there.

Jon studied the jacket as Jean shimmied into the window seat. The birds looked different—really different. When she leaned back, she acted as if something was there.

A pall settled over their seats. *Stay quiet. Listen.*

"This is too weird," Jean whispered, leaning into Spence. "The jacket moved and the birds changed. I checked in the mirror. That bandage guy knew—I swear *he knew*."

"Honey, you're just too conscious of it. Lean over—act like you dropped something. Let me check." Spence put on his glasses.

Jean leaned forward. She stared at the tiny airline logos on the seat, dangling her arm and swishing the air at nothing. She raised her eyes to Spence. His dark eyes registered disbelief; his expression, however, screamed panic.

"It knows something."

The jacket and those birds. Jon watched the Collinses' actions unfold beside him. Jean showed Spence the back of the jacket and wasn't searching for anything on the floor. Spence had gone silent. Jean stared out the window. Their body language signaled contemplation. He'd never seen two people more in tune with each other; almost merged DNA. No more banter, funny or otherwise, for the remainder of the flight to Newark.

Raleigh's head hadn't moved a millimeter since he'd returned to his seat the second time. He kept an eye on all three of them. *What the hell is going on?*

Jean's stomach dropped as the plane started its slow descent into Newark. She hadn't gotten up since she'd checked the fabric in the mirror the first time. An occasional twinge shifted the back of her jacket, but she tried to ignore it. She really wanted to stretch her legs but wasn't willing to take any more risks. *Is it still changing?* She decided to stay put for the fifty-eight-minute layover.

"Spence, I want to stay. Keeping the jacket out of view would be a good idea."

"I'm not comfortable leaving you here alone."

"I knew you'd say that. Make sure you have your passport and boarding pass. I made a list for the next leg." She handed Spence a piece of paper. "I won't go anywhere. I'll stay right here, right in this seat."

Spence read off the items. "Four large bottled waters, bag of almonds, packet of tissues, antacid, and ibuprofen. Anything else?"

She wrinkled her nose. "Bird seed? How about a dead mouse?"

"Not funny, Jean. Not funny at all."

As the wheels hit the tarmac, everyone shifted and powered up their cell phones. Jean heard the seatbelts unbuckle even before the plane finished taxiing. It bumped to a stop at the Jetway, and half the passengers jumped up to open the overhead bins. Jon stayed put. Raleigh remained still in his seat. Spence popped up, checking to make sure he had his passport, wallet, and boarding pass.

"Jon and that weird guy aren't leaving the plane. Are you sure you'll be okay by yourself?" Spence whispered.

"I'll be fine. The flight attendants will be here."

Please let me be fine.

"Be back as soon as I can."

The silence loomed for twenty-eight minutes. The flight attendants cleaned the open seats and reloaded the catering carts through the hatch doors in the galley. A maintenance worker in a yellow jumpsuit swished down the aisle to fix a malfunctioning seat. The plane rumbled as the refueling hose pumped to fill the tanks, and the sanitation hose sucked everything out. The back of her jacket shifted; she didn't. She tried to take a deep breath.

Jean reached up to swivel the air vent and spotted the first-class passengers emerging in the doorway. They turned left, instead of right. With near military precision, each one commenced the drill: place laptop on seat; speak louder than normal into cord attached to smart phone; slide wheeled carry-on into overhead bin, handle first; hand flight attendant suit jacket to be hung in front closet; and finally, slip into leather seat. Look important.

These passengers, with the weight of world problems on their shoulders, believed themselves to be the chosen ones. Their mission was to save all mankind. She gazed upon the scene like a time-warped voyeur, seeing herself only five months ago.

The memory evaporated as the next wave streamed on board, those passengers with frequent-flyer status. They launched themselves through the doorway like greyhounds lunging for the rabbit, eager to claim their prime space in the overhead bins. A small consolation prize for not being able to use their status to secure a first-class seat. She scoffed at this human predictability. She'd done that too.

Spence emerged into the cabin. Relief washed across his face when he spotted her still in her seat. He came toward her with a bulging plastic bag.

"I think I got everything," Spence announced, handing her the bag for an inventory check.

Digging through the contents, she stopped when she found a small gold box. As she opened the lid, four pieces of the most luscious dark chocolate released their rich, delectable aroma. The air filled with the scent.

"They're the 72 percent cocoa. I couldn't resist."

"You're a gentleman, just like Atticus in *To Kill a Mockingbird*."

"Yes, I am, Scout. Speaking of—everything all right?"

"Quiet so far, but I'm going to the restroom now that you're back. Why don't you let me out before the cattle call?"

The last wave of flyers—those who didn't travel often—would board soon. They would be a nightmare. She stood, shimmied by Spence's knees, and raced up the aisle.

Spence's mouth dropped open, as if a jaw screw had fallen out of its hinge, when he looked at the back of the jacket. The fabric had completed the transformation to become one enormous hawk. At least Spence hoped that was the end of the transformation—he wouldn't want it to become more ferocious. The bird looked vicious. The feathers gleamed in rich hues of brown, beige, and black; eyes focused and wary. The bird's thick talons—curved and sharp—gripped invisible prey. The noble predator had enlarged to fill the entire piece of fabric.

Jon and the bandage guy saw the change too. They both reacted when Jean walked up the aisle, so much so that the bandage guy pulled out his phone and snapped a picture. With his eyes trained on the restroom door, Jean slipped inside as the remaining passengers boarded the plane. Spence had to bob and weave to keep his focus. The crowd jammed the aisle, bumping their bags on the seats. He glanced over at Jon, who took in the whole scene.

Spence put away the earplugs. Better to have his wits about him for the leg across the pond.

Jean flinched at a *click* behind her after she passed the bandage guy's seat. She slid the lock on the restroom door and twisted in the mirror. She gasped. Her mind raced.

"Okay, big guy, what are you trying to tell me?" she whispered. "Just stay calm. Nobody wants to hurt you. Please don't hurt me, either."

Keep it together until we get to London.

After she washed her hands, she took off the jacket. She'd put it back on when she returned to her seat.

The door bumped into a sea of people. At the right moment, Jean joined the stream and inched her way toward Spence. His face was like the precious parachute cord swinging out of reach as she flailed in free fall. *Just get back to the seat.*

Her gaze shifted to Jon across the aisle. He stared straight ahead and had an odd expression on his face. Jon had seen the change in her jacket—she was sure of it.

A break in the boarding traffic. Out of the corner of his eye, Raleigh spotted Jean headed to the restroom again. He retrieved his phone and snapped a picture of the back of Jean's denim jacket as she went by. His stomach cramped, like he'd been sucker punched. A hawk—on her back. Fierce. The damned thing stared at him. *Impossible.*

Raleigh studied the picture to confirm it was true. He raised his eyes and stared at the seat. He had six hours to plan out the details. He'd go straight to Gerrod Barnes's office to show him the picture. *I can't tell him about the eerie transformation or he'll think I'm crazy.*

After meeting with Gerrod Barnes, he'd head to the museum and snoop around the Collinses' appointment with the curator. When they left the museum, he'd wait by the front door to get that jacket off Jean, one way or another. If he had to knock her down, too bad. He'd jump in a taxi and go right back to Gerrod's office. The Collinses didn't have any idea where he was going. Besides, they'd be delayed with reporting the theft, bogged down with paperwork, and Jean would be boohooing about her precious jacket being stolen.

Jean walked past his seat. He eyed the jacket. This wouldn't be easy.

Lost in the logistics of his plan, Raleigh wasn't even aware that the plane had pulled away from the gate and taxied to the runway.

Jon waited for the meal to be served before continuing to chat up the Collinses. Jean and Spence performed a ballet dance of trading items on their trays: she took his roll, and he took her bag of carrots; she placed the olives from her salad on his, and she added her candy bar to his tray. *Hilarious—just like Meg and me.*

"So, what are you researching in London?" he asked Spence as he peeled back the tab on his dressing container.

"We're going to the Victoria and Albert Museum to meet with one of their department heads this afternoon...or tomorrow, with the time change. Jean is a big fabric nut," Spence said. Jean bumped Spence's foot.

"We also love to spend time in the gift shop," Jean interjected, trying to keep her smile genuine. "The best shop of any museum in the world. I'm out of greeting cards."

"Long way to go for cards. Where do you like to stay? My hotel's on the north side of Hyde Park."

"We like the Copthorne Tara," Spence said, taking a bite of his salad. "Close to everything, quiet, and you can jump on the Underground to go anywhere in the city. A lot of the airline people stay at that hotel when they lay over. Our favorite restaurant is there too— Ffiona's—in Kensington."

"Follow the airline folks off a plane. Isn't that what they always say? Like if you want good Chinese food; look to where the Chinese eat, right?" Jon laughed and poked at the miniscule chunk of sweet-and-sour pork on his tray. "Are you going straight to the hotel? I can't check in to mine until three. I'll be a zombie."

"That's right!" Spence turned to Jean and bobbed his fork. "We have to meet Graham at four thirty. If we can't check in, we won't have time to get a nap or take a shower before we go to the museum."

"We can check into the Yotel for a few hours." Jean picked one of the carrots out of the little bag from Spence's tray. "We can shower and take a nap there." She leaned forward and wiggled the carrot at Jon. "You know, Jon, these things are not real. They're mush, formed and pressed to look like carrots."

"Really? I always wondered how they got those to grow all the same size," he said, laughing. "What's a Yotel? Some kind of hip-hop hotel?"

"Oh, no. We found it the last time we were here." Jean crunched her pressed mush. "You can rent a small pod to crash for a few hours. The rooms are tiny, more like a broom closet on a cruise ship. But after flying this long in coach, being able to get horizontal with no noise is heavenly."

"Cool, I'll have to remember that one." Jon smiled to himself. *Excellent!* Jean and Spence would be safely ensconced in a pod at the airport for a while before going to the V&A to meet with someone named Graham at 4:30 p.m. They were staying at the Copthorne Tara, not too far. He'd have time to follow Raleigh to the antiques dealer's office, and then tail him back to the museum. *Yes, stick to Raleigh.*

Satisfied with the plan, he wadded up his napkin and pulled up the video screen from the arm of the seat. He made a mental note to call the office as soon the plane landed. Coulter's car was a priority and new information might have come in about his financial transactions. But this connection with the Collinses added a twist. Raleigh received that wound at their house. Insider trading and breaking and entering—what else could he add to the list?

"Excuse me folks, I'm going to zone out with a movie for a while," he said and removed the headphones from the plastic bag. He browsed through the selections. His finger trailed along the video screen and stopped at the third icon. *Bad Santa* would get him revved for the holidays. He liked Billy Bob Thornton. The combination of a good movie and the prospect of Raleigh behind bars would make it a great Christmas.

CHAPTER 20

Across the Pond

As the plane approached the coast of Ireland, the morning sun glinted off the wings. The flashes were blinding at thirty thousand feet. The long descent started even before the pilot made the announcement. Sleep eluded Jean since they bounced around over Reykjavik. Spence dozed with his glasses teetering on top of his Eric Clapton biography. Deep breaths. *Let him rest as long as he can.* She plucked the glasses from his book and folded them in her lap.

As the flight attendants began their final arrival preparations, Spence flinched awake. She patted his knee. "Did you get some good snooze?"

"Yeah, I must have. I don't remember a thing," Spence said, rubbing his eyes with his thumb and forefinger. "What time is it?"

"Nine in the morning—London time." She gathered her purse, magazines, and the plastic bag from under the seat. "All quiet, but take a look." She handed him his glasses and leaned forward.

Spence yawned and adjusted them to focus. "Still a hawk."

"How do we explain this to Graham? We sent him pictures of the fabric. It showed three pheasants."

Spence gazed at her, drawing a blank. "I don't know, but that may be a good thing—another bit of magic to show him."

The door unsealed, and the seats emptied in front of them. The bandage guy stood at his seat, missing his turn to deplane. Jon waited for them to get out first. He talked on his cell phone, but as she moved into the aisle the word "shit" flew out and stuck in her hair.

After they gathered their bags and coats, she and Spence trekked up the long ramp to the international terminal, snaking toward customs. Jean stiffened. Three sets of eyes bored a hole into the back of her jacket. *Calm down.* She imagined the hawk protecting her. Oddly, after the initial shock, she wasn't threatened by the menacing bird at all.

Spence stood close behind her in the shortest line. They placed their passports on the counter.

The customs agent stared directly in their eyes. "Are you here on business or pleasure?"

"Pleasure," Spence said, his smile a bit over-the-top.

"Where will you be residing during your stay?"

"The Copthorne Tara...in Kensington," Jean jumped in, keeping an eye on her passport. The customs agent raised his gaze, stamped it, and hesitated. He examined her eyes again and turned to view the computer. Her heart bumped against her ribs. *C'mon let's go. Go already!*

"Any plans to travel outside of London?"

"No, just London."

"Have a pleasant visit." The customs agent slapped their passports on the counter.

Jean let out a long breath. She was looking forward to a nap and a shower after she called Mary about the hawk. The time was late in Portland, but Mary had wanted to be kept informed.

"C'mon, Spence. Y'off to the Yotel."

Mary hung up the phone and glanced at her alarm clock on the nightstand. The digital numbers clicked over to 2:15 a.m. Pins and needles didn't begin to describe her excitement after Jean and Spence had come to visit her with her fabric, and now she wouldn't get any sleep after that call. *A hawk?* She couldn't imagine what it meant. This was completely new.

Fidgety, Mary turned on the bedside lamp and pulled back the covers. She slid her chilly feet in her soft sheepskin slippers and put on her terry cloth robe. She scuffed to the kitchen. A cup of tea would help her to relax.

She sat in the living room and listened to Doc's old farmhouse clock tick until it released one lazy bong. Three thirty. So good of Jean to call. *These two people truly care about me...and they share my secret of the fabric.* She wanted Jean and Spence to be the ones to make her immortal. Her time. Keep them close now.

This afternoon she would arrange for the Milwaukie Manor van to take her downtown to Landrum & Sullivan. Her dear friend and lawyer, Don Landrum, was always willing to see her on short notice. With recent events, some changes were in order. Beneath her elation, fear gripped her heart about Raleigh being in London at the same time as the Collinses. Something didn't sound right at all. This was no coincidence.

CHAPTER 21

The Hawk

Graham Hollingsworth leaned on the information desk and chatted with the guest services representative while he waited for the Collinses to whirl through the revolving door at the main entrance. It was only 4:15 p.m. but he wanted to catch them should they arrive early.

This meeting would reveal the find of a lifetime or deliver the greatest hoax of his career. He was willing to take the chance. When he received Spencer Collins's original e-mail and viewed the pictures, he immediately recalled his fascinating conversation with Anhur Kumar from the Cairo Museum. They had met at a symposium held for textile conservation in Ottawa, Canada, back in 1997. Over dinner and drinks, Anhur described just such an artifact, which he had been in search of for many years. This fabric could possibly be the same. He shouldn't neglect to investigate. Out of habit, he smoothed his red silk tie, the one with the Spitalfields-inspired floral design, and ran his manicured hand through his short, gray hair.

Graham's gaze fixed on the revolving door. A man whirled in with a large bandage on his face, as if on a mission. He raised his eyes to the chandelier and grimaced, then smirked. *Curious.* Most newcomers didn't take notice of the massive blown-glass piece until they were leaving the museum. The man approached the information desk.

"Can you point me to the fabric exhibit, or do you call it department?" the man asked.

An American. He didn't know a whit about textiles, except for what he found on sale at Harrods.

"I'm sorry, sir, that particular exhibit is closed, in preparation for its relocation to Blythe House in Kensington. I apologize for the inconvenience. I'm sure you will enjoy the other exhibits," the guest services representative said and nodded to the opposite end of the lobby.

The man walked away, clearly upset. Graham's gaze followed him. He was entirely out of his element, but the choice of jacket was well done. How could he not be self-conscious about that dreadful bandage?

Jean Collins's face filled his view as she emerged from the revolving door. Her hair had been auburn when he'd met her in 2008, but he'd never forget those brilliant eyes. He stepped forward and extended his hand.

"Welcome, welcome! We meet again."

"You remember me after all this time? Wonderful to be here," Jean said and turned to Spence. "Was my hair brown or red when we were here before? I can't keep track." She turned back to Graham. "You've been busy this year. Congratulations on your acquisition of the new building for the exhibit."

Jean had read an article about the fabric exhibit closing for the next year to relocate to a separate building in Kensington. The move would allow the museum to consolidate the growing displays and expand the conservation studio. The Victoria and Albert Museum was known all over the world for its collections of important, and historic, fabrics and textiles.

They followed Graham through the cavernous marble lobby. As they moved toward the former exhibition area, the clack of their shoes echoed under the acoustic dome. She raised her eyes and imagined the enormous tentacles of the Chihuly glass chandelier were attached to a monster sea anemone descending to gobble her up. "That Puget Sound beast followed us all the way here," she whispered to Spence. "A sign."

"Maybe. A sign of *what?*"

"I must apologize for the untidiness," Graham said as he moved them toward a thick, crinkly plastic curtain. "We're preparing to pack the display fabrics. We must keep them away from airborne fibers. You would be amazed at the amount of dust brought in here by the thousands of visitors to the museum. An arduous process, indeed, but this allows us the opportunity to examine each piece for necessary repairs, prior to packing them. Any we find will go directly to our new, state-of-the-art studio for conservation work."

As Graham held back the curtain, Jean and Spence stepped into the closed area. She marveled at the stainless-steel tables set with magnifying lights on long arms, the many storage racks, and the huge rolls of bright-white, acid-free tissue. Lying on the far table was one of the expansive fifteenth-century Devonshire hunting tapestries. The woven scene was like a magnet. The tapestry pulled her forward. Without touching it, she inspected the intricate images of the Middle Ages, the elaborate royal ritual of the hunt. The scenes were both violent and elegant. Photographs of the tapestry could never replicate the detail and scale of its art.

"Ah, you're admiring one of our treasures," Graham said, beaming with pride. "This is just one of the four. This particular one is *Falconry*, the only one depicting a single hunt. When they're all together, the scenes measure over 40 meters, the equivalent of 133 feet. The tapestries give the viewer a fairly complete representation of royal life in the mid-fifteenth century. Quite amazing. Their fame is superseded only by their rarity. Tapestries of this size and quality didn't survive. Most are only referenced in archival papers. The museum acquired these stunning pieces from the estate of The Dukes of Devonshire." Graham clapped his hands together and moved to one of the empty stainless-steel tables. "So, my friends, where is this lovely gem you've come such a long way to show me?"

"Oh, sorry." Jean refocused her attention, remembering she too had a priceless textile, and turned to show Graham the back of her jacket.

Graham sucked in a breath and approached her. "Tell me you didn't sew this to the jacket. Did you? Not at all like the pictures sent to me."

"Part of the story, Mr. Hollingsworth—and please call me Spence. We must tell you—and this is going to sound crazy—the fabric changed. The three pheasants in the pictures I sent in the e-mail became this—one big hawk—on the trip over here." Spence pointed to the back of the jacket.

Graham stared at Jean, dubious. "Can you take this off?"

"I can do one better. It's not sewn in—only stuck in with Velcro. Originally, I tried to hand-sew the fabric into the jacket, but I couldn't get the needle through." She slipped her arms from the sleeves and showed Graham the back panel. "You can peel this out of the center."

"I see. Do you mind?" Graham moved in closer to inspect the seam. "Pull like this?" In unison, the conservation staff in the room shot up their heads, aghast at the ripping sound when the Velcro seams were pulled apart. "Back to work everyone! I'm not tearing anything over here." The staff visibly relaxed and resumed working.

Once the fabric was free of the jacket, Graham slipped on a pair of white gloves and held the corners to examine it.

"Remarkable! The stitches are invisible to the naked eye. The colors are infinitely brilliant and rich. I've never seen anything quite like this."

"Can you tell us how old it is?" Spence asked.

"I would normally expect warp and weft in the weave in ex-tremely old fabric, but I don't detect the technique here. The warp provides the foundation of a tapestry, running horizontally; the weft provides the color and pattern and is wrapped completely around the plain warp. The technique gives the piece strength and durability—as in the Devonshire tapestry over there." Graham nodded to the table on the other side of the room. "This fabric doesn't correspond to a traditional antique weave at all. No repeating of the design in the placement of the image. Yes, this is completely unique. I dare not say with precision how old, but surely older than any of us could imagine, predating Renaissance techniques. It needs to be thoroughly researched and analyzed; however, we won't be ready for this level of examination for another year." He paused and turned to one of the empty steel tables. "Give me a moment, please. I want to view this under this magnifying lamp."

Graham floated the fabric to the table with a large magnifying lamp clamped on the edge. Swinging the bright-white light over the fabric, he lowered the arm and gazed through the top. He examined the illuminated feet of the hawk; they resembled real three-dimensional talons. *Amazing.* He inched the lamp along the image.

"Hmmm...yes...hmmm." He was now completely focused. "The talons seem quite lethal...fascinating." He held the magnification disk closer to the fabric. Maneuvering it up to the tail feathers, he became even more intrigued. "The colors are impeccable; this bird looks as though it could fly around the room. The texture is...indescribable."

This made no sense. *Yes, Anhur Kumar must see this immediately.* He was taken aback when the hawk's head emerged into his view.

"The beak of this bird, most definitely, resembles real bone." He hovered the lamp over one of the eyes. He paused and stared, within one inch of his own. The huge, magnified black eye darted left, then right, and blinked. He gasped and smacked the light arm away.

"Mr. Hollingsworth? Are you okay?" Jean asked.

"The eye moved," he said in an urgent whisper. "You...you say the birds changed?"

"Yes," Spence said. "They disappeared and came back. After we got on the plane, the fabric faded to become this hawk. Jean sensed heat on the back of the jacket—movement too. I'm sure this sounds bizarre, but the former owner said it was magical."

Graham was certain Spence had no idea, at all, what they had brought to him.

"We only heard part of the history, Graham. The former owner, an elderly widow, told us what she knew," Jean added. "She said a man acquainted with her grandfather found it in an Egyptian tomb over a hundred years ago."

"Come with me to my office upstairs. We need to contact a colleague of mine at the Cairo Museum." He carefully folded the fabric in fresh tissue, grateful to have had the foresight to forward Spence's e-mail to Anhur Kumar yesterday. Anhur would be waiting for his call. Spence held the plastic curtain aside to let him pass. He whisked the fabric to the bank of elevators.

Raleigh lowered his museum map when he heard the curtain rustle. He stepped back into the recess behind a pillar. A distinguished-looking man with graying hair rushed past him. He held a tissue-covered bundle in front of him with white-gloved hands. He looked like a waiter carrying out a baked Alaska blistering with flames. *That man must be Graham Hollingsworth.* The Collinses rushed out behind him. Jean had the denim jacket draped over her arm.

Having overheard a good portion of the conversation, he was elated to find out the fabric was only held in place with Velcro. It would be easy to tear away and run to one of the taxis in front of the museum. All he needed to do was get a firm grip on the bottom and pull. Unsure of how long the Collinses would be upstairs, he'd wait on the steps for them to leave the museum.

Jean pulled Spence's arm and did a fast trot to keep up with Graham. The elevator doors dinged and opened. They stood aside to let Graham enter first.

"Three, please. My office is on three," Graham said. His gloved hands quivered as he held the fabric.

"Graham, is this an emergency?" Jean asked, thinking she should be more panicked. Or, was she just getting used to the bizarre circumstances?

"This may be, Mrs. Collins. Anhur Kumar can provide additional information. Are you able to change your plans to go to Cairo?"

"I don't know. Who's Anhur Kumar?" Spence asked.

Jean put her hand on Spence's arm. "Let's hear what this Mr. Kumar says before we unravel our plans at this point. We've been living with some strange happenings with this fabric. I understand this is your first experience, but I don't think there's any reason to be frightened."

"Oh yes, there may very well be a reason to be frightened." Graham stared at the elevator doors as if willing them to open.

Graham nodded for them to step into his office. He set the tissue-covered fabric on his desk and rolled off his conservator gloves. Without turning the pages of his Rolodex, he picked up the phone, hit the button for an outside line, and called a number. He fixed his gaze on the fabric as he talked.

"Anhur, my friend, I'm so pleased you answered your phone. As I mentioned to you in my e-mail yesterday, I have met with Mr. and Mrs. Collins this afternoon. They are currently in the office with me. The fabric is quite amazing, Anhur—if it is even fabric at all."

The elation on Graham's face changed to fear. Jean's own expression mirrored his.

"Yes, that's correct. Moved. The eye moved, Anhur. I swear," Graham continued, flustered. "And, I don't mind telling you, the experience was most unnerving. One moment while I locate a pen. Here we are. Yes, right."

Graham wrote down a time, a flight number, and an airline. Jean glanced at Spence, bewildered. He shrugged his shoulders.

"I hope so, Anhur. You will not regret this. Thank you. I will relay the information to Mr. and Mrs. Collins."

Graham hung up the phone and clapped his hands together. "Anhur Kumar is eager to see the fabric straight away. He is the executive director of the Cairo Museum and is making the arrangements, as we speak, for you both to fly to Cairo in the morning at 9:40 a.m. The Cairo Museum will assume the expenses for your trip. I trust this shouldn't pose a problem with your arrangements here in London. You mentioned you were staying in Kensington?"

"Yes, but—" Jean tried to catch up with Graham. *Go to Cairo tomorrow morning?*

"Go to your hotel straight away. This may, indeed, be the fabric Anhur has searched for his entire career. This fabric may be well over three thousand years old."

There was stunned silence. This was a new chapter, on top of a new chapter. She couldn't imagine anything three thousand years old, never mind having such an important artifact in their home. She cringed, picturing herself waving her arms and dancing around the living room with it to Beatles' songs.

"Now, I'm distressed at the thought of you leaving here with this in your possession, but I have no right to hold it. Mr. and Mrs. Collins, you must promise me you both will be on that plane tomorrow morning." Graham handed the paper with the flight arrangements over to Spence.

Jean nodded her head in a daze. *We're going to Cairo tomorrow.* Spence handed Graham the empty jacket, which was draped over the back of her chair.

He beamed up at them. "Let's get to work."

After slipping on the gloves and unfolding the fabric, Graham carefully pressed it back into place, eyeing the hawk eyeing him as he worked. When he finished, he handed her the jacket.

"Put this on, go to the taxi line in the front of the building and have the driver take you directly to the hotel. Kensington is only ten minutes away in traffic. Please stay there until you go to the airport in the morning. I wouldn't stroll around London with it if this were in my possession."

Jean stood, feeling like a scolded child expelled from class with a pile of homework. If they didn't follow the instructions, they'd be letting down a lot of people: Graham, this Anhur Kumar and, above all, Mary. This trip had taken on a life of its own, with her and Spence along for the ride. She slipped her arms in the sleeves and turned her back to Spence. "What do you think? Do I look like I'm three thousand years old?"

"Honey, you'd be beautiful at any age, especially for a well-preserved mummy."

"Do you have children?" Graham asked. As he studied their faces, he broke his professional demeanor and laughed out loud. "Did you mean a corpse or a mother?"

"Uh...a mother. Jean's been playing mummy to that hawk for the past fifteen hours."

"Yes, right—you must call me after you meet with Mr. Kumar. I'm sure he will contact me as well."

"We'll call you as soon as we can." The mood turned serious. "This is an amazing opportunity but also a pretty hefty responsibility. I assure you, we don't take this lightly."

"I'm afraid you don't know what you don't know, Mr. Collins. Mr. Kumar will, most assuredly, be able to tell you more." Graham tapped his desk blotter with his forefinger. "You have something important there. Yes, quite important."

"How can we ever thank you?" Jean said.

"Board that plane tomorrow morning."

Spence opened the office door. "C'mon, Jean. Once we get to the hotel we're on lock down."

As they prepared to leave, she raised her arms, with no small amount of trepidation, to hug Graham. She sensed the slightest hesitation in his embrace. He was afraid to hug her back.

CHAPTER 22

Taxi!

The low stone bench hugging the perimeter of the museum entrance offered a good vantage point from which to monitor Raleigh's movements. Raleigh sat on the second step down to his right. Jon glanced at his watch. A sunny day, albeit a little chilly. The hot European coffee tasted good. *Everything tastes different over here.*

To avoid being recognized, he'd changed out of his jacket and slacks in the lobby restroom: black sunglasses, khaki pants, white turtleneck, and heavy, navy-blue sweatshirt. His transformation into a tourist was complete.

Jon's gaze made a repeating triangle: the revolving door to his right, down to Raleigh on the step, and over to the line of black taxicabs in front of the building. The taxis idled, waiting for a generous fare to climb inside. Trails of exhaust raced to catch up with the chilly north wind. It was difficult to stay focused with a little girl, who'd just arrived at the museum with her parents, making noise next to him.

A voice he recognized made him turn his gaze to the revolving door. Raleigh turned too.

Jean Collins rotated through the glass panel, followed by Spence. The Collinses chattered and gestured as they descended the steps. They passed Raleigh, unaware of his presence. Jon shifted his gaze when the blond toddler screamed. Just laughing. She twirled her red mittens, attached at each end by a rope of yarn. Egged on by her parents' clapping, the little girl spun them to a blur and bumped Jon's coffee cup. The lid flew off, spilling most of the scalding liquid down the left leg of his pants. He snatched a napkin from her mother's hand and patted the spill.

A ripping sound. Jon jerked up his head. Jean cried in pain as she fell backwards on the stone steps. The little girl's voice changed from a giggle to a wail. Raleigh took off running toward the taxi line with the fabric in his hand. *He pulled the damn thing from the back of the jacket!*

Jon threw the cup aside. He jumped sideways around the screaming toddler and launched himself down the steps. Spence knelt next to Jean to help her up. He sprinted past them, keeping his eyes trained on Raleigh, who dove into the first taxi in line and slammed the back door. The taxi pulled away. Jon whirled his hand for the next car to pull forward. Behind him, Jean shouted, "That man! Dammit, stop him!"

Jean and Spence raced toward him. The empty flaps of her jacket rippled behind her as they caught air. "Get in here! C'mon!" he shouted. Spence dove into the backseat, followed by Jean. Ducking in behind them, he slammed the door.

"Jon, what the hell are you doing here?" Spence asked, incredulous.

"Follow that taxi!" Jean shouted at the driver, banging on the Plexiglas partition. "Go! Go! I don't believe it!"

"Trying to keep you two safe and follow that guy up there. *That's* what I'm doing," Jon said, seething. He was annoyed, more at himself than anyone else. "I'd have gotten him, too. Those stupid mittens spilled my damn coffee." He narrowed his eyes at the smirk on Spence's face, waiting for a smart remark to fly out of his mouth. "You think this is funny?" He glanced down at the soaked leg of his pants. "Keep following the taxi that just passed the Cromwell Hospital! It's going to turn right up at Holland Road. Can you get behind him?" The driver nodded, sped up, and jerked the vehicle back in the lane.

"No. Sorry. I'm just trying to imagine you in mittens," Spence said.

"How do *you* know where he's going?" Jean turned from the windshield and stared at him square in the eyes. "Jon?"

"Because I followed him earlier today—after we got off the plane." He punched in a number on his phone. "He's headed to an antiques dealer in Holland Park, on Goldhawk Road." Jon held up his hand. "We're coming down Cromwell from the V&A and going to turn right on Holland Road. Intercept at any intersection. You know where he's headed."

Jon ended the call.

Sirens. They were coming from several directions as both taxis raced down Cromwell Road. Jean focused only on the taxi in front of them. Her hand flew to her mouth when a voluminous streak of bright red splashed across its back window.

"My God! Did you see that? It's blood!" She whipped her head around to Spence and then to Jon. Stunned disbelief registered on their faces.

The taxi in front of them jerked into the next lane, nearly sideswiping two other cars. Jean grabbed the seat. They lurched to avoid being hit. The front taxi swung back toward the sidewalk and bumped up over the curb. The man in the backseat thrashed in and out of view. Another splash of blood splattered the side window. They gawked, in shock, as the taxi heaved over the curb, turned at an angle, and hit a metal signpost. A shower of sparks cascaded from the metal-on-metal impact. Its driver bolted to the sidewalk, leaving the door open. A spray of blood cascaded down the right arm of his shirt. He fell to the concrete and started to rock, as if in desperate prayer.

"Stop!" Jean banged on the Plexiglas partition.

In a panic, their driver squealed the tires and jerked to a stop behind the crashed taxi. Jon stuck his hand under his jacket and took out a gun.

"Put that thing away. Now! Nobody is getting shot today." She gave Jon a don't-mess-with-me glare.

Spence had his hand poised on the door handle. "Better listen to her!" He moved to get out.

"You stay right here!" Jon ordered, leaning around her to grab Spence's arm. Spence jerked away and sprinted toward the crashed taxi.

Jean shot across the seat and jumped out to follow him. Jon ran to catch up.

Spence opened the back door of the crashed taxi. All three of them stepped back in shock. A horror scene. Jon stretched his arm across Jean's chest to hold her, the gun raised in his other hand. She pushed his arm away. Jon's hand flew into the edge of the taxi door. Ignoring his cry of pain, she launched into the backseat. She squinted to blur the sight of the blood and spotted the fabric on the floor. She grabbed it. No sign of a live hawk, only the aftermath of its carnage.

The fabric pulsed with heat in her hand. The hawk's image bulged from the surface. She tried to push herself backward out of the taxi but realized she was lying on top of the man. His bloodied face was only inches from hers as he lay motionless. Panic surged through her body. She stared right at the bloodied bandage taped on the side of his left cheek. *The guy from the plane!*

A pull on the back of her jacket. Jean kicked her legs to scramble out. A hand covered the top of her head as someone gripped her elbow and lifted her free. She straightened and froze. *Jon!*

Clutching the fabric to her chest, she grabbed Spence's sleeve and signaled for him to run. "I got it! Let's get the hell out of here!" She bolted. Shock and morbid curiosity from the gathering bystanders blurred to indistinguishable shapes.

Her mind raced faster than she could run. Spence was on her heels. They couldn't afford to be delayed in making the trip to Cairo, but now they might be connected to a dead man. *How can we possibly explain any of this?*

Jean glanced over her shoulder. Jon was catching up. She jumped back into their taxi. Spence pushed her over as he dove into the seat after her and reached for the door handle.

"Go! Please, go!" she shrieked at the driver.

Jon stopped the door with his leg. He pointed the gun at the driver and ordered him to get out of the taxi.

"Stand on the sidewalk! Now!" The driver put up his hands and eased out of the car. "You wait until I tell you to move!" Jon slid in the backseat. He slammed the door and wiped the sweat trailing down the side of his face. "What the hell *is* that?" Jon pointed to the fabric scrunched under her arm. "What are you people into—voodoo or something?" He licked the torn skin on the back of his left hand and shoved the gun in its holster under his sweatshirt.

Jean locked her eyes on Spence. They both remained silent. Her pulse pounded deep in her ears. The fabric continued to heave but had calmed as she held it against her ribcage. She squeezed harder.

"Jon, please, we need to get this away from here," she begged. "We're going to Cairo with it in the morning. Tell the driver to get back in the car. Go with us to the hotel—we'll talk there." In an instant, her fear turned to defiance. "And, by the way, who the hell are *you*, Mr. I-Work-for-the-Airline?"

"I'm an FBI agent. I've been tailing that guy for the past two weeks." Jon pointed to the crashed taxi. The whine of a siren grew louder as an ambulance approached and stopped in front of them. Two black sedans followed and screeched to a halt.

Spence turned to Jon. "You're a G-man?"

Jon squeezed his eyes, as though he couldn't believe Spence actually said those words aloud. "Yes, I'm a *G-man*, and the man in the taxi is Raleigh Coulter. You know him?"

"Raleigh Coulter? *That's*—?" she said, shocked.

They stared a hole through each other, neither moving a muscle, not even to blink. For the first time in her fifty-three years she'd finally learned to shut up. Spence watched the silent volley between her and Jon, waiting for who was going to break. Jon lost. He turned his head to the plastic partition. All three of them stayed quiet. Their driver closed his eyes and whispered something in a foreign tongue.

The medics had pulled Raleigh out of the taxi. His face, hands, and legs were covered in blood; his clothes shredded and torn. One performed CPR on him as they rolled the stretcher to the ambulance. He appeared unresponsive. An officer tried to quiet the car's driver, who hadn't stopped wailing and rocking on the sidewalk. The driver pointed at Raleigh and then to the blood on his sleeve. The blood was Raleigh's. The other officers kept the gathering crowd from the scene.

"Look, I want—no, *I need*—to know what happened in that taxi! I have to explain this absurdity. What should I tell these guys who just pulled up from Scotland Yard? Huh?" As additional inspectors huddled at the scene, he turned back to her. "And you *are* going to tell me." Jon went silent; Jean and Spence remained frozen, their eyes doing a three-way Irish Jig. Finally, Jon blew out a breath. "You both go back to your hotel. I'll meet you in about two hours. Don't go anywhere, don't stop and shop, and don't go out to dinner. Wait for me to get there. Can you just do that for me, *please*? I have to meet with these guys at the hospital to find out Raleigh's condition. I want to talk to him." Jon moved to get out of the taxi but hesitated. He turned to her. "How's your back? You took a pretty wicked fall at the museum."

"I'll live, but we have to protect this." Jean held up the fabric. The hawk's image had begun to fade, and streaks of bright colors had appeared in the feathers. Jon's expression changed. He'd seen it too.

"Go! You'd both better be at the hotel when I get there." Jon climbed out of the taxi and slammed the door.

Jon stomped away, sucking the back of his hand. He stopped only long to enough to wave the driver back in the taxi.

"Go!" Jean shouted when the man was buckled in.

Spence gave the driver the address of their hotel. "Excellent driving, Nes…er," he said, peering through the partition to get a better look at the name on the picture tag.

"Thank you. I am Egyptian. We are accustomed to driving in, let's say, perilous conditions." He smiled in the rearview mirror. "My name is pronounced *Niece*. Means eagle in my language. What happened to our friend in the taxi?"

"What's the Egyptian word for hawk?"

"Horus. Same as for falcon." The driver eyes widened.

"Yes. Horus the Hawk—that's exactly what happened." Spence turned to Jean, and then back to the driver's image in the mirror.

They rode in silence the entire ten minute trip. The only sound was a *click* as Jean took a picture of the fabric with her Droid. The hawk had faded and the vivid colors of the pheasants strengthened.

Spence handed the driver two £100 notes as they pulled in front of the hotel. "Thanks, Neser. I think £50 per mile ought to cover it."

Thank God Spence picked up Ibuprofen. Jean lay supine in the tub and stared at the shiny, beige tiles around the bathroom wall. The pungent aroma of Spence's cigar wafted into the room from the balcony and mixed with the steamy air. She wrinkled her nose and swished her legs. The heat engulfed her lower back. Her tailbone already showed the first signs of a bruise from the tumble she took on the stone steps of the museum. The image made her cringe and her knees itch. Her head filled with the ripping sound of that Velcro.

"Room service time! How about the grilled chicken Caesar salad?" Spence asked, leaning his head around the bathroom door-way.

"Fabulous." She blew out a breath. *The fluffy bed sounds pretty good too.*

"By the way, the three pheasants are back. I thought you'd want to know."

Jean closed her eyes. The lure of the fabric was overwhelming, but the pain in her tailbone pleaded with her to stay in the warm water. She willed her limbs to move and winced as she eased herself out of the tub. She pulled a thick white towel from the metal shelf and stared at her wet form in the mirror. She sunk. The stress on her face was pronounced. Her eyes were swollen from the jet lag, which had settled in after the adrenaline of the afternoon's trauma.

"When should we expect Jon?" she called out. "I need to hand-wash the blood out of my clothes. They're all smeared from crawling in the damned taxi. Creeps me out to even think about it, especially since that guy was Mary's son."

"Don't talk about it...*please*. We probably have about an hour. I'll order us some salads and a turkey sandwich for Jon. He'll be starved. Then, I'll sit on the balcony and look out at the city we're not going to see while we're here."

"Fine, but we should call Mary first. I don't even know what to say to her about this...if we say anything at all."

"*We* need to call Mary? I think you want *me* to call Mary. I'll call her after I put in the room service order. You called her last time. Go ahead and wash out your clothes." He sounded worn out too.

"Deal!"

Jean poured a trial-size box of laundry detergent in the sink and ran the cold water. She turned off the faucet and swished her white cotton shirt. The water exploded in swirls of rust. She closed her eyes and listened to Spence's side of the call to Mary.

"Hi, Mary, it's Spence. We're going to Cairo tomorrow morning. The guy at the museum thinks the fabric really is Egyptian and over three thousand years old, just like you told us. I know. Mary, your son's here. Oh, you did? Well, he tried to steal the fabric from Jean— I thought you should hear it from us. Yes, still a hawk. It attacked your son. He's in the hospital. You heard me right...came alive. No, we don't know his condition. We had no idea he followed us here. I'm sure you'll hear from the authorities tonight. We're just fine. Yes, we have the fabric. We'll call you from Cairo."

"Is she okay?" Jean asked, examining the fabric when Spence hung up the phone. All three pheasants were back in their full, glorious color. The hawk had disappeared. One of the birds blinked at her; the other two remained still.

"Yes...and no. She didn't seem surprised about Raleigh. She was upset, but it was like she already knew something happened. She seemed more concerned for us. Isn't that odd?" Spence took a puff of his cigar and set it in a dish on the balcony.

"Hmmm...I'll get ready before Jon gets here. How about you pour me one of those little bottles of wine in the fridge? Let's talk about what we say to him."

Jon sprinted into the emergency room and stopped short at the admittance desk. "I need to see Raleigh Coulter," he said, breathless. He was brought in a few minutes ago." Jon flashed his badge.

An inspector, likely the one who had accompanied Raleigh to the hospital, stepped forward. He examined Jon's ID and nodded to the nurse.

"He's in room two, down the hall and to the right."

Without thanking her, Jon bolted down the corridor. He stood in the doorway, horrified at the scene. There were four people in the small room working on Raleigh in controlled chaos.

"I can't stop the bleeding! His chest is torn wide open. Ragged wound. More sutures! Quickly!"

"Doctor, his thigh is bleeding out. I'm holding it. I need a tourniquet! Straight away!" the nurse shouted.

"Get her the tourniquet. Dammit all! Press firmly to keep it closed." The doctor continued to press, stitch, and dab the chest wound.

The four of them worked in unison on different parts of the body. Jon continued to stare from the doorway, willing Raleigh to wake up. He'd never seen wounds so vicious. His hope of being able to talk with Raleigh tonight faded to nothing.

"What's this? Something in his leg...holding open the artery," the nurse said in panic.

The doctor pointed his lighted headgear to Raleigh's thigh.

"Good Lord!" He grabbed the forceps and pulled out a blood-covered curved object. He held it to the light. "A talon...a very large bird talon. Must be three inches long—sharp as a scalpel. This man was attacked by some kind of an enormous bird or a small dinosaur!"

The confirmation Jon feared most. *This happened. Still happening.* He'd never believed in the supernatural; stories that were the fodder for hyped-up cable programs on Halloween.

Jon found his voice and raised his eyes to the doctor. "Is he going to make it?"

"Questionable. He'll require several transfusions. Lost a massive amount of blood." The doctor sounded exhausted.

"I need to talk with him when he wakes up."

"*If* he wakes up."

As he turned to wait in the lobby, the alarms blared behind him. The signals pulsed from each of the patched monitors on Raleigh's head, chest, groin, and feet. Jon's gaze raced around the flashing screens in sequence and settled on the one with the flat line. He froze as the ugly, chaotic ballet began again.

After fifteen minutes, the group switched off the monitors and unplugged the machines. The IV drip needle was pulled from Raleigh's arm. The life-giving blood in the tube wasn't going anywhere. Raleigh was pronounced dead at 6:37 p.m.

"Can I have that talon you took out of his leg? I need it as evidence," he said, trying to make his voice sound official. "And I also need his cell phone. It's probably in his pants or coat pocket."

"You'll have no argument from me. Take this horrible thing out of here. This man is gone, regardless." The doctor wiped the talon and handed it to him in a tissue.

Jon put the bundle in his left pocket. He turned and lifted Raleigh's blood-soaked wool coat, draped over the side chair, and found the cell phone. He dropped it in the right pocket of his pants, suddenly more weighed down than the phone alone accounted for. *Technology and ancient magic.*

Jon wandered toward the emergency room doors. They parted upon his approach with a *shhh*. He stepped outside and stood under the canopy of the driveway. The coffee spill, almost dry now, still made his thigh colder than the rest of him. He took a deep breath. The chill of the air stung his lungs. The day's events had to be dissected with his colleagues at Scotland Yard, but that particular conversation would have to wait. The priority for tonight was to talk with the Collinses before they left for Cairo in the morning. His stomach growled. He was starved for answers.

Jon was a smart guy, smarter than most, but now he was sure he didn't know anything at all. A brown and white-striped bird flew above his head. It landed in the barren planter box next to the door. Jean and Spence had better be waiting for him. This time he'd get on the Underground for the trip to Gloucester Road. From there it was short walk to the Collinses' hotel. He wasn't up for a taxi ride. He fingered the talon in his pocket just to make sure...still there.

Mary replaced the phone receiver and padded to her patio door in her sheepskin slippers. The morning light, dark and gray, blurred the wash of rain over the river. If Raleigh had hurt the Collinses, she'd never forgive him. No one could ever forgive him. Yes, a good thing she'd gone to see Don Landrum first thing yesterday morning. The trip downtown was an exhausting task but a good visit, nonetheless. He promised to overnight the changes by close of business today. The delivery was due half an hour ago. Late.

Mary glanced at Doc's old clock in the living room, wondering what she could do until the package arrived. She turned on the television and switched the channel to the BBC. Something might be said about the incident in London. The satellite beep of the intro-ductory theme signaled the beginning of the newscast. She started the kettle in the kitchen. She straightened and leaned around the doorway. The tease of an interesting news item from London caught her attention. She stood in front of the television and listened to the thick British accent of the perky news anchor.

"A rollicking chase took place in Kensington today. A taxi pursuit unfolded outside the Victoria and Albert Museum, only to end in a blood-filled crash on Cromwell Road. The passenger in the taxi was taken to Charing Cross Hospital with life-threatening injuries. No word on his name or present condition. The injured passenger was an American, who arrived at Heathrow only a few hours previous. The American FBI and Scotland Yard, unusually present at the scene, had no comment. Two other Americans were also involved but fled before authorities could speak with them. More as this story develops."

Mary froze. Another call would be coming. Mary abandoned her teacup on the counter. She needed to be presentable when the delivery man arrived.

As she inserted the hair comb into her French twist, the front door knocker rapped two times. She pressed an errant hair into place. A legal-size box fell forward, abandoned inside the screen door. She took the box to the kitchen and pulled her utility scissors from the drawer. Slicing the perforation, just enough to solidly grasp the flap. The thick stack of papers, secured in a heavy binder clip, slid from the box. Her new will.

Mary dunked her teabag and took the documents to the living room. Sticky tabs labeled *Please Sign Here* dotted the right edges. She made sure the information reflected her exact instructions. She signed her name where indicated and placed the papers back in the original box, taped the flap, and pressed the stick-on return label.

Slipping on her rain jacket, Mary raised the hood and pulled the door closed behind her. She checked to make sure it was locked. No more lectures from Raleigh about her neglectfulness. She walked as fast as she could in the rain, the box under her arm, to the main desk of the Milwaukie Manor administration building. Her feet were wet and cold. The water splashed and soaked into her sheepskin slippers.

She'd completely forgotten to put on her rain boots. Each step squished and squeaked until she reached the entrance.

"Good morning, Monica," she puffed as the glass doors parted. "Can you make sure this goes out right away? This must be sent back to this address today."

"Oh yes, Mrs. Coulter. Not a problem. The next pickup is in an hour. By the way, onion soup is on the lunch menu. Your favorite."

"Yes, thank you. This is important. Yes, very important this goes out right away." She gave the receptionist a vacant smile, turned, and squished out of the glass doors. A wave of dizziness washed over her.

As she did a brisk walk back to her apartment, Mary hugged her jacket tighter. The rain had picked up its pace. She must remember to take her medication...Yes; she'd forgotten to do that this morning. First, she'd make some toast with blackberry jam. She couldn't take pills on an empty stomach. Maybe she'd get a call from Jean and Spence, or the authorities in London.

Mary marched past her apartment and turned the knob on her neighbor's door. Locked. Embarrassed at her mistake, she went back one door and unlocked it. A blinding light and a searing pain exploded behind her eyes. With her fingers wrapped around the handle, she fell forward. The last thing she remembered was whispering, "Med...i...ca...tion." The world went dark.

CHAPTER 23

What's Right? What's Wrong?

Jon scanned the hotel lobby, waiting for the clerk at the front desk to call the Collinses' room. He smiled at a group of pilots and runway-model flight attendants laughing as they came through the front doors. The logo on their navy-blue jackets had the insignia for China Sky Airlines. Should he wait around to see where they went to dinner?

"Room three-oh-three, sir. The elevator is across the lobby." The desk clerk nodded to the bank of shiny stainless-steel doors.

Jon stepped into the elevator and pressed the button for the third floor. A groaned approach. The mechanism wasn't so new. The floor made a slight bounce when he got inside. He stepped out and gazed down the hall. Spence waved at him from their doorway.

"We didn't go anywhere. Stayed right here. Come in, come in," Spence said, shaking his hand and slapping him on the back.

Jon stopped short. The jacket hung backward on the handle of the closet door: three colorful birds. *Did an eye blink at me?* From the balcony, Jean took a sip of red wine from a small juice glass.

"Hey, Jon! How's Raleigh?" Jean asked, stepping back inside the room.

"He's dead." He might as well put it out there, right from the start. "This situation takes things in a whole different direction for me—and for you two."

"Jon, we didn't do anything! He stole the fabric from us. We're the victims here, and so is Mary Coulter. This was an accident."

"The crash didn't kill him, Jean. He was torn to bits." He nodded toward the jacket on the closet door. "Why don't you fill me in on that thing."

"Kind of a long story," Spence said. "We ordered you an enormous turkey sandwich in this incredibly tiny fridge," Spence handed him a white ceramic plate with a turkey and bacon sandwich and potato chips, pickle on the side. Spence waved his hand along the rack inside the refrigerator door. "Would you also like me to line up seven of these lovely little bottles for you? You're going to need them. I guarantee you won't say you've 'heard this one before.'"

"The sandwich looks great. Thanks, Spence. I want to be dead sober when I listen to this." Jon rolled the chair from the desk. Jean and Spence sat on the edge of the king-size bed. Ravenous, he took an oversize bite of the sandwich and mumbled, "Shoot—I'm all ears."

Jean and Spence talked through the sequence of events of how they acquired the fabric: the estate sale, finding the old chest, and how they marveled at its unusual qualities. Jean described the shock of seeing the birds disappear, fly from the yard, and reappear again in the fabric. If he hadn't seen it transform with his own eyes on the plane, he wouldn't have believed them. Now he was sucked into the vortex of their story. He glanced over at the jacket on the closet door.

"So why did the fabric change?"

"Mary, Raleigh's mother said it's magical. The fabric has spiritual properties used to help those dying to pass on in peace...into immortality. She told us the stories but, like you, we want more answers."

"Well, guys, there was nothing peaceful about it today," he said, still trying to absorb the details.

"The fabric came from a tomb in Egypt," Spence continued. "That's why we absolutely need to go to Cairo tomorrow. Who knows? Maybe we awakened it when we opened the chest. Our cat acted odd too. Jean had to put the fabric in the trunk of her car to get it out of the house."

"When I called the estate sale company to find out more about the history, the owner gave me Raleigh's name," Jean added. "I talked with him for a few minutes, but got this weird, negative vibe. He knew I found something, and the whole atmosphere changed. Actually, I hung up on him. I guess I was right."

Jon considered how much to tell them about Raleigh. Best to be as truthful as they were being with him.

"Did you guys have a small purple towel go missing recently?"

Jean opened her mouth and glanced at Spence. "Yeah...we sure did. Pretty random, Jon."

"The towel was found in Raleigh Coulter's Porsche at the Portland Airport with his blood all over it. Raleigh Coulter was the one who broke into your house. You just confirmed that for me. Your cat clawed Raleigh's face when he got in to snoop around. I'm sure he was after that fabric because he thought it was valuable. He must have found your plans to bring the fabric here to London." Jon stared at the jacket, took another bite of the sandwich, and continued. "Raleigh needed money. I've been closing in on him for insider trading with his buddy at VEY Steel. He tried to cover himself. He'd racked up a huge debt. We got involved because the company believed there was a bigger problem. Still is. I think so. Greed at that level hurts people—a lot of people."

"Unbelievable!" Jean said.

"Creepy!" Spence added. "That jerk was in our house and went through our stuff."

"No—what you two are telling me is more unbelievable...and way creepier," he said.

"We have to keep this confidential," Spence warned. "The director of the Cairo Museum is waiting to see us tomorrow. He's the one person in the world who can tell us what this fabric means. We all witnessed the transformation. Lethal in the wrong hands. This is way over our heads...and yours too." Spence's voice became more frustrated as he spoke. "Can you imagine what would happen if the media got hold of this because of what happened to Raleigh? People panic about things they don't understand, especially the unexplainable. We don't want any part of this, and you don't, either."

"A political nightmare—for you." Jean interjected. "You're with the FBI. The FBI solves things. This is not solvable; nobody to blame. Believe me, they *will* try to find someone to blame. I've dealt with enough corporate politics to last a lifetime. This information would go straight to the top of the FBI, and then the bigwigs would retreat to the shadows. They'd rather lambaste you, or us, to avoid getting involved in anything this controversial. We'd be left for the jackals. Anyone who shows them the truth would be discredited, no matter how fantastic the truth might be."

They were right; most people wouldn't be able to accept this. He'd sound like a nutcase. Sometimes playing by the rules was the wrong thing to do in the long run. Messing with people's core beliefs, while trying to uphold the letter of the law, was rife with conflict. This knowledge would create a firestorm—an impossible one to put out.

"Maybe Mary was right, Spence. Some things shouldn't be questioned." Jean went quiet and placed her hand on Spence's arm.

Spence brushed off her hand and rubbed his face. "No...too late, Jean. The right thing is to keep going forward to Cairo. But we need to keep all of this between us. If the fabric is the lost artifact Graham Hollingsworth, or this Mr. Kumar, thinks it is, then it's not ours. The fabric needs to be under the protection of experts who understand and respect its power. I'm humbled, for sure—and respect the power—but I'm certainly no expert in these things. After what happened today, I can assure you, the three of us are not those people." He pointed to each of them in a triangle, himself last. "Jon, are you qualified?"

Jon's shoulders slumped, relenting to Spence's words. "No, I don't." He had to let them go to Cairo in the morning. "All right, but call me when you get back. I have to know what the museum says about those birds. I'm hooked too."

"I think we're in this together now, Jon," Jean whispered.

Pushing away the empty plate, Jon moved in a trance to the small refrigerator. He pulled out six of the little bottles from the rack in the door. He put two in his sweatshirt pocket, two in his right pant pocket, and two in his left. They clanked against Raleigh's bloodied cell phone. He bent down, one more time, and took the last one from the shelf. He broke the seal on the cap and downed the scotch in two swallows.

"Thanks for the drink," he said, closing the refrigerator. "Have a safe trip. Remember to call me when you get back. This isn't over, guys." He opened the hotel room door, stopped, and dug in his left pocket. "Oh...get a load of this. Found in Raleigh's leg." He spread the folds of the tissue. The three-inch talon sat in the palm of his hand; Raleigh's dried blood still caked in the grooves.

Spence sucked in a breath. "A hawk talon?"

"Horus," Jean whispered.

"Yeah, I'm keeping it."

They each gave him a long hug and clicked the door shut. As Jon walked down the hall, he heard the turn of the safety latch. Every step made him feel like he was floating as the Collinses' words sunk in. This case would change his life.

Jon stood at the elevator. Before he pressed the button, he fingered the razor-like point of the talon in his pocket. A curious tingle zapped his forefinger. He pulled out his hand and gawked at the deep, bloodless gash on the pad of his fingertip. As he stared at it, the skin sealed, with no trace of the wound.

His hand shook as he reached for the down button.

CHAPTER 24

Cairo, Egypt

Jean rolled down the window in the taxi and slipped on her oversize black sunglasses to block out the bright sunshine. She hadn't thought she'd need them on this trip, but was glad now to have tucked them in her bag at the last minute. The warm, humid breeze, surprisingly tropical, sailed across her face. Cairo was much greener than she imagined. Thousands of years of history zoomed by during the forty-minute drive from the Cairo International Airport. Sweat trickled down the back of her neck. Neither one of them had packed the right clothes for traveling to Egypt. The air was warmer than warm outside, and the jacket was hot. At least the entire trip from London had been quiet.

Within half a mile of the museum, the traffic came to stop. She craned her neck to find the source. *Just like Houston, and the people are just as frustrated. The universal language of traffic.* The taxi inched forward. Jean fidgeted when the orange stucco building filled her view.

"Maybe we should get out here and walk up to the museum. This is nuts to sit in this traffic. The building's right there," she said, squirming.

"Let's not find out. I don't know the customs here at all. I'm glad you bought that scarf at the airport, though. More women are wearing them than not."

"Good thinking." Jean pulled the scarf from the plastic bag and ripped off the tag, convinced she was overcharged. Wrapping the unadorned, turquoise linen over her head, she tossed the ends over her shoulders and adjusted her sunglasses. She pursed her lips in an air kiss. "How do I look?"

"Like a menopausal Jackie O." Spence laughed and pulled out a pack of tissues. "Here, wipe the sweat off your face."

Worse than a hot flash. She imagined herself hanging out of the window and waving her arms with the scarf sailing behind her.

When the taxi finally pulled up to the museum, Jean grasped the door handle. "C'mon Spence, let's go." She jumped out of the taxi, winced as her lower back gave her fits, and swung her purse over her shoulder. Her sunglasses slid down her face.

"You go on ahead. I'll pay the driver." Spence pulled out his wallet. "I have no idea how much to tip this guy. Egyptian pounds are different than English pounds. I'll meet you up in the lobby. Here, take your—"

"Should be about thirty pounds!" she shouted and ran up the steps.

Jean's gawk made an arc when she entered the cavernous lobby. Her mouth gaped as she took off her sunglasses and wiped away the beads of sweat from under her eyes. On each side of the lobby, two thirty-foot stone statues loomed above her, poised to squash her like a bug with their enormous sandaled feet. The seated forms of the Egyptian man and woman took her breath away. "This must be what an ant sees when I work in the garden," she murmured. Her gaze rose to the glass-domed ceiling. The shafts of light cast a yellow glow on the statues, making them even more ominous.

Seeking guidance in her humbled state, Jean's eyes settled on the information counter. An elegant, dark-eyed gentleman in his fifties, in a dark suit and red tie, had been studying her. Their eyes locked. He smiled with the whitest teeth she'd ever seen. The exotic air about him momentarily stopped her pulse. She was suddenly self-conscious when he took a step toward her.

"Mr. Kumar?" She extended her hand.

"Solid granite...the statues," he said, pointing upward. "I enjoy the expression on the faces of visitors when they first enter the lobby. I have been awaiting your arrival, Mrs. Collins." His hand met hers in a firm handshake. The warm blanket of his deep, smooth voice wrapped around her. "Please call me Anhur. I am so pleased to meet you. Where is Mr. Collins?"

Jean shook herself back into the moment. "I hope you haven't been waiting too long. Our plane was bit late, and yesterday...well, that's a another story." *Mister, you have no idea.* "My husband will be here in a moment. He's paying the driver. Do you mind waiting?" She glanced at the revolving door.

"I became somewhat worried when you called to say you were delayed. I am anxious to inspect the artifact. Did you bring it with you?"

As she unwound the scarf, Jean took a breath of relief. She turned around. "In the back of my jacket. I had regrets about carrying the fabric this way. Somebody tried to steal it in London."

Anhur made an audible gasp. "Ingenious. You are right. Many people would like to lay their hands on this...quite literally."

Jean spotted Spence struggling to get through the revolving door, bumping their carry-on bags as he pushed against the glass. It finally released him into the lobby. *I should have helped him.*

As he set the duffle bags on the floor, Spence glared at her. His expression changed when he raised his eyes to the stone statues. "Wow, this is amazing." His gaze traveled down and settled on Anhur. "I see you've already met my patient wife. I'm Spencer Collins—Spence, please. We've been looking forward to this meeting. Thanks for your help to get us here."

"Thank you for coming. Please, let us retreat from the public space. We shall move to our laboratory downstairs where we analyze and inspect the artifacts acquired by the museum. We are going to the elevators on the other side of the lobby. Please, follow me."

In the center of the laboratory, a row of technicians sat in front of a bank of computers, clothed in white coats and cotton gloves. They raised their eyes from brushing, tweezing, and researching various artifacts and nodded when Anhur walked in the room. Mr. Kumar had earned their respect.

"We conduct most of our conservation and documentation here. We also work closely with other museums, as most do not have the level of technical resources we maintain here." He didn't reveal any information to the group. *Curious.*

Anhur led them to a glass-walled room adjacent to the main laboratory. "This climate-controlled room houses a special light spectrum to ensure new artifacts do not incur damage during the initial inspection process. Also, we will have privacy."

As they followed him inside, the pronounced change in the environment was surprising: quiet and spotless. Even though the room was fairly large, its deadened acoustics felt intimate enough to share the deepest of secrets.

Jean dug through her purse and pulled out her Droid. "I can prove to you there are supernatural qualities in this fabric. Look at this—" Her finger swept across the screen, creating a slide show of the pictures. She handed Anhur her phone and leaned around his shoulder to describe each one.

"This is the original image showing three pheasants when I found the fabric; here's one where it's empty, right after the birds were in the yard. We don't have pheasants in our neighborhood in Oregon." She glanced at Anhur, and then to Spence for agreement. "And look at this one; a huge hawk when we got to London. The man who stole it from us is dead because that hawk *attacked* him. This last picture shows all three in the fabric again at our hotel." She blew out a breath and set the jacket on the table, spreading it out to show the fabric.

With hungry intensity, Anhur moved his finger across the screen several times. He glanced at the jacket. The fabric clearly showed three pheasants. Jean watched the birds watching Anhur—inspecting him, judging him.

"These are not pheasants, Mrs. Collins." He paused. "They are images of the sacred phoenix. Where the fabric is empty, someone, or something, has released their power." Anhur scrolled through the pictures again. "Yes, the magnificent phoenix."

Jean's eyes pleaded to Spence for guidance. He nodded and mouthed, "Mycroft."

She drew in a breath with immediate understanding. "Mycroft," she echoed.

"Mr. Kumar—Anhur," Spence said, hesitant, "one thing...was rather odd: our cat, Mycroft. He started acting strange when he was on the fabric. Jean didn't get a picture because there was so much commotion at the time, but he acted as though something alive was underneath him. We thought he was sick. Jean took these pictures *after* Mycroft crouched on the fabric."

"He looked really weird after there was a bang on the window," Jean continued. "He jumped up and ran outside. He was lying on a dead robin."

"Your cat knows more than you do." Anhur smiled. "I'm not surprised the transformation was revealed to your cat so readily. You do know, cats are revered and hold special powers in Egyptian culture. Receptive and sensitive creatures. I don't believe he was hurting the bird. Your cat helped it to die...and gave the bird immortality."

"What?" She stared at him, trying to neutralize the emotion, and guilt, of misunderstanding Mycroft's actions.

"Well, he certainly holds special powers in our house," Spence said.

"May I separate this fabric from your jacket?"

"Oh, yes." She jumped and dropped her phone in her purse. "I only stuck it in with Velcro." She started to disassemble the back of the jacket.

"I would feel better if you handled the fabric with these gloves. Let us not take any chances." He turned to the cabinet and pulled out three pairs.

"I think we've done nothing but take chances, Mr. Kumar," Jean said. "As Mr. Hollingsworth reminded us, we don't know what we don't know."

"You will soon, I believe. The gloves are not only a cleanliness issue, Mrs. Collins. Touch can be quite powerful."

Once the fabric was released, Anhur peeled away the Velcro strips. He worked in silence.

This man truly found his calling. Rare to find an executive administrator with so much focus and technical expertise. He took measurements, inspected the fabric with a black light, and swept a magnifying glass above the images. Finally he raised his dark eyes.

"Curious. The stitches are so fine they are nearly invisible. No, not made by human hands." Anhur tapped his finger on the magnifying glass. "The colors in the feathers are so true. Their reflective quality makes the birds seem...alive. Not a normal depiction of the phoenix in any form of Egyptian art of this period. I had a sense the birds were—"

"Watching you, studying you," Jean whispered.

"Yes. Quite unsettling to be judged in this way. We will need to conduct more sophisticated tests to assess its chemical properties." He narrowed his eyes as he thought of something. "There is a new piece of equipment we have acquired, which may help us."

Anhur opened a bottom cabinet. She was surprised when he pulled out what appeared to be a sophisticated, but small, video camera.

"Thermal imaging," he said. His expression equaled that of a young boy about to try out his first chemistry set. "By waving this camera over the fabric, a difference in temperature can be detected within one half of a degree. The screen captures the image. A cool temperature shows as white, warm will be pink, and extreme heat is reflected in red. Here, I will show you an example."

Anhur waved the camera in front of Spence's face and captured the image. They stared in amazement at the outline of Spence's head on the screen; the chin area was pink and the color graduated to red on his forehead.

"Amazing! Do I have a fever?" Spence asked.

"Perfectly normal. Heat rises and is released through the top of the head." He turned the camera toward the fabric. There was a moment of silence.

"Anything?" She stared at him.

"As I suspected. Quite marvelous."

As Jean and Spence moved to Anhur's side, their mouths fell open. The image showed three hot-pink birds surrounded by white, their heads tinged with red.

"They are alive. Three of them would also be significant—the sacred symbolism of the father, the mother, and the child. In legend, the phoenix will rise from the ashes and become reborn. Also, they will regenerate when wounded. This is an extremely significant moment."

Spence fingered the edges with his white gloves. "Can you tell us the story behind where it came from?"

"Yes, I owe you that, certainly." Anhur folded the fabric in a specially prepared, acid-free tissue he'd retrieved from the cabinet drawer.

"I will put this in the safe within my office and ask one of our guards to stand watch. Accommodations have been arranged for you tonight at an excellent hotel across from the museum on Tahrir Square." Anhur set his gloved hand on the folded bundle. "I expect you need a rest from your caretaking responsibilities. We will take, as you say, a field trip tomorrow morning to address your questions. At 9:00 a.m., we will fly approximately one hour to the Valley of the Queens."

"Don't you mean the Valley of the Kings?" Jean asked. An exciting next step, but leaving the fabric made her uncomfortable. Under the watchful protection of the pyramids, though, it might be a quiet night.

"I'm afraid not. The Valley of the *Queens* is on the western side of the mountain. The site is one and a half kilometers from the Valley of the Kings."

"And the fabric? You're sure it's safe here?" Separation anxiety crept in. Every waking minute of the past two weeks had been filled with protecting the fabric. She missed it already. The three of them had taken this journey. Now, just her and Spence.

"Safe in the safe. Do not worry."

"Excellent! We'll meet back here in the morning." Jean turned to Spence.

As if reading her thoughts, he whispered, "Tomorrow never knows."

Jean adjusted her lighted hard hat and checked the water bottle in the pocket of her sand-colored jumpsuit. She and Spence nodded to the security guard and followed Anhur beneath the six towering statues carved into the rock face of the entrance to the tomb. The thirty-three-foot stone figures soared above her. Intimidating. By contrast, the opening was small and unadorned.

Anhur led them down the eighteen steps into Nefertari's tomb. They landed in a close vestibule. While he had given them a thumbnail history during the short helicopter flight, the conversation had been drowned by all the noise.

"Welcome to QV66! This is the most elaborate, and important, of the tombs found in the Valley of the Queens," Anhur declared. He turned in a circle with his arms spread wide. "The tomb of Queen Nefertari. Originally discovered in 1904 by the Italian archeologist, Ernesto Schiaparelli, this tomb was closed to the public in 1950, and again in 1986, to undertake a painstaking restoration. Your country assisted in the effort to preserve this great work of art. The Getty Conservation Institute collaborated with the Egyptian Antiquities Organization to restore the historic images."

Gazing in awe around the small vestibule, Jean figured it only hinted at the surprises to come. The room danced in a carnival of shapes and goddess depictions of bright yellows, deep greens, brilliant reds, electric blues, and deepest blacks. The far doorway projected an infinity effect, as when two mirrors faced each other. The sequence of rooms ahead was brightly painted from floor to ceiling. The vision made her slightly dizzy. Spence waved at her to follow Anhur to the next chamber.

"Nefertari was the greatest, and most beautiful of the eight wives of Ramesses II of the nineteenth dynasty."

"You referred to QV. What does that mean?" Spence asked, his head turning as if on a swivel.

"All of the tombs carry a number to identify the inhabitant of their excavation. The KV or QV indicates their location, Valley of the Kings or Valley of the Queens."

As they moved forward to the next chamber, Jean raised her eyes and grabbed Spence's arm. "Check out the ceiling. Amazing."

Spence followed her gaze to the curved dome, painted in deep indigo, with hundreds of gold five-pointed stars made with single brush strokes. Each had been individually hand-painted, exquisite in their imperfection. The effect was like floating in space.

"Ah, yes, the ceiling. You will see the same ceilings in every chamber from here. Imagine these stars in darkness for over three thousand years. They shone their light for the first time in modern history in 1904. Come, our ultimate destination is the burial chamber. We can only be in the tomb for approximately one hour. The paintings are quite delicate, and even our bacteria-laden breath may have harmful effects on the art."

Jean wrinkled her nose. The damp, earthy air became cooler as they descended a second set of stairs. At the sheer mention of bacteria, she worried about dormant mold spores, laying in wait for a host, and the possibility of catching some ancient disease. As she gazed around with some apprehension, the remains of early desecration made her sad. At least the most impressive wall paintings had been expertly preserved.

"Guarding the entrance of this next chamber are two life-size goddesses: Neith and Serket. They welcomed Nefertari on her journey to the afterlife. These scenes are taken from *The Book of the Dead.*" Anhur stopped and pointed to the next wall. "This, my friends, is the stunning Nefertari herself, considered to be the most beautiful woman in Egypt. A goddess. Many believed she had transformative powers."

Transfixed, Spence stared into the hypnotic eyes of Nefertari's likeness. Jean imagined him spending days in here. When they visited museums, she usually waited in the gift shop while Spence wandered through the exhibits in a meticulous private ritual of absorbing small details on the placards. Obscure, trivial tidbits would fly out of his mouth, making them sound profound. She tapped his arm to keep him moving. Anhur had already entered the next chamber.

As they moved deeper into the tomb, the weight of the earth seemed to grow heavier as the passages narrowed. She squeezed Spence's hand. With each step, the damp walls closed in on her. Jean started to breathe faster, and her heart began to race. She willed herself to relax. She and Spence both suffered from claustrophobia.

"Are you okay?" she whispered.

Spence nodded, his face only slightly distressed. He mouthed back, "Let's keep going."

"We are almost to the burial chamber, Mr. and Mrs. Collins." Anhur sensed their discomfort.

The light from their helmets and Anhur's lantern cast an unearthly glow around the rich images of hawks, cranes, and hieroglyphic symbols. The images appeared to move on the walls.

"Here we have a depiction of Nefertari seated and playing a game of Senet. This board game depicts the gates of passing. A first complete set was found in the tomb of Amenhotep III. It resides in the Brooklyn Museum in New York, but I do wish we had the set back in Egypt. The image here represents a step in Nefertari's passing."

"We need to go to the Brooklyn Museum, Jean," Spence said as they proceeded through the passageway.

"We have arrived at the burial chamber, or the golden hall, according to ancient Egyptians. This is where the legend of the fabric comes alive...on these walls." Anhur's voice echoed off the carved stone as he swept his light over the hieroglyphics. "Let's start here."

Cavernous and eerily quiet, the room measured thirty feet in length and nearly as wide. Four elaborately decorated square pillars supported the ceiling. A hand-hewn stone bench lined the entire room, with notches cut on each wall.

"These pillars served as gateways for Nefertari to enter the underworld." Anhur raised his bright lamp. The queen's journey, in hieroglyphic relief, soared around the walls. "All of the images, throughout the tomb, embody the truths about Egyptian society and also the views regarding life and death. A world of opposition: good and evil, earth and sky, peace and war, man and woman. And then you have Isis giving Nefertari the breath of a new life. As she is about to step into the underworld, Isis holds her hand and places an ankh—the Egyptian symbol for breath, life, and spirit—to her nose. The gift of immortality is to be inhaled. Beautiful...yes?" Anhur paused and then continued. "All of these images of Nefertari, after she breathes from the ankh, are different—her lips are fuller, and her skin is richer in color."

"Spence, don't get any ideas. I'm not doing the Dance of the Seven Veils for you every night," she said, smiling at the élan on his face.

"Yeah...she's pretty hot."

Anhur smiled at their banter. "The notches you see in the benches—at north, south, east, and west—were used to house the magic bricks. They were placed here to protect Nefertari from the enemies of the god Osiris. Each brick held an inscription from *The Book of the Dead*. Behind one of these openings is where a glazed earthenware urn was found. I believe it to have contained the fabric you brought to me yesterday. Urns were known to conceal extremely sacred objects."

"What else did they find in this tomb?" Spence asked.

Anhur stepped toward the opening in the bench along the north wall. "The tomb had been plundered, most likely within a hundred years of Nefertari's death. Such a shame...such a sacrilege." Anhur went quiet and shook his head. "There were pieces from the lid of her sarcophagus, deep-red granite. A mummified kneecap—the only remnant found of the woman herself. The rest gone, I am afraid. Schiaparelli did find thirty-four figurines, thought to be servants who could assist in her transformation to become the god Osiris. Earthenware urns were recovered but, sadly, every one...empty."

"Not every urn, it seems," Jean said.

"Yes, you are so right. A pair of Nefertari's woven sandals, which escaped the looting, was found by Schiaparelli. They are currently on display in the Museo Egizio in Torino, Italy. Can you imagine how delicate her feet must have been?"

Jean smirked, waiting for Spence to make a smart remark. He didn't disappoint.

"If this were your tomb, Jean, they'd have found two thousand pairs of sandals in here."

She nudged him in the ribs.

Anhur smiled, but the mood turned serious as the three of them stood in front of the north wall. The hieroglyphic scene clearly showed images of Nefertari laying her hands on a rectangular piece of fabric. The pictures of the process came alive: the transformation of the birds; their flight into the sun; and, finally, their return.

"Your phoenixes, the graceful bird *benu*, regarded as the soul of Ra, the sun god. Also considered to be the representation of Osiris. Gods may take many forms."

"Like a hawk?" Jean asked. She pictured the lethal talon Jon had showed them at the hotel in London.

"Yes. You will see a number of depictions of Horus in life; Osiris in death. The god of sun, war, and protection" Anhur pointed to the image on the wall and resumed his description. "Through my research, I believe this fabric was created by Nefertari upon the death of her first-born son with Ramesses, Amun-her-Khepeshef. The time period we are in is approximately 1250 BC. From the recent exca-vation of KV5 in 1995, we believe the remains of Nefertari's sons have been discovered. They are currently being analyzed. Nefertari was completely devoted to her eldest son, sure of his position to become pharaoh. Many scholars concur that Amun-her-Khepeshef was struck down at the time of the Exodus in the battle against Moses, who assisted the Hebrews to flee Egypt. Only thirty years of age when he was killed."

Thousands of years of history, and myth, had come alive in front of them in one hour. She and Spence were awestruck and humbled.

"How do you know the fabric was created for her son?" Jean asked. The charge of sacred energy in the room made her voice sound disrespectful.

"Nefertari and Ramesses were devastated when their son came to such a violent end. We know this from other records in our archives. Ramesses II was quite elderly. Preparations for Amun-her-Khepeshef to become pharaoh, and ultimately to transform to a god, had already been made. I believe Nefertari created the fabric to release her son into the immortality promised him as the future pharaoh; a rep-resentation of her lasting devotion. She also prearranged her own release to join him. Until you presented this artifact to me yes-terday...only an educated speculation, but a lifelong quest." Anhur went quiet.

"Do we push for more?" Jean whispered to Spence. "I want more answers."

Anhur continued, unprompted, as he pointed to the images. "These hieroglyphs show the deep grief on Nefertari's face. Here is where the legend is revealed. Given the importance of the fabric, as indicated on this wall, we believed—no, I believed—it existed. I tried for many years to trace this artifact without success."

Jean stared at the wall's images, remembering Mary's description of events from her adopted grandfather. "Yes, we heard the story passed down to Mary Coulter. The man who found the fabric here was Edwin Seymore, a member of Schiaparelli's excavation team. It was given to Mary's grandfather in 1913 as repayment for a debt."

"I am pleased it was not bought and sold, as the fate of many antiquities, over these many years. The fabric knows, I believe...good hands." Anhur ran his hand lightly over the front of the hieroglyphs without touching the fragile images. "Sacred, magic objects were a tool, much like a stone grinder, an axe, or a water vessel. An exquisite work of art with a purpose, and never intended to be seen again by mere earthly eyes. The sacred fabric was to be interred here for eternity. Nefertari must have performed this ritual herself as Amun-her lay dying from his wounds."

"But how did she create the fabric, Anhur? And give it this unbelievable power?" Jean asked, almost afraid for an answer.

Anhur's dark, soul-searching eyes settled on her. He uttered the words that would change their lives.

"Why, my dear...magic, of course. Magic is all around you. To be found when you are not searching for it. I was not able to find this fabric for so many years only because I searched. I stopped and there you were; you brought it to me. Yes, certainly magic." Anhur turned back to the images on the wall. "Emerged from the shadows of legend. The artifact depicted here truly exists. It is...*magic*."

"What happens when the birds transform?"

"The god Osiris, the phoenix, takes the soul on and grants immortality to the worthy. You will return to the supreme moment of happiness in your life and remain in that state forever. If you are not worthy, well...not so pleasant an eternity."

Jean's view of reality changed with Anhur's words. She turned to Spence and mouthed, "Oh my God!" He nodded back.

The power of the fabric had to be protected. The world, as it existed today, could never handle a confirmation of this knowledge. Dangerous yesterday; today overwhelming. Apparently, Anhur read minds too.

"I believe we would all agree, aspects of our knowledge should remain private," He continued to stare at the hieroglyphic relief. "As much as I have studied this legend, I am convinced worthiness is a factor in its benevolence. This fabric is capable of many deeds—wondrous for the worthy and deadly to the—"

"Yes, that's definitely true," Spence interjected. "We witnessed Raleigh Coulter being mauled by the hawk in a taxi back in London. The fabric changed."

"I know nothing of this Raleigh Coulter. The phoenixes know who is worthy. The gods transformed to protect you. Magic is to be experienced every day, not displayed, or challenged and analyzed in a laboratory. Sadly, that is not the world we live in today."

"Are we worthy, Anhur?" she asked, wanting, but not wanting, the answer. "The implications of this are frightening."

"Oh yes, but you are. The fabric revealed its secrets and changed to protect you and Spence. The sacred hawk, a transformation of the god Horus from these very walls, was guarding you—protecting you. I would feel quite privileged, indeed, if it had exhibited such power to me." He turned away from the image. "Come, it is late. We should go back to Cairo. I am loath to leave the fabric for too long."

"Don't be upset at me, Anhur, but can I take a picture of the wall before we go? I want to show Mary when we get home." She pulled her Droid out of her pocket.

"As long as you maintain utmost discretion, and it emits no flash, I will ignore the request." Anhur held up his light as she snapped the picture.

After leaving the Collinses at their hotel to shower and change, Anhur returned to the museum to wait for them. The guard, stationed at his office door, returned to his post in the lobby. The office was still and quiet. Anhur stepped to the paned doors and opened them to a balcony lush with potted birds of paradise in full bloom. They stretched wide to reveal their vivid-blue, bright-orange, and red-spiked swords. A warm breeze swept through the doorway, circled around his office, and rippled the pages of his speech to the museum board. After today, a revision would be required. He showered and changed into a crisp white shirt and tan linen slacks.

"That was the afternoon of a lifetime," Spence said, stepping into his office. "The shower was hard to beat too."

"You don't think there were any weird, catchy things in that tomb, do you?" Jean asked, setting her purse on the side chair by the desk.

Anhur laughed. "No, I don't believe so. Teams of archeologists have worked in Nefertari's tomb over the years and, to my knowledge, have never been sickened."

Jean's cell phone rang and she excused herself. He glanced at Spence, and they both studied her expression. It changed from one of apology to anxiety.

"What? How is she? Where is she?" Jean asked the caller. "Yes, please keep me informed of her status. Thank you so much."

"Is everything all right, Mrs. Collins?"

"Well, no, not really. That was the director of Milwaukie Manor. The woman we told you about was taken to the hospital. She had a stroke. She's alive but not conscious. Her condition is critical."

"I'm so sorry. I hope she will recover." Anhur watched her face, curious.

Jean hesitated, as if she were carefully choosing her words.

"Mr. Kumar, I have a favor to ask. Mary Coulter, who originally owned the fabric, is quite elderly. She's a lovely person. We wouldn't be here at all without her. Can we use it to help her...if she's not able to recover?"

"I am more than happy to bear witness, but I'm afraid you must not take the fabric back to the United States for this purpose. As a valuable artifact, you would not be allowed to—nor should you—"

"No, no, I understand. What I mean is—do you think we can experience the transformation here, in Cairo, and have the fabric remain behind with you? Can we hold the power within us, and then release it for Mary when, or if, the time comes?"

Breathing a sigh of relief, Anhur pondered her request before responding. The potential of the fabric's magic was completely unexplored. In some ways, the Collinses understood more about its capabilities than he did, even after his years of intense study. They had actually experienced the phoenixes' transformation, both compassionate and treacherous.

He broke the tense silence. "Obviously, this is all too new to fully know with certainty. I believe you could hold the power for as long as you need for its intended, worthy recipient. You must focus on this woman as you place your hands on the fabric. You have seen the process depicted in the hieroglyphs." He set two forefingers on his lips and glanced from Spence to Jean. "Do as you ask...as long as I may document the transformation."

Anhur opened the safe and slipped the white cotton gloves over his hands, leaving two pairs on the cabinet. He retrieved the fabric and set it on the conference table. With great ceremony, he opened the folds.

"Quite exciting. How do you feel now, having experienced where this came from over three thousand years ago?"

"No words." Jean's voice caught in her throat.

"You do know, Mr. Kumar," Spence added, "this will be a gift to your museum. We aren't asking anything in return, only to use it for Mary."

"I do thank you both, more than I can properly relay." He bowed his head. "I am not sure I, or anyone, could ever put a price on this magnificent artifact. There are some objects too precious for a monetary value. We will make arrangements to give you proper thanks. Plenty of time for planning and discussion."

"May we celebrate another life first?" Jean pressed.

"Yes, of course. If you are amenable, I would like to record the experience." He stepped to a push button on the wall and pointed to the black bubble in the corner of the ceiling. "To help us in our study and documentation. The legend itself will be shared, but the true transformation will remain in confidence." He removed his right glove and pressed the button. "We are now recording."

"Spence, do you want to do it, or should I?"

"Let's do it together."

Jean raised her eyes to Anhur for guidance. The slight tip of his head signaled his approval for them to proceed. Her life would never be the same after this moment. The taste of food, magnificent; the garden, an explosion of aroma; touch, a thousand soft feathers; every sound, sharp and crisp; hues of every color, deep and vibrant. No small moment from here forward should go unappreciated. *Life is magic.*

Extending a long gaze at each other, she and Spence spread their fingers. The three phoenixes waited for their touch. She placed one hand on the chest of bottom phoenix; Spence placed his on the middle one. Together, their second hands met on the head of the third. Without saying a word, they closed their eyes. Her mind filled with the image of Mary on her patio, her rich life, and what they likely needed do for her when they returned to Portland. The little girl in the white dress of hummingbirds could go home.

The warmth began in her fingertips. The energy accelerated and spread up her arms. Her torso tingled. She sucked in a breath as a warm weightlessness engulfed her. Spence gasped too. She sensed Anhur move closer. The wings began to heave. Their fingers rolled as the phoenixes strained and lifted from the fabric. She opened her eyes. The images faded, as did the movement, and the birds disappeared. Spence's face beamed.

Overcome with emotion, Anhur wiped his eyes on the sleeve of his white shirt and turned his gaze to the open balcony doors. Jean's followed with eyes wide. Perched on the rail, all three in a line, sat the regal phoenixes. The birds radiated a brilliant spray of colors in the warm afternoon sun. Their heavy wings stretched to reveal shades of iridescent turquoise, gold, ginger, pumpkin, and chestnut. The phoenixes, with their deep red crowns, turned in sequence toward the office. The tilt of their heads signaled they understood their mission.

One after another, the phoenixes launched from the balcony and sailed in silence, with only the *whoosh* of their wings parting the air. Jean and Spence followed Anhur outside. The birds soared higher and higher in formation. They became pinpoints on the horizon. Anhur composed himself while she and Spence stood silent, holding on to the rail.

Jean grasped Spence's arm. "We have to go. They'll return to the fabric once Mary completes the process...*if* we can complete the process." She rushed back into the office. "Anhur, we need to be on the next flight back to America!"

"Wait for a moment while I call my assistant." He darted behind his desk. "She will make the arrangements, faster than by commercial means." Anhur picked up the receiver and talked quietly. He raised his eyes and smiled as he ended the call. "Yes, many advantages of having powerful board members at our disposal. One of them has a private jet, which we may be able to arrange. For an acquisition this magnificent, I do not think there will be an issue."

As they waited for the phone to ring, Jean's gaze followed Anhur as he moved to the conference table. He stared at the fabric. Only the scrolled green vines and flowers remained, looping around the blank space where the phoenixes made their home.

After a moment of silent study, he whispered, "This, my friends, has been a day for which I will always be grateful. You have given me, and all of Egypt, a gift beyond measure."

With white-gloved hands, Anhur folded the fabric of scrolling vines in the tissue and placed it deep inside the safe. The open door beckoned the fabric's return to a dark space. He spun the dial.

The chiming peal of the phone punctuated the air. He rolled off one white glove.

"Excellent! Wonderful news! We will have Mr. and Mrs. Collins at the plane within the hour." He hung up and motioned for them to gather their bags while he called the lobby to request the guard be sent back to his office. "Come, I will drive you to the private airport myself."

As they followed Anhur out the door, Jean tapped him on the shoulder and pointed to his hand. He still wore one of the conservator gloves. The glove landed as a soft white ball on his desk, right on top of the fluttering speech to the museum board.

CHAPTER 25

This Quiet Place

Anhur unlocked the door to his office after returning from the airport to drop off the Collinses. The guard was dismissed. He retrieved the fabric from the safe and spread the folds. Still empty. He sighed, recounting the years of arduous study and his exhaustive worldwide quest to find this artifact, but never dreamed it held secrets of this magnitude.

He'd nearly given up. Myths, legends, mysteries, dreams—yes—but the reality eclipsed everything he'd ever known about life. So ironic. This wondrous piece of history had been hidden in an old, wooden chest in Portland, Oregon. Two ordinary people had completed his long quest by merely trying to do what was right. He held out his hand. An inch of air was the only barrier between his fingers and the magic.

"You can never fail, if you never give up," he whispered.

The fabric would continue to be empty until the phoenixes had taken on its next charge. Transformed. Real. He buried his face in his hands and wept until the sun set. The sky darkened to indigo, revealing only the brightest of a thousand hand-painted gold stars.

Exhausted, numb, energized, and a bit pie-eyed, Spence followed Jean up the stairs of the private Gulfstream 650 jet. He poked his head into the cabin. Six seats, grouped in pairs; a sleek, luxurious penthouse inside. The engines whirred with a high-pitched whine, accompanied by the gracious welcome of a dark-eyed flight attendant. With her mysterious, exotic features, she might have jumped out of the hieroglyphs. He handed her their bags and settled into the soft, cream-colored leather seats.

"My name is Nailah. I will accompany you and Mrs. Collins to Portland. May I get you something to drink once we reach cruising altitude?" she asked with a knowing smile. "We ascend quite fast."

"Oh yeah, I think a drink is definitely in order," he said, swiveling the plush seat back and forth, practically turning a full circle. "Do you have bourbon?"

Jean turned to Nailah. "Right! I'll have a glass of cabernet. Thank you."

The door closed with a hermetic seal. The lights on the wings glowed red as they rolled toward the runway. With little warning, Spence's stomach bottomed as the jet cut through the air and soared straight up, as promised. He reached over the seat to squeeze Jean's hand to calm her nervousness. But when he glanced over at her, she was smiling and gazing out of the window. She betrayed no trace of the fear he had witnessed for the last thirty-two years of flying with her. This time he needed her hand.

Spence had never seen Jean this buoyant and calm. So much angst as they tried to serve up life hot and well prepared. Taking risks was their comfort food. His trepidation at starting a business faded as he studied her hand—full of magic. In his younger years, mixing personal passion with commerce seemed to be a conflict, a betrayal of his Midwest upbringing. Hard work was supposed to be hard work. Now, the work seemed easy. The north wind of uncertainty had been blanketed by the magic of possibilities that were tangible and imminent. His fingers still tingled. All coalesced when he had set his hands on the fabric. Together, they would do something important with the gift they'd been given.

As the plane leveled off, Nailah handed Jean a glass of red wine, and to him, a shot of Maker's Mark on ice.

Jean stared into the night at the ghostly peak of Mount Hood. The mountain grew more ominous by the minute. Having slept for only a few hours of the thirteen-hour trip, the pampering they'd received from a fine meal of roast chicken with dates, lentils, and an array of cheeses was a warm welcome back into US airspace. The entire flight had been quiet and peaceful, but the tingle in her hands served as a reminder of their mission.

"We need to get to the car and go directly to the hospital," she said. "If we stop by the house first, Mycroft won't understand our leaving again."

"Why don't you call and check on Mary's condition when we land?" Spence asked. "If she's holding her own, then we can go to the hospital in the morning."

"Sleep? There's no way I can wait until tomorrow to see her. I'll call as soon as we get low enough for a cell signal."

The course of the Columbia River led the jet on its descent. She attempted several times to connect but was unsuccessful.

"Don't we have to land before you can use your phone?"

"You can do anything you want on a private plane. Commercial rules don't apply." Jean jumped when her phone connected. "Here we go—I have three voice mails since we left Cairo."

The first message was from Jon Segert, checking on their progress in Cairo; the second was Linda, saying Mycroft had been fed and was fine. Her eyes grew wide on the third one: Milwaukie Manor.

"What going on?" Spence whispered.

"I asked the administrator to call my cell if Mary's status changed. He says her vitals aren't good. She's shutting down, Spence. I think I should call to get an update directly from Milwaukie Hospital."

When the call connected, she asked to be transferred to the intensive care unit. She studied Spence's face as she waited for someone to come on the line. *He looks different. Do I look different too?*

"Intensive care, may I help you?" The woman sounded friendly.

"Yes, I'm inquiring about the status of a patient. Her name is Mary Coulter. Can you give me an update on her condition?"

"Are you family?"

"Not exactly, but we're like family. We want to visit her, please."

"We're trying to reach her son, Raleigh. Do you know where he is?" the woman inquired.

"Yes, he passed away this week in London. Unfortunate." She relived the taxi scene in her mind. *Not unfortunate; horrible.*

"Well, I'm sorry to hear that. If you want to see her, you should come right away. We're doing everything we can, but she's not responding. When you arrive, ask for me, Alice Maxwell."

"We're on our way. Jean and Spencer Collins. We're coming from the airport in about forty-five minutes." She waved Nailah to their seats. "May we arrange for a car to meet us at the plane and take us to the hospital in Milwaukie? Time is of the essence."

"Yes, of course. Mr. Kumar instructed us to handle whatever arrangements you might need on your trip." Nailah made a quick retreat and knocked on the cockpit door.

When their eyes met, Spence gave her a scoldy glare.

"There wouldn't be time to fuss with the car tonight," Jean said in defense. "Going to the parking garage will slow us down by a good twenty minutes. We can come back up to the airport tomorrow to get the car."

"Don't you think that's taking advantage of the museum's generosity?"

"Twenty minutes seems like a long time right now. We need to focus on Mary, not on driving."

Spence nodded his agreement and stared at his reflection in the window.

Once the plane landed, Nailah unsealed the door and extended the staircase to the tarmac below. Jean spotted the town car pulling up near the stairs.

"Best of luck to you, Mr. and Mrs. Collins," the pilot said, leaning out of the open cockpit door. "A pleasure. We hope to be back soon to return you to Cairo. Mr. Kumar will be in contact."

They descended to the town car and stacked their bags on the seat. "We're going to Milwaukie Hospital," Spence said to the driver. "Takes about twenty minutes, but faster is better."

As they rode in silence, Jean reached for Spence's hand. Anticipation and tension combined to squeeze the air in the car.

Jean's words finally broke free. "What if this doesn't work?"

"It will."

She could hear the concern in his voice. Spence plucked at his front tooth with his fingernail.

They will come. Mary felt nothing. In her mind she moved her hands and legs, but they wouldn't respond in this quiet, dark place. The steady beep of the monitor was an odd, predictable comfort. She sensed the atmosphere change. Light, rubber-soled shoes squeaked as they came closer. A bag crinkled. Wheels rolling over linoleum.

"Mary?—it's Alice Maxwell, your nurse. The Collinses are here."

Yes, yes, please send them in. Her pulse accelerated and thumped deep in her ears. She sensed the monitor had reduced her emotions to rhythmic lines.

Jean's voice: "Does she know about her son?"

Yes...in my heart he's gone.

"She's been unconscious since she arrived," Alice whispered. "Hard to tell in these cases whether she can process information."

Mary relaxed as soft warmth spread through her hand. Fingers wrapped beneath her palm. The familiar softness of Jean's skin as when they shared so much together on her patio.

"Mary? It's Jean. Spence is here with me."

Urgency in Jean's voice, but a curious calm too. The long, lean fingers of Spence's hand grasped her fingers.

"We found out so much." *Brushing a wisp of hair from her forehead.*

"The fabric's transformation was on the wall in Nefertari's tomb, Mary." Spence's voice; smooth and deep. "The story you told us is true."

Spence is so full of life. He embraced this adventure.

Silent communication between Jean and Spence. Jean's voice: "Mary, this is a beautiful process...so beautiful. When you're ready you need to let us know. Spence and I both can do it. The birds are not pheasants; they're phoenixes. The director of the museum helped us to release them before we left Cairo. They've flown the fabric."

Do this for me, as I did for Doc and Birdie.

"Mary, we owe you so much." Spence's words, barely audible, were there.

Warm. Sincere. Yes, I have made a difference.

"Mary, we love you. The fabric is safe at the Cairo Museum. They'll protect it. We can help you to complete the process as you asked."

Soothing voices.

"Give us a sign, Mary."

I am ready. This is not living.

The heartbeat monitor fluttered, so much that the alarm started its annoying blare.

"Spence?" Jean gasped. "Put your hands on her face. I'll put mine on her chest and hold her hand."

Mary focused on their touch. *Like magic.*

Intense warmth, as if Charlotte's heated quilt had been wrapped around her. The tingle radiated in her face, and then spread in her chest. Hands of love had started the process that she, herself, had done so many years ago for Doc and Birdie. Her feet, warm for the first time in months. Her body relaxed as all the stress and aches dissipated. Raleigh's face eclipsed by Jim's, her loving husband. Sure, healing hands of Doc on her face as he gazed into her eyes. The soft, welcoming hand of the mother she knew only as a specter. *Charlotte? Is that you?* Doc and Charlotte wrapped their arms around her. A black Labrador tickled her feet. Wiley licked and nipped. Mary's image reached out to catch the end of his tail, whipping in a sparkling fan. She gazed back at the robin, unfinished in her embroidery hoop on the nightstand, soon to join her to fly and sing. Jean would finish it for her. A drop of water on her face. *A splash from the bird bath.*

C'mon, baby girl. Time for you to come home.

Been waitin' for you, Miss Mary.

Birdie? Jess?

Jean kept her hands pressed on Mary's chest. She opened her eyes and pleaded, "Her face, Spence, keep your hands—it's happening."

The alarm faded as the electric charge spread through their arms. The heat—their heat—combined and traveled across their hands.

The window! Jean turned her gaze in anticipation. Beyond her own reflection, a *tap, tap, tap* as the three phoenixes balanced on the recessed ledge. Flickers of ginger, orange, gold, and electric blue glinted in the glow of the dim light from Mary's room. Jean's eyes filled. A tear spilled on Mary's face. She couldn't hold back a process that now had a life of its own. The birds took flight from the sill, disappearing into the dark to complete their long journey. She wiped her eyes as the nurse ran into the room to investigate the alarm.

"Mary's gone, Alice. But it's all right. She's happy," she said, taking in a life-giving breath.

Jean stepped around the bed to Spence. They held each other in celebration of lives lived in love, Mary's and their own. There was so much ahead of them. Caretakers of something precious.

Alice struggled to silence the alarm as she stretched the phone cord from the wall. "Code blue, Code blue."

"Alice—Stop—unplug the machine." Jean reached for her purse on the chair and spotted a nearly finished robin in an embroidery hoop on Mary's nightstand. *Stitches Mary would never complete.* Someone had hoped for a different outcome.

"May I take this with me, Alice?" she asked, already folding the raw linen corners under the back of the hoop. She slipped the robin into her purse—a little piece of the former Mary to frame and hang on the wall.

"Yes, of course." Alice searched in vain for a pulse, and then disconnected the IV.

"Let's go see Mycroft, honey. He's waiting for us to come home," Spence whispered and stretched his arm to lead her to the door.

Jean leaned over Mary and kissed her on the forehead. "She'll be with us always."

"Forever."

Hospitals took on an eerie quietness at night, especially on Sunday. She held Spence's hand as they stepped in the elevator. The fluorescent glare inside was an assault, a sharp contrast to the soft light in Mary's room. As they ambled through the main lobby to the entrance, the automatic doors swooshed open. They climbed into the back of the waiting town car in the circular driveway. Spence leaned toward the driver, gave him their address, and said:

"We're going home."

On Monday morning Anhur Kumar rehearsed his new speech in the mirror one more time. He smoothed his gray hair into place and repeated the opening line of his address. Nothing said could speak as clearly as what he would show the archeologists, historians, benefactors, politicians and select members of the media gathered in the conference room. They were waiting. He needed to be at the top of his game.

Turning from the mirror in his office, he spun the dial to open the safe. He pulled on the white conservator gloves. Removing the tissue, Anhur placed the folded fabric on his desk. He took a deep breath in a moment of silent contemplation.

"Father, Mother, and Child," he whispered, opening each of the three folds.

Before him, the trio of magnificent phoenixes presented themselves with the flowering vines wound above their crowned heads. Their feathers pulsed with energy under the glow of the recessed lights, alert and curious. "My dear ones."

The phoenixes had taken on their last charge. From here forward, the fabric would be trapped in an alarm-protected, Plexiglas display case when the construction was completed for this once-lost artifact from QV66. A fortress of protection. No other way existed for the throngs of visitors to gaze upon its magnificence. The world was not ready for this magic.

Anhur refolded the fabric and walked the long hall to the conference room. The security guard held the door for him to pass. He placed the folded fabric in the center of the table and addressed the elite group. Raising his gloved hands, the chatter quieted.

"Today is an historic day for the museum, and all of Egypt, my distinguished colleagues."

Silence.

Anhur touched the fabric. A collective gasp. With each opening of a fold, rainbows of rich, iridescent colors radiated throughout the room. Beams of warm sunlight leaped and pranced across the surface, followed by an explosion of clicks from the cameras. The flashes created a strobe of reflection off the glittering plumes. The phoenixes' eyes fluttered to block out the glare.

CHAPTER 26

The Meaning of a Good Man

It was good to be home, a little numbing, in fact. As she changed into her sweats, Jean glanced at the duffle bags Spence had tossed on the bed. *They can be unpacked later.* She washed her face. So tired, too tired to sleep. In another life, the laundry would've been done.

The possibility of immortality altered her perception of time. She was reminded of when, as a six-year-old child, she'd asked her teacher what was behind the stars. "Eternity," the teacher had said.

Unsatisfied with the answer, Jean had pressed for more. "What's after eternity?" The question drew a blank stare, then a pat on the head and a scoot of her behind. The fact no one answered the question haunted, and scared, her for years. Now she had an explanation that made sense: *magic.*

Jean cracked open the sliding door and took in the crisp rush of piney air. As she brushed her teeth, her gaze fixed on the solar lights around the yard, fading with the strengthening ghostly glow. The sun would soon emerge through the trees, but predawn light was special. Still and quiet outside. The air, charged for the primal ritual, carried the birds' calls in a thousand different tongues.

Jean glided the door shut and padded to the kitchen. As the coffee machine burped and puffed, she eyed the phone sitting in its base. Dread washed over her as the digital display flashed its numeric red warning: Thirty-two messages. The limit had been reached.

She listened to the first three messages; all reporters requesting interviews, their pens poised to turn something lovely into a carcass. They were ready to ravage and pick apart what had happened. Someone from the museum's board must have leaked their names without honoring their request to stay anonymous. But they'd have to trust that Anhur had kept his word not to discuss the transformation experience. He was trustworthy. Or, maybe some of those messages were about Raleigh. Her stomach squeezed at the thought.

"Not now," she said aloud. The automated voice instructed her to replay, save, or delete. She unplugged the phone from the wall.

The steam swirled behind her as she stepped to the living room with two mugs. Spence had lit the fire and placed a chair in front of it, though he wasn't in the room. Mycroft had taken up his favorite spot. So relaxed with his legs and tail draped over every side of the chair. Full of dinner—maybe breakfast—Mycroft was sound asleep, set on slow toast.

"We know what you know, big guy." She gave Mycroft nod of respect.

Where is Spence? Jean turned, with the two mugs in hand, and gazed out the wall of windows. The winter pansies, planted only a month ago, were now a carpet of speckled color in the gray light. They reminded her of spilled Chiclets. She spotted Spence on the patio and listened to his muffled voice. He laughed and talked as he tossed hazelnuts to three squirrels poised on their hind legs. Sun peeked between the trees, illuminating the scene.

She stood and watched him as the coffee lost its steam.

That afternoon, Jean sat in the living room by the fire after she, Spence, and Mycroft enjoyed a long morning nap. Spence chattered on the phone with Jon Segert while she completed the final embroidery stitches of the robin's breast feathers. The fabric had changed Jon's life too. He shared their secret. The three of them were now glued together with magic. She looked forward to meeting Jon's wife, Meg.

Between downpours, the sun teased and receded behind the clouds, a taunt of the final remnants of fall. Mycroft settled in next to her and pawed the thread as she listened to Spence play back the litany of messages she'd ignored last night.

God, he has more strength than I do. Each reporter's voice requested an interview as Spence played them on speakerphone and then hit DELETE. Some praised the donation of the fabric; others inquired about the incident with Raleigh in London. She stopped the needle mid-stitch on the twenty-fifth message. Spence turned up the volume.

"Mr. and Mrs. Collins, this is Don Landrum with the law firm of Landrum & Sullivan, LLC. I would like to set a time for you both to come in to meet with me regarding the estate of Mary Coulter. Please call me as soon as possible."

"Jean! Did you hear that message?"

"Yes, I did. Can you call him? At this point, we're not committed, so anytime this week's good," she said and pulled the last pumpkin-colored thread through the hoop, knotted it, and snipped the end. "I'm done! Mary would be happy with this." She unlatched the frame, smoothed the linen, and blew out a breath.

The robin is free. Couldn't have done it better myself.

"Mary? Was that you?" she murmured.

"What did you say?"

"Nothing. I think Mary...just spoke to me."

"Well, after I call this Don Landrum guy, I think Mary would tell us to pick up the car from the airport. I'll follow you home in the Mini Cooper."

"What do you think he wants with us?"

"No clue. With our luck, Mary's probably giving us that chest back. Oh, and when I talked to Jon, he said he's making progress on the insider trading case. The investigation isn't over, but he doubts we'll have any involvement from here."

"I won't breathe easy until he's got it wrapped up. What if they try to pin Raleigh's death on us? This doesn't feel over to me."

CHAPTER 27

The Robin is Free

"Jean, don't get worked up. This is another adventure," Spence said, opening the glass door of the office building. "What's the matter?"

Spence pushed the button for the fourth floor. Jean made a concerted effort to stop biting the inside of her cheek.

"I've had plenty of adventure over the past two weeks, thank you! I'm upset about the whole Raleigh mess. Do you think we need a lawyer?" she said.

"No, I don't believe so. This meeting is about Mary. But if we do need a lawyer, we'll be in the office of one in about two minutes."

The elevator opened in front of two richly paneled mahogany doors. She closed her eyes, pushed the one on the right, and stepped into the law office of Landrum & Sullivan.

The attentive receptionist, in her sixties, sat behind the counter. Her graying hair was pinned in a smooth bun, and her hazel eyes appeared magnified behind her rimless glasses. Jean could tell the woman had worked at the firm for decades.

"Good morning! Jean and Spencer Collins—we're here to meet with Don Landrum." She tried to make her voice sound cheery.

"Oh, yes. Please have a seat. Mr. Landrum will be right with you."

Jean sat next to Spence and fiddled with the small plant on the side table. She picked off the yellowed leaves and scrunched them into a ball in her left hand.

Spence thumbed through a vintage car magazine. He glanced up at her every few seconds over his reading glasses.

She mouthed, "What? I'm fine." He shook his head.

"Mr. and Mrs. Collins? Mr. Landrum is ready for you." The receptionist escorted them to the office.

Don Landrum, easily in his seventies, was tall with a bushy head of white hair in need of a haircut. His vintage eighties jacket, meticulous in its tailoring, was overly dry-cleaned. He stood and moved from behind his mahogany desk to shake their hands and motioned them to the two leather guest chairs. His kind brown eyes were more like those of a country doctor who made house calls than a lawyer.

Jean and Spence sat and stared at him, then at each other, bewildered by the invitation.

"Mary Coulter has been—was— a client of mine since 1969, the year her husband, Jim, passed away. I was a young man back those days." Mr. Landrum paused. The air filled with sparkles of unspoken memories. "She was one of my first clients when I started the practice. This is a sad day for me. Yes, well, Mary came to me recently to talk about you two. She held you both in high regard."

"Mr. Landrum, we've literally known her for less than three weeks," Jean said.

"Indeed, but you and Spencer clearly impressed her. If she liked you, then I like you—simple as that. So, let's get to it, shall we?" Mr. Landrum slid a stack of papers in front of him. "Mary's son, Raleigh, is unable to fulfill his role as executor of her estate. He preceded Mary in death only this past week. Tragic. This particular responsibility now falls to me." He raised his eyes with an expression akin to satisfaction. Apparently, Don Landrum wasn't a fan of Raleigh. "Mary named you both as her contingent beneficiaries in the event of her son's death."

Jean whipped her gaze to Spence. His mouth popped open in shock.

"Mary had a considerable estate. Outside of her personal affects, which includes a 1963 Thunderbird and the house in Irvington on Nineteenth Street, there are cash investment funds, worth approximately $1.2 million. They're made up of a combination of stocks, bonds, CDs, and money market accounts. Her son, Raleigh, managed her investments." Don glanced up, pressed his lips together, and continued. "Mary also owned an historic home in Richmond, Virginia, which is the asset she wanted you both to have—regardless of whether Raleigh remained alive. Mary inherited the Virginia home from her father, Dr. Beaumont Gaines, when he died in 1945. She never sold the property, as she wanted to provide for Birdie, the family's housekeeper. When Birdie passed away in 1948, Mary rented the home to a host of families. The property provides a nice income and is fully unencumbered. Since 2000, a couple has been running it as a successful bed-and-breakfast inn. Now you, as the new owners, can decide whether you want to maintain the status quo, sell it, or even move in."

"I...I don't—Mr. Landrum, this is all quite unexpected," Spence said, still processing the words.

"The best things are, aren't they?" Don's warm smile faded. "I loved that woman. I'd do anything for her. I hope you do something good with what she's done for you."

"No doubt," Jean interjected. "I expect we'll keep things status quo. I doubt we'll be moving to Richmond, Virginia. We certainly don't want to upset the current family." She glanced at Spence. "I mean...since the inn is doing so well."

"Yepper depps! My thoughts exactly," Don Landrum said, thumping the edge of his desk.

Jean opened her mouth in surprise. No one, besides Spence and his mother, ever said yepper depps. Silly—so Spence. He smiled back at her but his lip quivered.

"Well, that's it. The rest are details, details. We can deal with those in the coming weeks. I'll overnight you some initial paperwork to sign in a couple days. We'll include the return shipping label. Or, don't be a stranger and drop it off in-person." Don stood and shook their hands. "I hope you'll attend the funeral this Saturday at eleven. I'll e-mail you the directions of where to go."

Like robotrons, she and Spence drifted out of the office, through the lobby, down the elevator, and to the parking garage without saying a word. They sat in the car. Jean opened her left hand. The wad of dead leaves from Mr. Landrum's plant was still in her palm, gummy from sweat.

Jean set out two glasses and popped the cork on the Australian Shiraz they'd been saving for a special occasion. Her gaze followed Spence as he strolled to his humidor in the dining room and picked out a saved Cuban cigar. He ran the length under his nose and lit it over the downdraft in the kitchen island. He poured himself a glass of wine.

"Don't you want to let that breathe for a few minutes?" she asked.

"Nope, just fine." The smoke wrapped around his words as he puffed into the vent. "I'm calling Bill tomorrow. I talked with a guy who wants to sell his entire album collection. Thousands of albums—really good ones too."

"We need to sit down with Bill and Linda. We owe them an explanation after everything we've been through. I think they, of all people, could handle it."

"What about Phil and Patty?" Spence said, narrowing his eyes.

"Oh, no, you've got to be kidding. If we tell Phil, Portland will become the estate sale capital of the world. While you and Bill ramp up the store, though, I'm going to extend my sabbatical. Maybe we should make a trip to Richmond soon. Let's not tell the renters we're the new owners. We'll book ourselves in as guests under another name. Wouldn't that be a blast?"

"A blast!"

"Do you want to be immortal, Spence?"

"I think we have plenty of living to do right here."

She hesitated. "I'm sorry, but I don't think I can go to Mary's funeral. Let's remember her the way she was, when we all sat together on her patio. Maybe she's enjoying the view of the river right now. I bet we'll get to talk with her again. But there are a couple of things I want to take to the funeral home before Saturday. Give me a minute."

"Agreed." He gave her a sly smile. "We can pay our respects to Mary when we see her in Richmond. You know, we'll have to lug that chest over here *again*. We're getting that damned thing back. Isn't that wild? I'll put on some music."

While Spence stepped to the den to search through his albums, she retrieved Mary's embroidered robin from the hassock. She raced to the guest room in her stocking feet and pulled the white box from the closet. Lifting the lid, she set the robin on top of the little dress. She carried the box to the garage and placed it on the front seat of the Volvo.

As Jean emerged through the doorway, she heard The Who's *Tommy*. The song "I'm Free" soared around the kitchen in full splendor. She gave Spence a mischievous glance; he gave her a knowing smile. With a running start, she surfed across the bamboo floor on her socks stuck with pine needles and grabbed the edge of the granite island to stop. She picked up the glass of wine Spence had waiting for her. It should be ready to drink now.

EPILOGUE

Susan Kent had been a freelance reviewer for Bed-and-Breakfast Magazine for over fifteen years. A cushy job. It didn't get any better than flying all over the country to spend weekends in beautiful homes; some simple and charming, others elaborate and gaudy. She couldn't remember ever being this excited, though, to come home and write her review. Her weekend in Richmond, Virginia, was unlike any other experience of her career. Normally it took a few days for her to gather her thoughts. This one would be different.

She tossed her bag on the bed in her condo in Portland's Pearl District, overlooking the Willamette River. She snatched up her computer and rushed to the living room.

With her fingers poised over the keyboard, excited to write, a new realization gave her pause. How on earth could she write this without ruining her credibility? Ignoring the professional warning, Susan clicked the keys.

The Old Gaines House
Richmond, Virginia

I am always intrigued when guests of B&Bs report sightings of specters or unexplained noises in the night. Until this past weekend, those luring promises have never been fulfilled. They are usually marketing hype for the brochure to increase bookings. All of my skepticism evaporated, however, after the life-changing apparitions I experienced in this beautiful Victorian home. Go to the Old Gaines House in the spring. The gardens are immaculate. From your comfy, overstuffed chair in the living room, buttery red wine in hand, you are welcomed by a rolling wave of pink, lavender, purple, and white from hundreds of hyacinths around a grand bird bath. Do yourself a favor—stay until 5:15 p.m., when birds of all kinds gather to splash and preen. But there is more. With my own eyes I saw them. The other guests witnessed the apparitions too. An old Southern gentleman in a string tie and glasses appeared, followed by a dark-haired woman in a wispy blue dress. They each reached out to clutch the hand of a little girl with a sweet face and bouncing, mahogany curls. Her bright-white dress, with tiny hummingbirds around the waist, billowed as they swung her back and forth. She giggled as a black Labrador jumped to catch her legs. The child released herself and ran to the bird bath in front of the window, not more than ten feet away from me, and scooped up a robin from the water. She set it in her mother's hand. The three of them turned and strolled through the garden, the robin still balanced, unafraid, in the woman's palm. The dog trotted behind them, wagging his tail. They faded and eventually disappeared. Spend a very long weekend at the Old Gaines House. The roast chicken is the best you'll ever have, anywhere in the world.

Susan shut her laptop. She dipped her teabag in a mug and gazed out the window at the twinkle lights rippling across the surface of the river. She reflected on that ghostly family's life, beyond the description in the brochure. Had they experienced anything this fantastic?

Author's Note

Every senior living complex mentioned in the book is fictitious. However, there are several wonderful businesses and institutions, which are very real. Powell's Books is one of the best independent bookstores in the world and is an inspiration to any writer. There are a few other favorite Portland businesses mentioned: Rich's Cigar Store, Ray's Ragtime, and Jake's Grill; they all make life a little better.

The Victoria and Albert Museum in London is world-renowned for its collection of historic textiles. While the character of Graham Hollingsworth is purely of my imagination, it is true the Textile Exhibit is expanding to Blythe House in Kensington to accommodate their growing collections and valuable conservation work. I wish them much success. The V&A is a jewel in the British crown, and I can't wait to see it again.

While the Cairo Museum is a fictional museum, the other museums cited for housing several Egyptian artifacts are real. The tomb of Queen Nefertari is one of the most magnificent discoveries of Egyptian art in the Valley of the Queens. The description of the tomb, as discovered in 1904 by Ernesto Schiaparelli, is accurate. The character of Edwin Seymore, the north wall of the burial chamber, and the legend of the fabric, as described in the book, are purely fictitious. While the historic details, related to Nefertari, Ramesses II, and Amen-her-Khepeshef, are true to what information is available in public records, the fictitious legend of the fabric was incorporated to support the story. Unfortunately, the tomb of Nefertari is closed to the public due to its fragile environment, but there are several virtual tours one can take of the tomb on the Internet. Give it a go...and dream.

Finally, go to www.stitchesthenovel.com to see Jean and Spence's playlist of great music!

About the Author

Courtney Pierce lives in Milwaukie, Oregon, with her husband and bossy cat. *Stitches* emerged from her own magical history, which encompassed a twenty-year career as a sales executive in the Broadway entertainment industry. She became transformed by the magic of fiction from a theatre seat in thirty-two cities for touring Broadway shows. On the other side of her transition from corporate life, she has had the wonderful support of The Attic Institute, Willamette Writers, Pacific Northwest Writers Association (PNWA), the Northwest Independent Writers Association (NIWA), and Indigo Editing & Publications to develop her career as a novelist. Courtney's short story, *1313 Huidekoper Place*, was selected for inclusion in the 2013 *NIWA Short Story Anthology of Speculative Fiction*. She is currently in the Hawthorne Fellows program at the Attic Institute and will be on the board of NIWA in 2014. *Stitches* is also a showcase for her other passions: music, fine art, international travel, ancient history, and sewing exquisite fabric.

Follow the progress of the *Stitches* Trilogy at:
www.stitchesthenovel.blogspot.com

The magical journey of Jean and Spence Collins continues in *Brushes*, the second installment of the *Stitches* Trilogy.

www.ingramcontent.com/pod-product-compliance
Lightning Source LLC
Chambersburg PA
CBHW050511260626
47157CB00004B/1273